# PASSIONATE ABRASIONS

## A NOVEL

I0553627

## John Lewis Smith

LEWIS MUSIC

This novel is entirely a work of fiction. The names, characters and incidents portrayed in it are the work of the author's imagination. Any resemblance to actual persons, living or dead, events or localities is entirely coincidental.

First published in 2016 by Lewis Music

http//:www.lewismusic.co.uk

Copyright © John Lewis Smith 2016

All rights reserved
The moral right of the author has been asserted

Front and back cover design and illustrations
by John Lewis Smith

ISBN: 978-0-9933111-1-6

**To**

The friends and fans of Fyrm Fouroux

## Acknowledgements

I wish to thank my friend, Tom Young, for the help and encouragement he has given me in relation to the writing of this book. I am also grateful to my nephew, Adrian Smith, for his advice concerning the medical condition of one of the characters.

# Chapter 1

Harold awoke with an exquisitely painful erection. Desperately, he clung to the fading image of the woman with good posture who, without doubt, was responsible for the benign protuberance in his pyjamas. He could not remember what it was that she had been doing to him that might have accounted for his current state of excitement. As he turned to silence the alarm, the mistress of his dreams faded from consciousness and the day kicked in.

Harold's wife, Veronica, lay sleeping by his side. He shook her roughly by the shoulder as he got out of bed; she was congenitally immune to alarm clocks. In the shower Harold attempted to recapture the thread of the dream from which he had been so rudely awakened, when his reverie was interrupted by an impatient hammering on the bathroom door.

'Harold, will you get a bloody move on! I want a pee and you've locked the fucking door.' Veronica was always at her best first thing in the morning.

'Alright. I'm coming, I won't be long,' Harold replied, grumpily.

'Well, hurry up. I'm desperate,' shouted Veronica, banging on the door one more time for good measure.

Harold turned off the shower, grabbed a towel and, after a quick rub, slipped into his bathrobe. As soon as he opened the door Veronica barged past, shoving him out of the way as she did. Harold padded off in the direction of the bedroom to get dressed. He felt thankful for the fact that the sound of Veronica farting was, to some extent, attenuated by the hiss of the shower.

Harold sat in the kitchen, chomping on a piece of toast and marmalade while casting an eye over the newspapers. Veronica, somewhat bedraggled, appeared in the doorway and pointed herself in the direction of the fridge. She had the habit of dragging her slippers across the floor with every step. As usual, she wore a white towelling robe. It was tightly belted at the waist, as if to prevent too much anatomical anarchy.

'What's happening tonight?' she said.

'I don't know. I might be late from work. Are you going to cook?'

'No, I did pasta last night. Why don't you do something for a change? Honestly, Harold, you're a bone-idle git sometimes.' She looked at him with what was, for her, a relatively modest degree of contempt, as she sipped her orange juice.

'OK. I'll pick up a few items on the way home.' Harold put his mug and plate into the sink, took hold of his bag, and deposited a solitary peck on Veronica's cheek. There was no concession to the double-sided embrace, despite the fact that they were Francophiles.

He eased the car away from the kerb and allowed his mind to wander as he turned right, heading for the riverside campus. He braked hard as a couple of cheeky schoolkids sauntered defiantly across the road in front of him. Had they known the level of Harold's commitment to daydreaming at the wheel, they would doubtless have thought twice before engaging in such seriously suicidal behaviour. As he waited in the queue of cars backed up on the access road to the bridge, the woman from his dream popped back into his mind. A smile of recognition crossed his face. She was Julia Rivers and Harold knew her from the university. She occasionally acted as a visiting lecturer on the marketing course. Indeed, she had been at a meeting he had attended earlier in the week and had sat directly across the table from him. He remembered that she had been wearing a smart black business suit and a white shirt. She had said little but when she did speak there was, as always, a measured seductiveness in her manner that Harold found more than a tad exciting. At one point in the meeting she had caught him staring at her but she had shown no embarrassment. Quite the reverse. She surreptitiously winked at him and then held his gaze until, unnerved, it had been he who had felt compelled to look away. She had been known, from time to time, to join Harold for a coffee and a chat after attending these tedious meetings.

Harold parked his car and walked up to his office. He logged onto his computer and waited for the system to fire up. He settled down and began to check his emails. It wasn't long before his eye chanced upon a circular from the Vice-Chancellor. Given the dire rumours that had been doing the rounds he felt compelled to read it.

He skimmed rapidly through the crass banalities of the opening gambit and quickly found the meat:

*... and it is therefore necessary to adjust our staff expenditure and other outgoings in line with the prevailing academic market forces. By trimming back now we will obviate the need for total closure in the future. This strategy will hone our competitive edge and ensure success in the long-term...*

Harold didn't want to read any more at that moment. If it confirmed what everyone had been saying at the pub the other day, he needed to be somewhere alone to think about it. They were saying that voluntary redundancy and early retirement deals were likely to be wheeled out within the next week or so. The unspoken threat was that if not enough people agreed to go, compulsory redundancy notices would follow later. Harold was one of the oldest members of the psychology department and there would be considerable pressure brought to bear on him to take the money and go. He had to get out of the building and get off campus as fast as he could. He checked his diary and found that his teaching was blocked into afternoon sessions but all classes had been cancelled for the student union annual general meeting to take place. This was a stroke of luck. His mind was made up in a trice. He printed out the V-C's email, skimmed over the headings of the others to make sure there was nothing that couldn't wait, and then closed down his computer. He decided to drive to the coast. He stuffed the email about redundancy into his jacket pocket, picked up his bag and locked his room. He walked on past security and out of the building, trying not to inhale too much of the cigarette smoke that inevitably hung in a pall over the main entrance. He brushed past the tobacco addicts who were huddled together for support and carcinogenic company. They stood in silence, shifting their weight from one foot to another. It took him several minutes to find his car. This was not unusual since he could never remember where he parked the bloody thing.

Harold headed off campus and drove up the coast road to a secluded spot on the cliff tops. He parked his car facing the sea and looked about him. To his right stood an old-fashioned lighthouse, now a museum doing home-made teas in the summer months. Gulls wheeled in the airstreams at the cliff face. Their screeching reminded him of the frequent trips he had made to the seaside when he was a boy. He wound down the car window and listened to the sound of waves pounding on the beach. He inhaled the salt sea air.

He unfolded the print-out of the Vice-Chancellor's email and read it from start to finish. It soon became clear to him that his head was going to be on the block. He was slightly puzzled by the fact that he didn't appear to feel at all angry. If anything, he took it fatalistically. The melody of the song *Que sera, sera* drifted into his mind. Still, he felt that such a momentous communication carried with it an implied permission, if not a positive exhortation, for him to go home and get drunk, be it the middle of the day or not! He picked up his mobile phone and dialled his friend Trevor's number.

'Trevor Lamb.'

'Hi, Trev. It's me, Harold.'

'What can I do for you, my old mate?'

'I've just read the email from the V-C. It's a bit of a bugger.'

'Yeah, right. Nothing we didn't expect, though. Don't you reckon?'

'I know, Trev. I'm pretty sure that I'll be for the chop.'

'You don't know that, Harold. It might never happen.'

'Maybe. Still, I don't suppose you fancy a pint or maybe a bottle of wine round my place, do you?' Harold asked plaintively.

'What, now?'

'Yeah. I'm in need of a daytime piss-up.'

'Harold, there's nothing I'd like more but I've got classes all morning and bloody meetings all afternoon. Back to back from here to fucking China, mate.'

'OK, Trev. Just thought I'd ask. I'm a bit low right now.'

'Harold, take it easy. I'll call you tonight and we can go for a pint, mate.'

'Cheers, Trev. You're a gent. See you later.' Harold put an inauthentic spring in his voice for the benefit of his friend.

He turned his thoughts to the immediate demands of domestic trivia: he needed to get some food for the evening meal. He started the car and threaded his way towards his favourite supermarket. Once he arrived, he shopped as if on automatic pilot. He tossed a bag of green salad into his cart, along with some new potatoes, strawberries, mushrooms and a couple of lemons. He found himself wandering down the poultry aisle and paused to collect a packet of chicken breasts, when he suddenly became aware that he was being addressed.

'Dr Hake, what are you doing here? Should you not be at the university?' Harold looked round and realised that it was Julia Rivers. She was smiling at him knowingly.

'Oh! Hello!' he said. He felt flustered by her.

'I think you're skipping your classes,' she chided.

'I'm not, honestly,' he replied. 'I haven't got any teaching today and, anyway, I've just read the Vice-Chancellor's email about redundancy. I'm not in the mood for the university.'

'I heard a rumour they were about to clear out some of the dead wood. So, you think they might give you the chop? You poor old thing,' replied Julia.

Harold was taken aback by the fact that she should say anything to indicate that she might be remotely concerned for him.

'What are you going to do?' she asked.

'I'm going to buy some wine and get drunk,' he replied.

'I meant in the longer term.'

'I haven't thought about that yet. It's too early. I mean I don't know for certain that I will be let go. Although, to be honest, it looks very likely,' he said.

'You be careful. You mustn't let yourself go to pieces.'

'No. I mustn't do that. I know,' he replied.

'Take care!' she said and then, leaning toward him, she kissed him lightly on the cheek. He watched her walk away in the general direction of frozen vegetables. Somewhat surprised by this encounter, he shuffled off to choose his wine.

Harold stood in line at the checkout. He glanced over to his right and noticed Julia further down the line of tills, settling her bill. His queue moved ahead and he started to stack his stuff onto the conveyor belt. When he came to push his trolley out to the car park, he could see Julia packing her bags into the boot of her car. She occupied the bay next but one to where he was parked.

'Let me see what you've got in there,' she said, as Harold approached. 'You've bought three bottles of wine! You can't possibly be left to drink them on your own. You'll end up getting depressed.'

'No I won't,' said Harold.

'We'll drop your car off and you can come round to my place and have a drink of wine there.'

'Are you sure that will be alright? How will I get back home afterwards?' asked Harold.

'Taxi,' she replied.

Harold stowed his bags.

'You can jump in with me once we've dumped your car,' she said.

They drove off in convoy. Once out of the car park Julia followed Harold on the main road towards his home. Eventually, he indicated to turn right, and drove down the access road towards his house. There was a pleasantly suburban feel to this part of the city and a reasonable sprinkling of trees lined the streets. Once again he indicated, and turned left. He pulled up outside his house and watched Julia in his rear-view mirror as she parked behind him. He got out and walked back to Julia's car.

'I'm just going to take my bags in. It'll take me a little while to unpack them. Do you want to come in?' Harold said.

'No, I'll wait here for you but don't be too long!' she said as she wound up her car window.

The house was empty; Veronica was at work. Harold quickly put his food away. Then he dived into the bathroom for a quick pee and a squirt of deodorant. Something in the back of his mind told him he shouldn't be doing this but he took no heed of it. He wondered whether he should change his clothes. On balance, he figured that would take too long. He closed the front door and got into Julia's car. She revved the engine as he sank into the passenger seat.

'Hold on tight!' she smirked. She roared off down the street, and opened up the throttle as soon as they joined the motorway. Harold touched his seat belt for reassurance; a pair of rubber pants might have been a sensible precaution. She followed the ring road for a couple of miles and then turned off into a district on the outskirts of the city that had the feel of a country village. The houses were well-painted, the hedges were well-trimmed and the cars parked in the driveways tended to be top range models, no more than a couple of years old. Julia turned into a side street and parked beside a modern Tudor-style house. This was far more upmarket than where Harold lived. Still, lucrative business consultancies and a lack of kids meant she could afford fast cars and fancy housing.

'You bring in the shopping while I see to the alarm system,' she said.

Harold carried her bags into the kitchen.

'Put them on the worktop for me, there's a good boy.'

Harold did as he was told and then sat at the kitchen table. He waited. He could still walk away now. Nothing had yet irretrievably changed. Nothing apart from the fact that he was likely to be forced into premature retirement. He sat rooted to the spot. With every second that passed he came nearer to having his decision made by default. He tried to force himself to stand up but he couldn't move from the chair. The more he tried to make himself go back home, the more enticing became the thought of staying. He heard Julia's heels clicking on the floorboards: busy, efficient steps, ringing out like staccato bursts of machine-gun fire. He pulled out his mobile phone and retrieved the number for the city taxi company. Julia was coming back. He could hear her steps returning along the corridor. He had about ten seconds in which to take the evasive action that would preserve the status quo in his humdrum life, messy as it was. He held his breath, vacillating at the point of bifurcation.

Harold had hesitated a moment too long and he knew he would not be able to leave now that Julia had entered the kitchen once more.

'Can you cook?' she asked.

'Yes, I can. I make most of our meals at home,' said Harold.

'There's an apron on the hook by the door.' Julia pointed as she said this.

Harold took off his jacket and tied on the blue and white striped apron.

'Very Master-Chef,' she said, drolly.

Harold glanced around the kitchen. It was certainly more upmarket than the one in his house. He let his fingers caress the dark granite top of the central island, with its gently curving corners. He looked enviously at the touch-controlled ceramic hob and marvelled at the elegance of the of bow-fronted storage draws. He opened a pair of double doors, about the size of his wardrobe at home, and found a perfectly organised pull-and-swing larder staring him in the face. He felt that he could fall in love with a kitchen like this!

'What do you want me to cook?' Harold enquired.

'I don't know. Rummage in my bags and have a look at what I've got in the fridge. I'm sure you will think of something. Meanwhile, get that bottle of Chardonnay open and pour me a drink,' said Julia. She crossed over to one of the wall cabinets and removed two crystal wine glasses which she handed to Harold. He then poured the wine.

'Here's to my possible redundancy,' he said.

'Yes. Cheers. Could be the first day of the rest of your life and all that!' Julia clinked her glass against Harold's, walked over to the window, and eased her body into an old-fashioned wicker chair. Harold listened to the satisfying sound of the wicker creaking slightly as her foot moved up and down, he presumed to an imaginary beat. The toe-caps of her high-heeled boots were exceptionally shiny; they caught the light as she crossed her legs. Suddenly, he became aware that she was watching him.

'Why are you blushing?' she enquired.

'I don't know. Am I blushing?'

'You were staring at my legs. Weren't you?'

'Yes. M-more your boots, actually,' he stammered.

'Do you have one of those fetishes? Is that what is making you blush?' A smile played over her lips; she appeared to relish Harold's embarrassment. He attempted to change the topic of conversation.

'They're very smart. Fashionably stylish. Shall we have some spinach?' He produced a green packet from the bag.

'Yes, that sounds healthy.'

'It might not be, by the time I've finished with it.'

'Well, so long as it tastes good, I don't really mind.' She took a sip of her wine. ' What are you going to do, anyway?'

'I think I'll cook it down, squeeze the water out and then get it to take up some butter and cream. Perhaps grate some nutmeg into it,' Harold replied.

'I was asking about your life, not the spinach.' She said this in a flat tone of voice.

'I don't know exactly. As a last resort, I could do some counselling. Maybe a bit of freelance consultancy or even some part-time teaching. I haven't had time to think it through.' He knew his reply was lame; he wasn't very good at selling himself.

'I can probably get you some work here and there.'

Harold was surprised by this act of encouragement and generosity. 'Could you?'

'It wouldn't be much. I have a few clients who might be persuaded to give you some market research. It would be questionnaire design for the measurement of attitudes to consumer goods. That sort of thing. You might get a bit of data collection and possibly analysis too, if you are lucky. Compared to what you are used to, the pay would be good,' she said.

'I suppose I am technically capable of doing that sort of thing. I mean, I have the skills but it would bore me stiff.'

'You may not be in a position to pick and choose. I didn't know you were a counsellor or therapist?'

'I had a semi-dodgy diploma in that area before they tightened up on the qualifications and training, nationally. I got in by something they called the 'grandparenting' scheme. It was a kind of truce for the oldsters who had feeble but vaguely accredited qualifications. I have kept up the minimum stuff I need to do to remain on the books, as it were.'

'How amazing! Are you good with a woman lying on the couch?'

'That entirely depends upon the quality of the legs exposed.'

'So, a letcherous therapist!'

'Well, Freud did bang on about sex rather a lot, you know.'

'I should have thought *banging on* was a rather unfortunate expression, in the circumstances,' said Julia.

Harold chortled as he put the spinach into a large pan. 'Be that as it may, I might be able to take some counselling hours from Anthea Partington. Do you know her?'

'Yes, I do,'

'All she wants to do nowadays is her aromatherapy massages. I could do some hypnotherapy for her: smoking, weight loss, things like that. Nothing too demanding.'

Harold shook the pan and quartered a couple of oranges. He turned the heat up and prodded the spinach with a large spoon. The water began to run out and he drained it into a colander, expelling as much of the green liquid as he could. He tossed some butter into the empty pan and tipped the spinach back in. As soon as the butter had been absorbed, he started to feed it some double cream. The spinach acted like a sponge mopping up as many calories into itself as Harold cared to offer it. He was not very good with calories; he was not a prudent cook. He poured himself another glass of wine and topped up Julia's. She took a sip and then walked over, behind Harold. He felt the weight of her body as she leaned against him. Her arms encircled him; she grasped her hands around his waist and gave him a gentle hug.

'Is that nice, Harold?'

'Very nice,' said Harold. 'In fact it is just what I needed!'

'Well, you're upset about all these threats of redundancy. You need a bit of cheering up.'

Harold turned around and smiled at Julia. 'I do indeed!'

Julia briefly stroked his cheek. 'Let's have this lunch, then.'

Harold plated up the food. They ate in the kitchen, informally, at the small table that nestled against a window onto the garden.

'So, does your consultancy work keep you busy?' Harold asked.

'Oh, yes. I have as many clients as I can handle. I built things up over the years. At first I did more teaching and university work but I don't really need to do any of that anymore. I keep in touch here just to keep my fingers on the pulse. Apart from that, it looks good on my publicity brochure.'

'Is it mainly local work?'

'I do have some local clients, but a lot of the time I have to travel. Sometimes I have to go overseas.'

'And you don't mind that?'

'No, I have always enjoyed it. I would not want to be in sales, living out of a suitcase all week. But meetings in London and occasional trips abroad are fine. I usually take a book to read for the times I am on my own, travelling.'

'What do you like to read?'

'Something not too demanding. I like page turners. I'm not too fussy about genre or author, although I don't like science fiction or fantasy.'

'So, you pick up something from the book shelves in the shops at airports and railway stations?'

'Yes, that's about it.'

Harold nodded. 'I should do more of that. I'm getting a bit fed up with all the academic tomes that I have to read. A lot of it is complete bullshit, you know.'

'I can imagine. Still, if you get made redundant, you won't have to read that shit anymore.'

'That's true. At one time I thought I might write more of it when I retired, but now that I am close to getting the opportunity it no longer has a pull on me.'

'Maybe you can find some interesting things to do with your time, if they do kick you out.'

'Yes. Maybe.' Harold sighed.

When they had finished the food, Harold collected the plates and rinsed them at the sink. Julia walked across the kitchen and placed her arms around Him. He turned, wiping his hands on a tea towel hanging from a nearby hook. The thought crossed his mind that he really should have been home alone or sitting in some dreary pub, quietly getting drunk and maudlin. Julia relaxed her hold, and leaned back slightly.

'Are you comfortable with being here, Harold?'

'I'm not sure. Today has been rather strange, so I suppose being here is another part of that strangeness.'

'But all that is mainly about work and redundancy, isn't it? I mean, it occurs to me that you are a happily married man. Is that not the case?'

'Well, that is the official line, I suppose. Actually, you have put your finger on another area of my life that is not going too well at present.'

'You said your wife was not at home when you took your shopping in earlier on.'

'That's right.'

'So you don't need to be rushing off home right now?'

'Not really. She won't get home until later this afternoon.'

'What does she do?'

'She's a teacher.'

Julia strengthened her grip around Harold as they hugged, leaning against the kitchen worktop. 'Something tells me you would rather be here with me. Even if it is a bit naughty of you.'

Harold smiled and nodded.

'Let's go upstairs, and just see how we feel,' said Julia, taking Harold's hand and leading him through the door. When they reached the bedroom, Julia turned to Harold and said, 'I'm told that it is far from cool for a man to leave his shoes and socks on in this sort of setting, so why don't you take them off and put them over there beneath the chair.'

Harold found himself bending down to attend to this. Julia had already begun to remove her own clothes.

'I think you want to take your trousers off for me now, don't you?' Harold fumbled with his belt.

'Oh, do get a move on, Harold. It's not that big a deal.' She bent forward and unzipped his jeans as she said this. Gradually clothes were shed and Julia drew Harold over to her king-size bed . She settled him onto his back and put an extra pillow under his head.

'Is that comfy?' she asked.

'Very comfy,' Harold replied. Julia lay down beside him and rested her forearm along the length of his thigh. Harold felt her hand beneath his testicles. The room was very quiet. Almost nothing was happening. The pressure she applied to his scrotum was barely perceptible. She slowly moved his balls around her cupped hand. He had experienced nothing quite like this before. Harold felt time grind to a halt beneath her palpation. She had not touched his penis. There was a coldness about the situation. It was almost clinical.

'You're becoming a little erect, Harold.'

'This is weird,' said Harold.

'It's different. I don't expect it is like when you are at home with your wife, Veronica.'

'You can say that again.'

'I think you need someone like me.'

'Do I?' said Harold.

'You know you do.' Julia stroked Harold's cheek as she said this. Harold sighed when he felt her hand on his penis. This did not turn him into a rutting beast; rather, he gave the appearance of laying back and thinking of England. His pleasure was more conceptual than carnal. He noted that his seduction was something that was happening to him, as opposed to anything that he might be causing to happen. To some extent this assuaged his guilt.

Harold felt that he would have liked a little more foreplay, but Julia obviously thought this sort of thing to be a frivolous waste of time. She had, by this time, mounted him and she now began to move her hips.   She showed a singular determination in forcing life into the vintage body that lay shuddering beneath her thighs. For the first time in many a year he was very nearly in top gear, although the wheezing gasps that emanated from his lungs suggested that the Grim Reaper might well come before Harold did. Julia, who by now was well into her stride, began slapping his face from side to side in time to rhythmically delivered Karate grunts. He was therefore somewhat relieved when she switched her hedonic strategy by deploying both hands in frantic clitoral stimulation. For Harold, the relief from pain more than made up for the humiliation of knowing that she demonstrably held his sexual technique on a par with a pile of camel dung. Harold, in an attempt to get into the spirit of things, flung his arms forward, grasping a cheek of Julia's buttocks in each hand. He hung on to her so tightly that the laws of biological mechanics now lifted him up towards her. She grabbed his shoulder with one hand, tearing her nails across the flesh of his quivering back. At last, bellowing like a farting hippopotamus, he came. They crumpled into a sweaty heap of body parts, strewn across the double bed.

At first, there was only the sound of heavy breathing. Gradually the ownership of arms and legs was established and the bits and pieces of corporeal being were once more reassembled into two distinct and separate Gestalts. Since Harold's tantric skills were negligible, the pubic interconnection remained intact for no longer than a minute or two. Harold went off to the bathroom to clean himself up. When he returned he found Julia wrapped in a toweling robe, sitting on the bed.

'Well, Harold, what am I going to do with you now?' she said.

'I don't know. I think I'd better get back.' He started to put on his clothes.

'I may want you to come and see me again,' said Julia.

'Will you? Oh, I don't know. When?'

'I'll email you at work. It will be sometime when it is convenient for me and not necessarily when you want to come. Do you understand? As far as we are concerned, you exist for my pleasure and not the other way around.' She spoke like a lawyer going over the details of a contract.

'What if I don't want to?' said Harold.

'Don't be silly Harold. You know you want to.' She said this with a bored air of finality.

'Yes. I suppose I do,' said Harold, with a note of resignation in his voice.

'I'll call you a taxi,' Julia said.

'It's ok, I'll do it.' He pulled out his mobile phone and made the call. 'Should be here soon,' he said. 'I'll see myself out.'

'I'll be in touch. I shall expect you to come when I say. No excuses.' She stood up and put her hands in the pockets of her bath robe.

'Alright. I'll go now. Bye.' Harold raised his arm a fraction as a token gesture of farewell. He slammed the door shut and got into the cab.

They hadn't kissed goodbye, despite the fact that their sex had been so very intense. There was something chilling about what they had done; it was passion without warmth but he had liked it. He sank back into the seat of the taxi with a smug, satisfied smile on his face. It was only as he started to pass the more familiar landmarks of his neighbourhood that his complacency became troubled by pangs of guilt and anxiety. He had to go home. There was no way around that fact.

## Chapter 2

Harold walked through to the kitchen. Veronica was sat at the table, reading the newspaper.

'You're home early,' he said.

'Timetable and rooms cock-up,' she replied. 'Anyway, what are you doing? Skiving off, I shouldn't be surprised.' Having glanced in his direction, Veronica turned her attention back to the paper.

'Not exactly. We got an email confirming the redundancies. It's just a matter of time before the individual letters come out. I didn't feel like doing much work today.'

'So, they're going to kick you out?' she said.

'Looks that way,' Harold replied.

'You'll have to find something else, then. I'm buggered if I'm going to slog my guts out just so you can laze around the house and go down the pub with your mate Trevor.' She turned the page of her newspaper and began to studiously avoid looking at him.

Harold was not entirely surprised by her response, given that they had not been getting on too well lately. She had recently been promoted at the school where she worked and they had always kept their finances separate. He had not been expecting charity.

'I'll sort something out. I'll do a bit of freelance,' said Harold.

'You'll need more than a bit if you're going to pay your share of the household expenses,' she said, 'and don't forget Emma's still got another year to go before she graduates.' Emma was their daughter who was completing a degree in media studies at university.

'I know, I know. Give me a break, it might not happen. I don't know for sure that it'll be me. We only just had the general announcement today.' Harold went to put the kettle on for a cup of tea.

'So, what have you been doing? I see you've been to the supermarket.' Veronica gestured to a plastic bag containing some of the things Harold had dumped onto the table earlier when he was in such a rush to get back to Julia in the car.

'Yes,' he said, 'I went round for a drink with someone from work.'

'Well, it wasn't Trevor because he was on the phone for you half an hour ago.'

'No, not Trevor.' Harold hoped that she would drop this line of interrogation; he was feeling evasive.

'So who were you having a drink with?' she asked.

'I bumped into Julia from Business Studies. She does some part-time lecturing on the marketing course,' Harold said lightly, 'I don't think you know her'.

'Well, why did you bring the shopping back and then go out again?'

'We went round to her place. She gave me a lift, so I didn't have to drive.' Harold was sweating a bit now. 'I only needed a taxi back home, that way.'

'I see. And where does this Julia live?' Veronica was no longer pretending to read her newspaper; she smelt a rat.

'Fenwell,' replied Harold.

'Very nice, too.' Veronica made a passable attempt to convert envy to scorn as she uttered these words.

'Yes, she's got one of those houses in Clanbrough road.'

'Very pricey!' said Veronica. Harold breathed a sigh of relief. A conversation about house prices might be terminally boring but at least it was safe territory.

'Trevor was thinking of moving up there as an investment,' he said.

'Where's he going to get the money for that, then?'

'I think his Mum died last year and he and his sister split the proceeds from the sale of the family home.'

'Alright for some,' said Veronica.

Harold put some milk in his tea and sat down. 'Might call Trevor back and see if he fancies an early pint.' On the surface, this sounded like a harmless enough declaration of intent but in practice it was an oblique request for permission to be out of the house. In the normal run of events this would be denied if Veronica had anything else in mind for Harold to do.

'Has he got one of those letters, too?' she asked.

'I shouldn't think so,' said Harold. 'His lot are flavour of the month right now.'

'Pity you're not.' She said this with an edge in her voice. 'Still, I don't think you've ever been that, Harold. Have you?' She never hesitated from showing her disappointment in Harold's poor career performance.

'No, I guess not.' Although Harold was prepared to allow himself to be berated over his flagrant lack of ambition, on balance he would have preferred a more extended discussion of property prices.

'What's that mark on your neck?' Veronica enquired. Harold felt a chill run through his body.

'What mark?' he asked, stupidly. He stepped into the hall to look in the mirror on the coat stand. 'Oh, I probably cut myself shaving,' he said.

'Right! On that nice electric razor I bought you for Christmas, I suppose.' Sarcasm was something Veronica reserved primarily for Harold. 'Here, let's have a look.' She got up and walked over to examine the evidence. By now his face was beginning to colour. His stomach started to churn. 'That's a bloody love bite, Harold Hake!' She spat her conclusion out with venom. 'What have you been up to?'

'It wasn't anything much. Julia and I got a little tipsy at lunchtime and started fooling around a bit.' Harold thought that an early confession might constitute a good damage limitation strategy. He could put up with being in the dog house for a day or two.

'I don't like the sound of that one bit,' said Veronica, 'Who started it?'

'She did,' he said. 'I think she wanted to cheer me up and take my mind off redundancy.' Dressing it up as an act of mercy was a bit feeble but it was the best he could do for the moment.

'I'll bloody cheer you up, my arse.' Her mood was turning ugly. Harold needed to get away from her before she pushed him any further.

'Look, it wasn't anything. It was like you at your Christmas party last year. You had your hands all over that new geography teacher, from what I heard.' Attacking was always a risky tactic for Harold, it could so easily backfire with Veronica.

'That is entirely different. Everyone was doing it and it all happened in public in the staff common room. I did nothing in secret.

You went to her house and came out with a fucking great love bite, Harold.'

He could see a vein pulsing in her neck. She was getting very angry. He had to get out. 'I've told you, there wasn't anything in it. I'm going upstairs to get changed and then I'm going down to the pub to meet Trevor.' He shut the kitchen door and went upstairs to their bedroom. He picked up the phone and dialled the number. 'Trevor, it's Harold. Look, mate, I want to get out of the house for a bit. Do you fancy a pint in the Cracked Bell?' Trevor said that he did. Harold put the phone back in the cradle. He had time to change his shirt before he left for the pub.

Harold opened the wardrobe and ran his hands over the row of shirts hanging neatly from the rail. He picked the one in dark blue on the grounds that the colour matched his mood. There was no need for a tie; he was only going for a pint. He laid his shirt on the bed and walked over to the window. He looked out on his garden as he took off the dirty shirt and threw it in the laundry basket. The bedroom door opened and Veronica walked in.

'Have you seen my green socks? You haven't got them mixed up with your stuff, have you?' she asked. For some reason, Veronica always wore socks to go with her jeans.

'No I don't think so. Why don't you have a look in my drawer?' Harold was being extremely cooperative and polite. Laundry was easily as good a topic of conversation as house prices. He turned to look out of the window at their garden, squinting slightly against the setting sun. The sight of the pink cherry blossom calmed his mind slightly. He heard Veronica open a drawer in the wardrobe, followed by another as she started going through his socks. Harold turned to the bed to get his new shirt. The sunlight caught Harold's back and bathed it in a warm golden hue. The room had become very still. He noticed out of the corner of his eye that Veronica was staring at him and the blood was draining away from her face.

'You lying bastard!' She spat these words at Harold with menace in her voice. 'Look at your fucking back, you pig.'

Harold turned against the mirror and looked over his shoulder. He knew he was doomed the moment he saw the three inflamed scratches etched across his shoulder blade. He had been branded with Julia's claw marks.

He felt like a drowning man whose life was flashing before him in an instant. He recalled that he had always had sensitive skin and how, when he was a child, he had sometimes woken up in the morning with the most intricate patterns spiralled across his body, caused by scratching in his sleep. What might amount to a barely visible abrasion on most people's skin could became an angry welt on his. He stared at his reflection in the mirror: the physical evidence of Julia's emblazoned moment of ecstasy.

Veronica straightened up as he slipped the shirt on to cover the evidence of his transgression. He was aware of her raised arm but he took no evasive action. He stood still, petrified in his guilt. The silence of the moment was shattered by her hand smacking his face hard. His head spun to one side under the force of the blow and his cheek burned. Beyond the stinging pain, he felt the emasculating humiliation of being slapped by a woman in anger. Had Veronica not pushed him towards the door he may well have dwelt upon the cultural meaning that was packed in her punch.

'You disgusting little shit.' He realised Veronica was not through with him when he received a very unpleasant clip to his ear. She pushed him again in the small of his back and he tumbled down the stairs, almost losing his balance. When he reached the hall he put his hand to the wall to steady himself and half-turned to look at her. She was leaping down the stairs, two at a time. While the sureness with which she moved her limbs might have been down to yoga classes, the malevolent competence of the kick she aimed as she flew into the air at the bottom of the stairs undoubtedly had more to do with Tae Kwon Do tricks, picked up as an undergraduate on a women's self-defence course.

Harold fell to the floor, winded. For the second time that day, a woman straddled his prostrate body and rained blows to his head. He brought his arms up to ward off the attack.

'You expect me to let you live here? You think I'm going to pay your bills while you fuck with some whore from Fenwell? You fucking little turd!' As she delivered her vitriolic stanza, she thumped his shoulders with both fists in unison as each word exploded from her lips. 'You total fucking shit'. She made up for the limitations of her poetic vocabulary by the movement of her body which she arched and coiled like a deranged timpanist as she pummelled the breath out of the decrepit hulk lying beneath her.

Suddenly she stopped hitting him and got up. Harold saw her reach for his coat, hanging on one of the hooks by the door. She threw it at him on the floor. 'I want you out of this house, you fucking worm.' She was breathing heavily and something told Harold that it was only self-control that was keeping her from putting him in hospital.

'What, now?' he said.

'Don't bloody argue. Get out!' She opened the front door as she said this. Harold began to scramble to his feet.

'What about my stuff?' he said, weakly.

'I want you to go right now. Anything else you can sort out later. But you are leaving, this minute.' She stood, arm outstretched, pointing to the road. Meekly, Harold stumbled out, tucking his shirt in as he went and pulling on his coat: bewildered, hurting and humiliated. He tottered down the road in the direction of the Cracked Bell, limping slightly as he went. He gingerly opened the door and made his way over to the corner where Trevor had a table.

'Have you been mugged, Harold?' said Trevor, rising to greet his friend.

'Yes and no. Veronica turned nasty. She kicked me out, literally.' Harold slumped into a chair as he said this.

'I'll get you a drink, mate. You look like you could do with a double whisky.' Trevor went to the bar to order the drinks. 'You're going to have a lovely black eye tomorrow,' Trevor said, looking at Harold as he set the drinks on the table. He settled back to listen to Harold's tale of woe. Harold briefly sketched out the events leading up to his getting kicked out of his own home, abridging the encounter with Julia to the bare essentials.

'If Veronica hadn't seen the scratch marks, I'd have been alright,' Harold concluded.

'But you wouldn't because you would have been round to see that Julia again the minute she snapped her fingers. You'd have been caught out one way or another.' Trevor tapped his finger on the table for emphasis as he delivered his assessment of the situation.

'I suppose you're right,' said Harold. 'But what am I going to do now? That's the question. I haven't even got anywhere to sleep.'

'Look, I'd offer you a bed at my place but my sister and brother-in-law are stopping over. They're out seeing some of their old mates tonight. You can have the couch if you like,' said Trevor, adding the offer of the settee somewhat tentatively as an afterthought.

'No, I don't want to be any trouble. I don't think I'd be much fun tonight, anyway. I must tell Julia what's happened. I might see if I can stop with her. I'll go round when we have finished our drinks,' said Harold. Trevor nodded.

'I think I've blown it with Veronica, and I can't undo that. You know, she had very little respect for me before, and now I think she just hates me. Her anger was filled with disdain, almost contempt when she was hitting me, Trevor. I don't think she likes me anymore. I am starting to wonder if she ever did. Perhaps my unconscious knew what it was doing when it took me to Julia's this morning,' said Harold. He smiled, ruefully.

'So you think this Julia, of the gorgeous figure, actually likes you?' Harold detected a note of thinly disguised surprise in his friend's voice.

'That would appear to be the case,' said Harold. 'I've been getting really fed up at home with Veronica, anyway. She just nags all the time. It's no fun, Trevor. It's been no fun for bloody years. It's just something I've put up with. She doesn't need me and she doesn't care for me. She just needs someone to swear at and find fault with.'

'You're not going to tell me that Julia needs you?' Trevor's tone was incredulous.

'Veronica needs to have a loser around the house in order that she can feel as if she is a winner. So my function was to soak up the shit, so she could think she was a rose.' Harold had moved onto beer by now and he slowly sipped his pint as he developed his analysis.

'But what's that got to do with Julia?' said Trevor.

"I get the impression that Julia knows she's a winner; it never occurs to her that she might be anything other than that. She doesn't need to use me as a point of comparison against which her own success can be judged.'

'So what does she use you for?' asked Trevor.

'It's early days. We only got together this morning. But I think I can see a difference. Julia needs someone who she can control so that she can get a sense of her own power.'

'You're losing me Harold. Don't start the psychobabbling,' said Trevor.

'It's easy. Veronica needs a failure, out there, so she can feel good about herself by comparison.'

'Go on.' said Trevor.

'Julia needs another person to be in close symbiotic union with her so that she can express her feelings of superiority and witness their manifestation in the flow of her everyday life. Nobody can achieve dominance in their domestic domain, unless they have someone who can enable that through their submissiveness. That particular coin has to have both sides present or it cannot exist.' Harold was becoming less sure of himself now.

'Sounds a bit weird to me, Harold. You take it easy.'

'I've got to talk to her again. I must sort something out,' said Harold, fumbling in his coat pocket for his mobile. Trevor sat sipping his beer while Harold spoke to Julia briefly and then ordered a taxi. They sat in silence to finish their pints. Trevor glanced out of the window,

'Here's your cab, Harold.'

'Right. I'll call you.' Harold got into the car and left his friend standing on the pavement shaking his head in bewilderment.He was barely conscious of the journey and before long he was ringing Julia's bell.

'My God, Harold, what have you done to yourself?' said Julia as she opened her front door.

'I had a bit of a fight with Veronica. Well, she had a fight with me, to be more honest. It was a one-way affair,' Harold replied.

'Come in and sit down. That eye looks very nasty.' She led him through to the sitting room and Harold brought Julia up to date with what had happened.

'So what will you do? Are you going back home tonight? Maybe Veronica will have calmed down,' said Julia.

'No, I couldn't face that. Trevor said I could sleep on his couch if necessary but he's got family staying over. I don't know what to do.' Harold sighed, 'I suppose I couldn't stop here with you for a bit, just until I can sort myself out?'

'Stop here with me!' echoed Julia. 'Well, that's a novel idea.' Julia got up and walked over to the window. She appeared to be thinking through the implications of what Harold had said. While Julia paced to and fro, Harold sat quietly. Eventually she stopped and turned to him. 'You can't just doss here with me,' she said with a smile playing over her lips, 'but maybe you could have a base here, as a paying guest, to use a rather old-fashioned term.'

'That might be easier said than done. May I respectfully remind you that I more or less got made redundant, this morning.'

'So if you can't pay with cash maybe there are other ways you can earn your keep.' Julia seemed to be enjoying herself. Harold failed to see where the conversation was leading.

'How could I do that?' asked Harold.

'You could do the cooking. Are you any good at all the other stuff, the cleaning and the shopping, that sort of thing?' asked Julia.

'I often do a lot of that at home. Perhaps I should say *did*, to be more accurate.'

'So I could give you a roof over your head in exchange for you being my domestic servant. Of course, it would be on a very temporary basis. Neither of us know how things are going to turn out, either with you and Veronica or you and me. We will have to take things a step at a time. But for those days, or perhaps I should say nights, when you are here, you will earn your keep in the fashion that I have outlined. How about that, Harold? I have a feeling you might enjoy it.'

'I'm not sure I've got any choice,' replied Harold.

'Oh, there's always choice, at least at the beginning. Of course, once you have made your choice, there may be very little thereafter,' said Julia. She ruffled his hair as if he were a young schoolboy and let out a little laugh. 'And it's not just my domestic needs you will have to satisfy, is it Harold?'

Harold grinned, 'I guess not.'

'So what do you say? Do you want the job, Harold?' Julia asked.

'Yes, I think I do. Thank you,' said Harold.

'I shall expect you to do as you are told, Harold,' Julia said. 'Everything will have to be done to my satisfaction. Can you cope with that?'

'I think so,' said Harold.

'I'm not sure that you fully realise what you are letting yourself in for,' said Julia.

'I think I know what you want. Let me try,' Harold replied.

'Very well. I'll take you on trial at first. You can spend a few nights here and then see what the living arrangements with Veronica turn out like. If I'm dissatisfied or have any cause for concern, you'll be out,' said Julia, 'Do you understand?'

'Yes, OK. What should I do about my things? Should I go back home and pick some up tonight?' asked Harold.

'No, you can arrange to do that tomorrow sometime. It's quite late anyway. You can make do this evening.' Harold nodded.

'That's settled then.' Julia sat in a chair across the room and surveyed Harold.

'Your clothes are in a bit of a state,' she said.

'I know,' said Harold.

'My brother has left some of his stuff here with me; he's abroad and moving flats. He's about your size and I think I should be able to find a few items to tide you over until you get your own things tomorrow. Well, a pair of trousers, maybe a shirt and a jacket. I don't think there is any underwear or pyjamas. I'll have to improvise something for you on that score.' Julia smiled wickedly. 'Anyway, make yourself a hot drink while I run a bath for you and sort something out.'

'I thought I was going to be the one who ran baths and things like that,' said Harold.

'Oh, you will, my darling. You will. Have no fear of that. But tonight you need to be looked after and you will put yourself in my hands.' She reminded Harold of a ward sister he had had a crush on when he had been in hospital as a kid. It was the fusion of the military and maternal attitude in her tone of voice. The possibility that Harold should do anything other than what she said was ruled out by her bearing and deportment. She was in charge; he was the invalid. Already she had left the room and Harold could hear her busy feet moving about upstairs. Cupboard doors clicked open and banged shut; water was cascading into a bath; curtains were being drawn.

Then Harold suddenly caught the sound of a woman's voice singing; it was Julia. She had a rich powerful voice and it brought a smile to Harold's face as it floated down from the upper reaches of the house. She was singing the blues in a style not dissimilar to that of Bonnie Raitt. Her singing showed him another side of her that did not come through when she was being Ms Super-Bitch Bossy-Boots. Harold could feel a warmth of emotion in her singing that was well hidden in the dominant persona she had so far shown him. She sounded happy. Harold knew that it was possible to sing the blues and sound happy at the same time, since he was also a master of the art. It had not crossed his mind that Julia might genuinely be pleased about the current developments. He knew there had been a powerful, if strange connection between them this afternoon. He heard Julia calling him.

'Harold, bring your hot drink upstairs with you. You can have it while you are lying in the tub.'

'OK. I'm just coming.'

'I hope you're not, you naughty boy.'

Harold smiled: she even made bad jokes. Maybe this could work out after all. He climbed the stairs.

The bathroom was large and womb-like. The only sources of light were the flickering candles that Julia had placed around the available flat surfaces. They gave off a herbal fragrance that made Harold sniff for more as he entered the room. She was wearing a black pencil skirt and a white blouse. The fact that she was dressed more appropriately for office than boudoir contributed to the surreal nature of the experience for Harold.

'Let's get you out of these clothes, Harold.' Julia removed his jacket and began unbuttoning his shirt. Harold put his hand to her waist but she moved away from him to put his shirt, along with his jacket into a plastic sack. He began to feel as though he was being put through a decontamination procedure.

'Take off your jeans and panties, Harold, and give them to me. And your socks. We can get these clothes cleaned up tomorrow.' He did as he was told and stood naked before her, feeling not a little embarrassed. Julia put the bag of clothes against the wall and turned to look at him.

'What's all this then?' She gripped his love-handles and poked his tummy. Harold was currently on the brink of corpulence; it could go either way. 'I think I'll have to get you into shape, my Harold.'

'You think I've got a crap body, then?' Harold said, with some sadness.

'I don't think that at all, Harold. No, you just need a bit of trimming down and honing up. Nothing too drastic.' Harold was not sure he liked the sound of this. Julia laughed at his frowning face. 'Don't worry, Harold. It won't hurt. Or perhaps you'd rather it did.' Again the laugh. 'In you get now.' She gestured to the bath and Harold lowered himself into the bubbles. Although he often saw bubbles in his bath at home, he had never actually been submerged in them; the bubble bath was always for Veronica or Emma. They would have taken the piss if he had tried it. Veronica would never have let him forget it. She would have thought it far too effeminate for a man like Harold. Yet Julia seemed to regard it as perfectly natural.

'You look very sweet, Harold. Is it hot enough for you?'

'It's wonderful, Julia,' said Harold.

'Just one more thing. You need some music. I think you look like a string quartet man. That will be your bath music for this evening.'

'You're quite sure it won't be Handel, then, because I can't stand his water music,' replied Harold. Julia laughed.

'No, you will get the Mozart whether you like it or not.'

'You mean I can't choose? I can't have a bit of Bach, then?'

'Harold, the whole issue of choice is inappropriate to your situation. If I think you need some Mozart, then that is what you will get. Stop fussing, now.'

'Well, I quite like Mozart, actually.'

'There you are. Just relax.' She left the room and shortly afterwards the Mozart started to play through the extension speakers fitted to the bathroom wall. The door opened again and Julia returned. She brought a stool to the side of the bath and sat down, facing him. 'What did you make yourself to drink, Harold?'

'Cocoa.'

'Very romantic, I must say.' She smiled at him as she picked up the cup and offered it to his lips. 'Here, have a sip.' He sat up and tried to take the cup from her.

'No, you can't hold it, Harold. You'll get bubbles all over it.' Harold settled back to get comfortable and let Julia feed him some of the cocoa; it was still pleasantly warm, if not hot.

'What a day this has been,' Harold mused. 'Perfectly humdrum this morning, then thrown out of house and home by nightfall.'

'Are you upset? Would you rather we hadn't bumped into one another at the supermarket?' said Julia.

'I do feel guilty when I think about Veronica and what I've done to her and Emma. I'm the rat; I've destroyed the family. They will survive but our family is dead and gone, as of today. And it was all my fault.'

'What's the worst thing about that, Harold? What's the thing that you would most like to fix, if you could?'

'The worst thing? Hmm... I don't know what's going to happen. I don't know whether I've been kicked out permanently. If I have, I shall miss being at home when Emma comes for a weekend or when she stays for a week here or there in her vacation times. It may sound silly but I'd like to keep up that chocolate-box image of a happy family on her visits. I mean, Veronica and I have been pretending for her sake for a number of years now, so it's not as though that would be anything new.' Julia stroked Harold's cheek with her finger.

'Why don't you talk to Veronica about that and see if you can sort something out? She might think it would be a good thing to do for your daughter's sake. Emma could still be told that you were not living there all the time but it wouldn't be so final if you were around when she visited.'

'Sounds a bit strange to me,' said Harold.

'As far as Veronica is concerned, it would be as if you were a sales rep, on the road a lot, or maybe one of those guys who work on the oil rigs. When I was growing up the girl next door's dad worked on one of those old-fashioned light-ships out at sea and he was gone for two or three weeks at a time. You never know, she might like that sort of arrangement.'

'But what about you? Do you not want me to be here? Are you being kind to me tonight because of what happened this afternoon when really you want to get me back home?' Harold asked this with no animosity in his voice. He was curious; he couldn't quite understand where Julia was coming from.

'Harold, you might find this rather odd but I want you to be happy.'

'But you don't want me lying around here, cluttering up your bath space. Is that it?'

'No, Harold, that is not it. I shall make allowances tonight because you have had a difficult day but in future you will not be permitted to talk yourself down like this. The only person allowed to make criticisms about Harold Hake, in this house, will be me. And I shall enjoy doing that when I think you need it. But if you try to do it, I shall punish you.'

'And how will you do that?'

'Oh, Harold, I'm sure there will be many, many ways. But rest assured, they will all be ways that you will crave or enjoy, my pet.'

'Hang on, this is weird. Am I to understand that you want me to live here for a while but kind of still keep one foot in my family home?'

'I think that's what you want to do, Harold, and so that's what we will do, providing you can fix it up with Veronica.'

'I just don't get it,' said Harold.

'Harold, it is not important whether you get it or not. Look at me.' Harold turned his head a fraction and stared into Julia's eyes.

'Do you trust me?'

'Yes.'

'Did you have to hesitate before you gave me your answer then?'

'No.'

'Then everything is going to be just fine. You don't love me yet but you will come to do so.'

'Will I, Julia?'

'Yes, Harold, I shall make sure of that when you are ready. There's no rush. I have all the time in the world.' Strangely, Harold did not find himself resisting what she said. He lay there taking in her words but barely processing them at the conscious level. He felt almost entranced.

'But why are you doing this, Julia?'

'You won't understand, Harold. I have been looking for a man like you for a long time and it struck me in the supermarket this morning that I had found him in you. I shall do everything in my power to make you feel good and to feel happy. But I shall have the power; you will have none in our relationship.'

'That's hardly a progressive attitude to adopt in this age of egalitarian relationships.'

'Indeed it isn't. Our relationship will be far from politically correct, Harold. I shall devote myself to your well-being but I shall have complete control over you. You probably won't like it at first but you will get used to it and then you will scarcely remember what it was like before. It will all be so easy and natural in the end.'

'And what do I have to do?'

'Nothing, Harold. Just lie back and enjoy. Now, I have some work to finish. Here's a towel for you and you can wear this robe when you have done. I've put a rather large, pink babydoll nightdress out for you on the bed. An old school friend of mine called Monique left it here, and she is a rather big girl! Anyway, I think it should fit you alright and it will do for tonight. You will have to go and get some clean clothes from your house tomorrow. Give me a shout when you are in bed and I'll come and say goodnight to you.'

'Haven't you got something a bit more suitable I could borrow?'

'No, Harold, you will wear the pink babydoll.'

Harold sighed. 'You don't want me to sleep with you tonight, then?' he asked, wistfully.

'No, Harold. You will sleep in the spare room. That will become your room. Then when I want you to come and sleep in my bedroom, it will be like a special treat for you. It will be better that way.'

'Will it?'

'Trust me, Harold. Everything will be just fine.'

'OK. I will. I'm too tired to argue.'

'Of course you are, Harold. And it wouldn't do you any good if you did, would it?'

'I guess not.' Julia got up and left Harold to finish soaking in the tub. When he had dried himself, he found his way to the spare bedroom and, almost without thinking, got into the pink babydoll PJs that Julia had set out for him. He was too tired to worry about it. 'Julia!' Harold called, as he climbed into bed. He lay on his back, head and shoulders slightly raised upon the pillows, and waited.

'You look snug,.' said Julia, as she swept into the room. She was wearing silk burgundy pyjamas. Harold was disappointed; he had expected something more diaphanous.

'Have you got an alarm on your watch, Harold?' she enquired.

'Yes, it's digital.'

'Then put it on for 6.30. You can get up and have a shower. You can choose some clothes from this wardrobe here; there should be a jacket and a pair of trousers that will just about fit you. They belong to my brother, as I said. There is no underwear for you but I have found a rather sexy pair of black lace panties, also left behind by my friend Monique. You will have to make do with those until you collect your own stuff later tomorrow.'

'Oh, Julia! Do I have to?'

'Yes, darling. Think of it as a perk. I am reliably informed that some men would pay good money for such an experience.' Julia laughed.

'When you are dressed, I want you to bring me up breakfast, in bed, at 7.00 sharp. I'll leave a note in the kitchen saying what I want. You might as well start earning your keep straightaway.' She raised her eyebrows when she finished speaking, as if to ask him if he had any questions.

Harold set his watch, 'Do I have to get up then? It seems a bit early,' he said.

'Yes, you do. At least, you do if you want to stay here with me. Those are my terms,' she said. She was sitting on the side of the bed, leaning over him. She was behaving more like a mother than a lover, rather a strict one at that. Suddenly, Harold felt tired. A lot had happened to him today. He had already been beaten up physically by one woman and he did not have the strength to endure a verbal battering now.

He sighed a meek 'OK, if you say so.'

'I do, Harold. And now it's time for lights out. Come along, snuggle down.' She kissed him on the cheek as she patted his duvet and pillows. Then she switched off the lamp. She remained sitting on the side of the bed when Harold turned over onto his side and began to settle down for the night. He was very tired and barely registered the fact that Julia's hand was sliding up his thigh. He feigned sleep, hoping not to do anything to disturb the flow of the moment. When he felt the light touch of her fingers upon his cock he let out a sigh, even though he had not entirely ruled out the possibility that he could be dreaming. Biology took its course. He came and then she left, mopping up before she went. At no time did she remove her pyjamas. Harold could live with that; a woman's vagina was not always a comforting place for a man with penile dementia.

Next morning Harold woke at 6.00 a.m. He showered, got dressed and prepared Julia's breakfast. Then he climbed the stairs, with her tray in hand: scrambled egg with fresh chopped chives taken from the herb garden, toast, freshly squeezed orange juice, and a cup of tea. He knocked.

'Come in,' called Julia, who was sitting up in bed. Harold put the tray on her lap.

'Sit down and talk to me about what you have to do today,' she said.

'I guess I'd better phone Veronica and arrange to pick up some of my things,' Harold said.

'Well, don't bring too much. Remember, I want you to square it with Veronica so that you can go back at weekends sometimes when your daughter is home. You must leave some things there to maintain a presence. So don't bring more than one carload over here.' Julia's expression suggested that he would be in trouble if he exceeded his quota.

'Then I ought to see Anthea and start to make some plans for the future, if I want to do some counselling.' He sounded scarcely more enthusiastic about this than he would have had he announced that he was going to visit the dentist.

'Have you got to go to the university today?'

'Yes, I've got to chair a meeting this afternoon. Some nonsense about developing new degrees bridging the gap between media studies and psychology.'

'So, sounds like a busy day for you. That's good. I don't want you getting up to mischief.' She looked at him sternly when she said this. 'And you can cook dinner for 7.00 tonight.'

'OK. What do you want?' Harold asked.

'I'll have your home-made fish cakes, with a green salad on the side,' said Julia. Harold had foolishly bragged about his cooking skills yesterday while he was in the kitchen with Julia, unpacking her shopping.

'Wow, that's very precise! Veronica could never make up her mind about what she wanted to eat,' said Harold. 'Do you want cod or salmon in the fishcakes?'

'Cod would be good. It will be expensive but keep a note of how much you spend and I will refund you. Once we get organised I will arrange for you to have a petty cash box for household expenses,' said Julia,

Harold looked taken aback. 'Amazing! I actually quite like that idea.'

Julia smiled. 'You can wait for me downstairs while I get ready and then I'll drop you off on my way into work.' She dismissed Harold by pointing to the door.

Harold phoned Veronica to tell her he would be round to pick up some things. She sounded as though she had calmed down a bit and told him that she was going to work early and he could call in after she had left.

Julia came downstairs. She was wearing a charcoal skirt and matching jacket, with a crisp fitted lilac cotton shirt. Her black court shoes made her look serious and business-like. Harold slipped his hand inside her jacket, cupping her breast in his palm.

'Harold, behave yourself. I have to go to work now.' She grasped his wrist and smacked his hand playfully as she pulled it away from her breast, rather reluctantly in Harold's opinion. Of course, Harold had a degree in wishful thinking. They left the house and Julia drove to the top of Harold's street.

'You can walk from here,' she said.

'Ok. I'll see you this evening,' replied Harold. He leaned over and kissed her on the cheek.

'Remember, just the essentials. Don't bring too much stuff!' she called out.

Harold waved goodbye as he crossed the street. Julia drove off. He unlocked the door and walked into the silent house. He stood where only yesterday he had lain on the floor, taking Veronica's blows. He glanced in the hall mirror and inspected the evidence; his eye was purple, if not actually black. He sighed as he made his way up the stairs to the bedroom. His strategy was to pack some clothes into suit cases and then to pack some of his books and papers into cardboard boxes. He could get some from the supermarket at the same time as he bought the fish and salad for Julia's dinner. He opened the wardrobe and started to fold his clothes. He was a neat packer. The bottom of the case he lined with small objects: belts, underwear, ties. Then he made a layer from his shirts and topped up with jackets, jeans and trousers. He filled two medium-sized cases in parallel, which lay open side by side on the bed. Finally, he stuffed some shoes and trainers down the sides of the cases. He was about to close them when his eye alighted on the small wooden box in which he kept his jewellery. He had very few items: some rings, a stainless steel bracelet, an old pair of cuff links. He opened it and saw the ring Veronica had given him. It now shared the same status as the wedding ring from his first marriage that lay next to it in the box. He felt that two rings just about summarised his adult life; he could hardly expect a third at his age. He put the box in one of the cases and closed them up.

Harold left the cases in the hall and went to the supermarket to get some cardboard boxes. He parked in the slot where Julia had been on the previous day. It was as if he wanted to convince himself that it all really had happened. He even passed through the same check-out.

Back home he went into his study and started loading up the boxes with his books. He chose a few essential reference books for what might become the next phase in his working life: a textbook on counselling techniques, a statistics bible, something on questionnaire design, and a couple of general textbooks on psychology. He then put in a handful of old favourites before adding two or three novels that he had not got around to reading. Next, he went to the kitchen. He opened up the cupboard containing a mixture of crockery and glasses. He picked out his favourite mugs and was about to close the cupboard when he saw his 'World's Best Dad' mug. It had been a fathers' day present, many years ago. He left it untouched and quickly shut the door, as if to shut out painful memories. He started to feel depressed and needed to get out of the house. He packed the cases into the boot of the car and then went back for a final inspection. He kept seeing more things that he should take. He put his laptop in the hall and then put a selection of CD ROMs into a bag, along with some software manuals. Then he picked out about 20 CDs from the music collection. Next, he put his guitar into its case and chose a few songbooks. He placed them, together with his favourite chord dictionary, into one of the boxes.

The whole exercise was getting out of hand. He hadn't realised how many material possessions he had accumulated over the years. He kept reminding himself that he needed to leave enough stuff to make it seem like a base for himself if Veronica did agree to let him back at weekends from time to time. The act of packing felt like a ritual, providing some sense of closure to his marriage. As rituals go, it was a tawdry affair compared with the wedding ceremony that had marked the commencement of their married life. He wandered into the bathroom and put some basic toiletry items into a bag, along with his electric shaver. His body shook. He found himself crying. He couldn't stop. Huge tears were streaming down his face. What had he done? He felt sure he would miss Veronica in some strange way. He didn't over-intellectualise his plight; he just sobbed and felt sad. It was some time before he managed to dry his eyes and blow his nose. He washed his face in cold water and that made him feel a little better. 'Right. I've gotta get out of this place, if it's the last thing I ever do!' He sang out loud, adapting the lyric from the 1960s hit song by the Animals.

The car was piled to the gunnels with a reasonable sample of the detritus of his life. He took the road out towards Julia's house, and was soon parked in her drive unpacking his stuff. The room she had allocated to him was large and it offered good scope for storing most of his stuff. There were shelves that, with a little re-arranging, could take his books. There was room in the closet to hang most of his clothes. He put the remainder in one of his suitcases and stowed it on top of the wardrobe. There was a little desk for his laptop. He took his guitar out of its case and lent it up against the wall in the corner of the room. He took his CDs down to the sitting room and put them in a neat pile near to Julia's. He would ask her where she wanted them when she came home. He was surprised by how quickly he had unpacked. He made himself a cup of coffee and then called Anthea on his mobile phone. She sounded pleased to hear from him. He told her that he had left Veronica; he gave her an abbreviated and expurgated version.

'Are you alright, Harold?' she asked.

'I'm a bit shaky but I'm holding together pretty well under the circumstances,' Harold replied.

'That's awful. What are you going to do? Where are you? Do you want to come round for a chat?' Her questions often came in threes, although that was the only characteristic she shared with London buses.

'Chat would be good, Anth.' Harold always shortened her name. He thought that the 'syllablectomy' cut through the fact that she was posh.

'Look, I'm at my clinic and I've got a client coming in soon. I'll be free at noon. Do you want to come up to Harley-Streetville?' She loved to aggrandise the suite of rooms she had rented on the cheap from her father in a dilapidated old building downtown.

Harold smiled, 'That would be great. I'll see you then.' He put the mobile back in his pocket and finished his coffee. He then fussed over where to keep things upstairs in his room until it was time for him to go.

He parked his car and made his way up the stairs to Anthea's consulting rooms. He rang the bell and waited. The door opened.

'Harold, darling.' She threw her arms around him with the sort of determination that suggested this would be a major hug. Harold allowed himself to relax into the warmth of her body. There was no attempt to kiss and all hands, arms and legs behaved themselves impeccably. They were powering platonic warmth into one another with great force and skill; it took an alumni of the 1970s encounter group culture to do this without feeling. After swaying imperceptibly, rooted to the spot for what seemed like an inordinately long period of time, they commenced the disengagement procedure. Stepping back, head slightly to one side (complementary angles from the vertical), they sighed.

'Aah, Har-rold. Mmmm.' Anthea wrinkled her face as if chewing on a lemon when she delivered her empathic noises.

'Anth...' said with falling intonation, a little shrug, and a barely noticeable shaking of the head in disbelief.

'Come in, you poor darling.' She put her hand round his shoulders as she guided him along the corridor to her office-cum-consulting room.

'Anth! You've got a bloody couch!' Harold marvelled.

'I know. Don't you think it's good, darling?' She went over and patted it. 'I went to the Freud museum in London last year and I just knew I had to have one.'

'I didn't realise you were into psychoanalysis, Anth,' said Harold, with a puzzled look on his face.

'Well, I'm not really, Harold. Good heavens no! But it's nice to have some of the trappings. Sets the scene. I mean when my clients go to the dentist they expect to be put in a dentist's chair. So why not give them a couch when they come here for counselling?' Anthea sat at her desk and motioned Harold to sit opposite her. 'So, poor old Harold. That nasty Veronica has sent you packing, has she my darling?' She sat back in her chair as if hoping for Harold to tell her all the juicy bits.

'True. We haven't worked out the practicalities yet. But that is only part of my problem at the moment,' Harold said. 'I'm also about 90% sure that I'm going to be made redundant from the university. I think it will be dressed up as an early retirement deal.'

'Never! Oh, Har-rold. They can't do that to you? Surely not. I won't let them, my darling.' Anthea frequently slowed the progress of their conversations down with displays of solidarity interwoven with moments of gross emotional outpouring. Harold hadn't the time or energy to prolong Anthea's outrage-and-empathy performance.

'They can and it's highly likely that they will,' he said. 'I'm going to try a bit of freelancing, to make ends meet, if I can.'

'Yes, well, absolutely, darling. Why not?' said Anthea, 'What sort of things are you going to do?'

'I don't know for sure but I thought I'd be eclectic: go for everything and anything I can get my hands on,' Harold said.

'Go on, my darling, tell me more,' said Anthea.

'Might do some market research jobs for Julia. Trev said he might be able to line up a bit of part-time teaching for me. And I even wondered about doing a bit of counselling on the side.' Harold speculated as to whether Anthea would take the bait.

'That's very interesting, darling, because I might be able to help you there.'

'Might you?' said Harold, trying to sound as if the idea had never crossed his mind.

'I've been getting a lot more into my aromatherapy stuff, Harold. And I've got all this space! Far too much for little old me. You wouldn't come in and take some of my clients off my hands, would you?' asked Anthea.

'That would be terrific, Anth. But I'm not sure that I could rent a room from you or anything,' Harold said.

'Oh, no, don't worry about that. I can set up a room for you and we can put your name on the door but you can be operating on my behalf, as it were. Besides, I only give Daddy peanuts for the whole floor. He's waiting for development to hit the area and then he'll sell up and make a disgustingly large amount of money, I expect.' She said this with the bored air of someone accustomed to having more money than is good for them.

'Are you properly accredited, my darling?' she smiled sweetly at Harold, denying him the opportunity to take offence, adding, 'Hope you don't mind me asking,' for good measure.

'Amazing as it may seem, I am still technically competent, even if I have been hanging on by the skin of my teeth these past few years,' Harold said.

'Well, what I have in mind for you is all pretty boring stuff, Harold, darling. People trying to quit smoking or lose weight, mainly. Occasionally I get someone coming to me with a recommendation from Dr Brighton's stress clinic in the big practice out at West Road but they are not officially referred on by him.'

'So what do they want?' asked Harold.

'It's usually helping to build their confidence, maybe a bit of assertiveness or general social skills. Again, nothing too demanding.' She smiled at Harold to reassure him that even someone with his abysmal level of competence might be able to manage her cases. Harold was never completely sure whether she patronised him intentionally or not.

'That sounds brilliant. If I'm for the chop, I think I'll get to know by the end of this week. I might even find out later today. I'll get in touch sometime next week if I need to and we can sort the details out then. If I'm going, I'll fix it so I can get started before I've fully worked my notice out at the university. They'd probably let me go early anyway,' Harold said.

'Good. Well, part of me hopes that you will be released from that dreadful place as soon as possible. Then you can come here and we can work together. It will be such fun,' she said.

Harold said goodbye and drove back to Julia's house.

## Chapter 3

Harold was sitting on Julia's maroon leather Chesterfield, drinking mint tea. He listened to the sounds of the house: the shudder of the fridge kicking in and out of its thermal cycle, the measured ticking of an old-fashioned clock in the hall, a slight creaking of the timbers as they strained against the gusting wind. Everything contributed to a tasteful and calm ambience. His own house, while not being untidy, would have achieved at best a lower second as a design project: its décor was passé, the curtains competed in a jarring fashion with the lampshades, the ornaments were either too big or too small for the positions they occupied. Julia bestowed the effortless taste of her middle-class upbringing upon her possessions and her home, and she had the money to pay for the extra care to detail that translated her ideas into such a pleasing and complete Gestalt. Veronica furnished her house functionally and economically; she had no time for posh crap. Julia created a serene environment; Veronica powered hers with a harsh, raw energy. Harold found it difficult to separate the furniture from the personalities. He glanced at his watch; it was time to start preparing the evening meal for Julia.

Harold ambled into the kitchen and looked around for the apron he used previously. It was nowhere to be seen; all he could find was a French maid's pinafore, hanging on a hook by the sink. He slipped it over his head. After all, there was nobody else to see him and he found it amusing in a titillating sort of way. He peeled a couple of potatoes, halved them, and put them into a pan of salted water to boil. As he went to the fridge to get out the cod fillet he had bought earlier, the doorbell rang. It was Julia, laden with flowers, briefcase and a plastic carrier bag.

'Take these and put them in a vase, there's a darling,' she said, thrusting the flowers into Harold's arms, 'and put the bottles in the wine rack.' She delivered her orders crisply but with a smile playing on her lips. 'Love the pinny, darling.' She leaned into Harold and kissed him on the cheek while she transferred the bag she was carrying to his hand. Then she turned and put her briefcase down. 'What traffic!' she said, walking to the hall table to flip through her mail. 'Bloody circulars!' She marched into the kitchen and threw them into the bin. 'Doesn't anyone write letters any more, Harold?'

'When was the last time you wrote a letter? It's all text messages and emails now,' Harold said. 'Today, the paperless office; tomorrow, the paperless home. That's what Trevor thinks.'

'Does he? Well, why have I just thrown all that paper in the bin?' Julia sat down at the kitchen table. 'Have you got everything sorted out?' she asked.

'As much as can be expected,' said Harold. He put the fish into a large pan, covered it with boiling water, tossed a bay leaf in for good measure and turned the heat down low.

'Did you speak with Veronica?'

'She's been out all day but she says I can see her first thing tomorrow morning. I'll have to see how it goes then. At least she will have had a couple of days to calm down. How about you? Has it been all work?'

'No, not entirely. I did meet with one of my clients but she had just returned from a holiday in South Africa and so we went out for some coffee and she told me all about it. She went to a game farm and had the most amazing adventures in the wilds with rhinos, lions and all those sorts of scary animals that you and I only read about in books,' said Julia.

'That sounds exciting. I'm not very good at holidays.'

'Nor me. I have too many things I like doing at home and I'm not fond of travelling,' agreed Julia.

'I hate the whole thing of airports and long flights and getting bored and waiting for your food and waiting to go to the loo,' said Harold.

'Of course, if you came with me, you would have to look after everything for me,' Julia replied.

'I think I could cope with that. Presumably you would tell me what you wanted me to do and then I could see it as a project to get on with,' Harold mused.

'That's right. You would be a sort of travelling companion for me, as if we were in the Victorian era.'

'I guess if we construed it in that fashion, it would be a completely different experience, don't you think?' said Harold.

'I think that this is something that has distinct possibilities.' Julia paused to look out of the window. She seemed to be weighing something up in her mind. 'So tell me, what are you doing for your holidays this summer?'

'I don't know. Veronica and I hadn't settled on anything. We were just going to drive up to Scotland, I think. That's not going to happen now,' said Harold.

'No, I don't suppose it is,' Julia replied. 'Well, don't despair. You can be my travelling companion and sex slave. We'll go somewhere together. You can drive me and take my bags into the hotel and give me massages and all that sort of thing. Are you good at reading aloud?' Julia asked.

Harold was surprised by the pace at which a tangible plan seemed to be taking shape, but he did not resist the idea. 'I am, actually,' he said, 'I always enjoyed having to read aloud in school, and I read to my daughter every night when she was little.'

'Excellent. I can picture you now, facing me, sitting naked in a velvet chair at the foot of the bed, reading out loud from a classic novel of my choosing.' She threw her hands out wide above her head and laughed. 'There will be a little table by your side upon which will stand a glass of red wine. I can just see you reaching for it and taking a sip, sharpening the tension of a cliff-hanging moment for me. Wonderful! Would you like that, Harold?' She smiled at him with glee.

'I can't quite explain it but I think I would, in a strange sort of way.' Harold was puzzled by how easily he slipped into the role Julia carved out for him. At root, he liked her a lot. She laughed so easily, too. It felt pleasant and seriously irresponsible to put himself into her hands. There was nothing rational about it; he intuitively trusted her.

'I shall organise something. It won't be until later in the summer because I have too much to do for the time being,' she said.

Harold drained both fish and potatoes and mashed them together. He popped in a pinch of cayenne pepper before he seasoned the resulting mix and then made his breadcrumbs. He threw together a green salad, the only concession towards culinary pretentiousness being the addition of a chopped and peeled peach, scattered casually across the lettuce leaves.

Julia was staring at Harold as he prepared the food. 'You do look ridiculous in that outfit,' she said, pointing to his pinafore.

'I thought I looked rather fetching, myself,' said Harold, wiggling his hips.

Julia guffawed with laughter. 'Harold! Is that supposed to be sexy?'

'Indeed,' he said while raising and lowering his eyebrows provocatively, 'did Madame not find it so?'

'It looked to me as though you had got an itch up your bottom, my boy,' she said.

'I don't suppose there's any chance you'd scratch it for me?' he asked.

'Oh, very well,' she said in a bored voice. 'Come here.' Harold walked over to where she sat. 'Turn round, then! I can't scratch it if you are facing me!'

Harold shuffled about. 'Aah! What bliss,' he said, as Julia poked her forefinger into the material of his trousers, somewhere in the region of his bum. 'Don't stop, don't stop! This is ecstasy,' cried Harold. He was getting a fit of the giggles.

'Oh, get on with your cooking, you big buffoon.' Julia smacked him on the bottom as he moved away. Harold winced. On the face of it, they were just fooling around, having an innocent bit of fun. But every now and again, it felt as though a line were tentatively being crossed. He was excited by this. He thought about those times as a kid when horsing around imperceptibly turned into a fight for real. So, too, with Julia.

He patted his fishcakes into shape and put a large frying pan on the stove. He poured in some olive oil and waited for it to heat up. He rolled the fishcakes in flour, beaten egg, and the breadcrumbs. He was very quiet as he did this. From time to time he glanced up to look at Julia. His bottom was smarting slightly. She gazed openly and steadily at him, watching his every move.

Harold turned the fishcakes with a slice as they sizzled in the pan. 'Glass of wine?' he asked.

'Yes, let's have some Beaujolais. Who cares if it goes with fish or not,' she said.

'Your wish is my command,' said Harold, glugging the wine into a couple of glasses. As he leaned across the table to offer Julia one of the glasses, she grabbed his wrist firmly.

'I want you to drink to that with me, Harold. Think of it as an alternative to the marriage vows. It can be our slogan, a ritualistic recognition of our new arrangement.' Her mouth was smiling but her eyes were intense. Once again, Harold wasn't quite sure whether she was joking or not. She was very good. If he backed off, she could retrieve the situation by chiding him for not getting into the spirit of the humour. But something told him that she was serious.

'My wish is your command,' she said, clinking Harold's glass.

'Amen,' said Harold. Given that he was an atheist, the sacrilegious reply also provided him with a way out of embarrassment, should she accuse him of taking the oath too seriously. Harold served the fishcakes, put some dressing on the salad and they sat down to eat their food.

'I might get some counselling work from Anthea,' said Harold.

'That's good. When's that going to happen?' she replied.

'Could be within a few weeks,' said Harold.

'I'll see what I can do on the market research front. There might be something coming up from an old mate of mine called Penny Charlton. She is a lawyer by profession.'

'Great. What's that about?'

'Don't know exactly. Sounded a bit wacky when she mentioned it. A bequest from a market gardener's widow who wanted to commission work into improving the image of green vegetables or something,' Julia said.

'Sounds like a total waste of time and money but if it's her money paying for my time I could be persuaded that it's an excellent notion,' said Harold. 'In fact the more I think of it, the more I am sure I could generate great enthusiasm for such a project.'

'I'm sure you could, Harold,' said Julia.

When Julia finished her meal she pushed the plate away and leaned back in her chair. 'Harold, pour me another glass of wine, there's a good boy.' She said this in such a flirtatious fashion, he was out of his seat almost before the words had left her mouth. 'I'm going up to get changed. I want you to tidy up in here. Then you can sit and read or something. I'll send you a text message if I want you.' With that, she got up and left, pausing only to kiss him lightly on the cheek.

Harold started clearing the dishes. He didn't think about what he was doing; he worked almost automatically. When he had finished, he went into the sitting room and settled himself down on the settee. There was something very odd about what Julia was doing to him. At first he had thought that she was a cold fish. He had to admit that he found her to be beautiful but now he had discovered that she had a great sense of humour, too. Apart from that she seemed to be rather creative, in a sexually perverted sort of way. He couldn't get over how relaxed he felt with her; none of the tension and endless competition he had endured with Veronica. He was curious to see how things would develop between them.

Stretching out on the leather settee, Harold started to read his novel, the story of which was set in the wilds of Northumberland. The hero was driving his lover to a remote holiday cottage and, before long, Harold could feel himself racing through the countryside, as the suspension of disbelief took effect. Then he began to daydream. He couldn't help wondering whether he and Julia might not be on such a journey at some point in the future. A bleep from his mobile phone cut off his reverie prematurely. It was the anticipated text SMS from Julia.

*Harold! Make me a nice cold drink (no alcohol). Then take off your clothes and bring it to me on the stainless steel tray from the kitchen.*

Harold stared at the message. He didn't know what to make of it. A strangeness was creeping into his life. Without much thought, he found himself getting out of the chair and wandering towards the kitchen. Already his mind was moving ahead to solve the problem of what sort of a drink to make Julia. He opened the fridge and let his eyes rove across the contents. There was a large pot of yoghurt and, hidden beneath a flat packet of smoked salmon, a plastic box of fresh raspberries. He ladled about 200 ml of the yoghurt into a bowl and topped it up with slightly less milk. Next, he tossed in a generous handful of raspberries and closed the fridge. He found some honey, stirred in a good spoonful, and gave the resulting mess a good whiz with the hand blender. He checked for taste, poured out a glass, and put it on the tray. Then, as if he were in a hypnotic trance, he took off his clothes and placed them neatly on a chair in the kitchen. He picked up the tray and climbed the stairs.

Julia was lying on the bed, with her back propped against a small mountain of fluffy pillows. She flipped the duvet to one side, thus stopping Harold in his tracks. She was wearing a dark green silk nightdress; the hem just about reached mid-way down her thighs. Her long white legs lay straight out before her, lazily crossed at the ankles. Harold was stunned by her beauty. He noticed that the varnish on her toenails matched the colour of her nightdress.

'What have you brought me, then?' asked Julia.

'A raspberry lassi,' said Harold. 'I hope you like it.'

'Mmm… that sounds delicious.' She took the glass from the tray that Harold had offered up to her, and sipped the drink.

'Oh, this is very good, Harold.' She drank some more. 'I like that very much. The raspberries are not too sharp.'

'I put a little honey in to deal with that.'

'What a good idea. I'm going to enjoy having you around to cook for me, I can see that. Didn't you make one for yourself?'

'Oh, I had some downstairs in the kitchen when I was testing it for taste and texture,' Harold said.

Julia looked at him and then slowly beckoned him with her finger. 'Come on, Harold, hop into bed with me.'

Harold leapt in; he didn't need to be asked twice.

Once in bed, he lay on his back. He was bewildered by the situation. He berated himself for not paying closer attention to the details of the Karma Sutra when he last read it, some twenty years ago. He almost shrank into himself to take up less space in the bed. He was not unhappy, unhinged might be a better word. Gradually, he became aware that Julia was watching him. Cool as a cucumber she sat still, sipping her drink, head inclined towards him. He became more and more self-conscious. Julia leaned across him and placed her glass on the bedside table. As she stretched to put the glass down, her breasts pressed lightly against his face. Just as he was wondering whether to risk his luck and bite a nipple through the satin lingerie, she sprang upon him like a cat out of hell. She shrieked with laughter and spread-eagled herself atop him, with the assurance of a kamikaze gymnast. He felt her fingers mercilessly digging into his ribs. The woman was actually tickling him! And she was bloody well succeeding. He started giggling helplessly and flailing his arms in a half-hearted attempt to defend himself. Suddenly she stopped and lifted herself up astride him to her full height. She had her fingers entwined in his; she held his hands above his head. Slowly she dropped her head down for the kill, looking into his eyes all the time.

'I want you, Harold,' she said, menacingly. Well, of course, this just made Harold laugh even more loudly. But she continued to look him in the eyes and as her head came closer to his, he felt her breath upon his face; he stopped laughing then. Her nose was so close to his yet she did not touch. He could almost feel her lips against his but she roamed around his mouth as if she was looking for the right place to make her incision. Shades of Whitby flitted through his consciousness at that point. He made a half-hearted attempt to raise his hands and flip her onto her back but gave up before his knuckles had barely left the bedlinen.

'Oh! Poor Harold. Did you want to come on top, my darling?'

'Well, you know, hunter gatherers and all that.' Julia shrieked with laughter.

'And I'm a preying mantis, and you'd better start fucking praying, my darling.'

Suddenly Harold felt both the soft and hard parts of Julia's body pressing into his flesh. He was aware of hands taking colossal liberties in all corners of his physical being. Yet his consciousness floated above the fate of penis, anus, and nipples. Julia's jaw worked life into Harold's middle-aged and under-used lips. Her tongue was relentless. At the slightest symptom of withdrawal her hands snaked up his body to grip his chin or his ear, immobilising him in a second. Harold maintained a dignified, if resigned, attitude to the assault across the totality of his erogenous zones. One by one they fell to her insistent probing and nibbling. At last she was done with all the fucking about and honed in on the fucking *per se*. He lay on his back feeling his cock hard and proud in her flesh. Slowly his hips were drawn into the rhythm she entrained with her pelvis. Gradually, grunt by glorious grunt, it became no longer possible to determine exactly who was fucking whom, although the smart money would doubtless have been on Julia being the prime mover. The cries emanating from Julia's mouth, on the infrequent occasions that it became unwelded from Harold's lips, indicated that she had lost all conscious control. Her behaviour appeared to be governed by the *Goddess of Fleshly Thighs*. Harold nearly went weepy at one point when the palms of his hands appeared to be fused to Julia's buttocks. The said buttocks pounded relentlessly as she smashed herself against his groin. He heard Julia start to come. Her lungs powered a discordant wailing that set his teeth on edge. His attempt to hold back was entirely pointless. Capitulating, he joined with Julia in the exultant cacophony of her ecstasy. Afterwards, he clung to her. It was a while before he stopped panting and started to breathe normally. Julia clung to him with equal ferocity until, gradually, they relaxed into the warmth of post-coital cuddling. At this point she started nuzzling him, kissing his ears and stroking his hair. He clasped his arms around her body and held on to her as if for dear life. They stayed like that for what seemed like an age. Eventually, she kissed him and rolled over on to her side. Harold plumped the pillows. They shuffled up the bed to make themselves more comfortable. Harold draped an arm around Julia's shoulders. She settled her head back against his neck. They moved closer together, arms entwining and coupling with intimate ease.

'Harold, I'm going to look after you. You do know that?'

'Yes, I suppose you are.'

'It's alright, you don't understand it. But that doesn't matter.'

'Ok,' he said. And then he drifted into one of the most wonderful sleeps he had ever had. Indeed, that evening would stay with him for the rest of his life. An experience that was paradoxically momentous and ordinary at the same time. After all, a lot of folks make love. His last moment of consciousness was filled with the pressure of her lips upon his mouth as she said 'Goodnight, Harold.' All he said was 'Mmmm'. Not a bad word, all things considered.

Harold woke up to a note on the pillow; Julia had already left for work. He showered and dressed quickly, since there was much he needed to do today. He phoned Veronica to confirm the meeting they had arranged yesterday. Within half an hour he was driving across town towards his house, except he no longer felt sure that he could think of it as 'his' house. He parked and walked up the drive. He went to put the key in the lock, out of habit, but stopped at the last minute and rang the bell. In that simple act he was forced to accept the reality of the situation that he had brought upon his own head.

Veronica opened the door and stood, defiant, chin held high. Her look drilled into him. Although the door was wide open, her frame barred his entrance. She said nothing but looked menacing.

'If you hit me again, Veronica, it will be lawyers, if not the police.' He didn't know where this voice was coming from but maybe something deep inside him was beginning to tell him that there were other ways of being. He was already revising his opinion of how happy he had been in this house, anyway.

'You'd best come in, then.' She looked slightly taken aback. It was as if the right to hound and bully her husband had been stolen from her.

'Can we have a cup of tea in the kitchen or something?' asked Harold, 'I want to talk through some things about Emma and stuff.'

'I can't think that there is much to say but if you must, go through.' Veronica spat her words out. But they signalled a moody sulkiness, rather than the anger that Harold might have expected. They sat on opposite sides of the table, mugs in hand. Harold stared out of the window, into the middle distance.

'I might be the guilty party but our marriage has been nothing short of a sham for many years now,' said Harold. 'That's something that I think we have partly hidden from ourselves and definitely tried to hide from Emma. We both love her in our different ways.' Harold paused to sip his tea. 'And I think that is what has made us keep some semblance of hearth and home together, despite our differences, our hostilities, and even our mutual apathy.'

'Bloody hell, Harold, what's brought all this on?'

'What do you think? It's time for me to take stock; you do what you like.'

'So what's all this got to do with aught?'

'You don't love me anymore. You have despised me for years. I was just a convenient punch bag for you. I helped you let off a bit of steam now and again. The fact that I've gone hurts your ego but not your heart.'

'I don't know about that.'

'Oh, come off it, Veronica! Look me in the eye and tell me that you love me.'

Veronica shuffled her feet and studied her hands.

'I assume you want a separation?' said Harold.

'Divorce more like, you sneaky bastard.'

'What about Emma?' Harold stirred his tea and waited for her reply.

'She's not a little kid anymore. I'm sure the two of you can see each other if you want,' replied Veronica.

'Yes, but how would that work? And what are we going to say to her?'

'I don't want you going and upsetting her.' Veronica pointed her finger at Harold, menacingly. 'Not in her last year at university'.

'So, do you want to tell her we are getting a divorce? Is that what you are saying?'

'Slow down Harold. Do you really think that fancy bitch is going to want you sniffing round her pussy for more than a couple of weeks? I think not. She'll replace you with some young stud before the month is out, you mark my words!' Veronica spat her words out with great disdain.

'Maybe she will and maybe she won't,' said Harold, defensively.

'But don't think I'm going to let you back here as soon as she's done with you. Oh no! You're going to have to beg your way back in here on your bended knees, my lad.'

'But you want me out now?' Harold was having difficulty following Veronica's logic.

'Of course I do, you stupid bastard. How do you think I feel?'

'Well, if I'm out what are we going to tell Emma?'

Veronica paused, looking out of the window. She seemed to be thinking things through. After a while she sucked in her breath through her teeth and said, 'I'll tell you what we'll do. We'll tell her that things have been a bit difficult and you are staying over with your mate Trevor quite a bit. She'll understand that we need to take the pressure off to give us some space to sort ourselves out. But we'll say you'll definitely be home for her when she comes back to visit and that. She's hardly here nowadays, even in the university vacations. You can get your bloody arse over here and sleep in the spare room when she comes home.'

'Won't she kind of see through that? I mean we are not exactly going to be all smiles and cuddles, are we?' Harold looked puzzled.

'Well, we'll just have to make an effort. We'll see how it goes. Once she's left college I think we might as well go for divorce if things are no better, but we'll keep it quiet with her until then. And there's no need to make a song and dance about it with the rest of the family, either.'

Harold thought about this. They had both moved around in their jobs, even before they met one another, and neither of them had any immediate family living within a couple of hundred miles. A certain amount of vagueness on the telephone, coupled with the occasional white lie, should do the trick. He looked at Veronica.

'If that's what you want, I suppose we can give it a try,' Harold said, 'but can she come to stay with me at Julia's sometimes?'

'I've told you, already. I don't want that fucking bitch anywhere near my daughter, do you hear?'

Harold felt resigned to the deal. There would be endless awkwardness and bitter negotiations, but in the end he would be able to come back here sometimes to play happy families. He didn't give a fuck as to how inauthentic that sounded. If it prolonged the sense of togetherness with Emma for just another year, that was all he wanted. She would doubtless realise very early on that things were not as rosy as they could be but she had probably worked that out years ago. They would all be a year older and wiser by the time the full impact of the broken marriage hit them. And by then, Emma would have begun to carve out an independent existence for herself. The next year would provide something of a buffer; it would act as a period of transition. Harold noticed that Veronica was talking again.

'And let me tell you that when I say the spare room, I mean the spare room. If I catch the faintest whiff of your body approaching my room, I won't be answerable for the consequences, you miserable pile of shit.' Veronica paused only briefly to catch breath. 'I will inform you when these weekends will take place for our cosy family get-togethers. If I ever get wind that you are trying to organise the fucking schedule with Emma, the whole bloody charade is off. Do you understand?'

Harold smiled to himself when he realised that she even wanted control over the access schedule.

'I need to pick up a couple of items from upstairs. Is that OK?' he asked.

'Well, don't take all day, Harold. I've got things to do and I want you out before I get started.'

Harold collected some socks and a couple of ties. As he left he called 'Bye' but he didn't wait for her answer. He felt relief as he got into his car and drove away. By and large, it could have been a lot worse.

Harold took the road into the university. By this time of the morning he had missed the queues onto the bridge. In fact he was the only person driving over it and he allowed himself to glance sideways through the steel structure, onto the view of the river below. It was high tide and there were one or two fishing boats at anchor. He brought his gaze back onto the road and took a right down towards the quayside campus. It was later than usual, for him, and he had to drive around the car park twice before he found a space.

He puffed slightly as he climbed the spiral staircase to the fourth floor of the building. It was a light modern building and the whole of the wall facing the river was given over to glass. Each time he circled round a spiral in the stairs, he looked out onto the concrete structure of the atrium, with the river merely a stone's throw beyond. He could see the fishing boats more clearly now. He had once thought about running away to sea on a fishing trawler when he was eighteen but he never did anything about it. Looking back with hindsight, he doubted he would have lasted more than five minutes.

Harold settled himself into his office and checked his watch. He had about twenty minutes before his appointment with the boss and so he decided to grab a coffee from the machine along the corridor. He wasn't sure what he wanted from this meeting. Not that he would be running the agenda. When he was younger, he had read about mid-life crises and how people reach a point where they have to acknowledge they have not achieved all they had set out to do. With the arrogance of youth, he had never believed that this would apply to him. Somehow, he would be different. Now, sipping his coffee, gazing at the river flowing below him, he realised that this simple truth was about to be confirmed to him. In a few minutes he would almost certainly learn that his degrees of freedom to act in that regard had expired. No point in delaying the moment; he went down to see the boss.

'Harold, good of you to come at such short notice. Have a seat and make yourself comfortable. Can I get Angela to bring you some coffee?'

'No thanks, Gavin, I've just had some.'

'Fine. Well, it's good that we can have this little chat. Times are rather uncertain at present, as I'm sure you know. To be honest, Harold, I've been having a right set-to with the Vice-Chancellor and the directors. I mean, I've cut my budget to the bone over these past two years and it's been people like you, Harold, who have had to bear the burden.'

Gavin paused to look Harold in the eye and smiled, briefly, in what Harold presumed was a pretence of heart-felt appreciation. The problem was that Gavin Strong smiled compulsively. He did it when he had good news and he did it when the news was bad. In fact it wasn't so much a smile as a grin. And when you are being told something nasty, it isn't nice to have it served up with a Gavinian grin. Gavin shifted his posture crossing and uncrossing his legs.

'*Here it comes*,' thought Harold.

'What I wanted to talk to you about, Harold, is the crisis that the university is facing at present. I'm sure you will be aware of just how bad things are, from the Vice-Chancellor's letter.'

'You mean how the affairs of the university have been so flagrantly mismanaged that the whole bloody ship is about to sink?' said Harold, smiling back at the Cheshire cat.

'Harold, I don't think it is going to be helpful if we go down that path. I can tell you lots of stuff about decisions that have been made in Europe that are affecting us. We are now in a global market, given the internet and the information technology revolution, and we are competing internationally in a way that we never dreamed would be possible even ten years ago. And then we have all manner of funding problems from our own government. And the introduction of student loans hit our university much harder than it did some others. So let's not get too bogged down on the historical and global pressures that have put us in the current situation.'

Harold shrugged his shoulders and leaned back in his chair waiting for Gavin to go on.

'Harold, I'll come straight to the point. I have to trim staffing by about ten to fifteen per cent. I've looked at the enrolment figures and your group isn't doing too well at the moment. I could cope with the over-staffing if we were in a strong position generally, but we are not.'

'You must be joking! We can't be over-staffed!' said Harold, incredulously.

'I'm afraid it looks that way, Harold. And I've checked my figures with Brian. I don't think anyone expected student recruitment to drop in your area but it has done, Harold, for the second consecutive year.'

Harold was surprised by this. He clearly hadn't been paying attention to what was going on in the dreaded staff meetings. This was one of the negative consequences of being a daydreamer! His line manager, Brian, was so anally retentive he felt sure that the figures would be correct if he had checked them. He kept his mouth shut. No point in arguing when he was on a hiding to nothing.

'Well, Harold, it's not rocket science. If we don't have the bums on seats, we don't have the money coming in to pay the staff. It's as simple as that. And right now there isn't any money coming from anywhere else, in your case. So ten to fifteen per cent of a group of about fifteen staff looks like one or two bodies to lose. I can probably argue my way out of two full staff reductions, and in any case I might be able to persuade someone to go onto a half-time contract. But I think one person has to go.'

Gavin paused. Harold remained silent. Gavin pressed on:

'Harold, it's just that you are the oldest member of staff by about 10 years, at present. Now, I could get rid of one of the youngsters but that would mean compulsory redundancy. But if you were to agree to it, we could try to find you an early retirement deal. What do you say, Harold?'

Harold felt he ought to put up a bit of token resistance:

'What if I don't want to go?'

'Well, as I say, I think I shall be in the position of having to lose one member of staff and I don't think the directorate will want to wait for the next person to hand in their notice, either. Things are getting ugly and there is no enthusiasm for natural wastage by the folk upstairs. And if I'm going to be making somebody redundant, Harold, your name will be in the hat alongside everyone else's. There won't be an early retirement deal for you if your name comes out of that hat, if you see what I mean. I'm not putting any pressure on you, Harold, but I do have to make sure you know where you stand. Basically, I'm saying that I think I can sort some kind of deal out for you if you volunteer to go. If you don't, then there will be no deal and you take your chances along with everyone else.'

Harold sat quietly, staring at his shoes. He could pretend to take his time and think it all through but he knew the moment was ripe for him to go. He couldn't be bothered with lengthy cost-benefit analyses. It was an intuitive decision. He looked over at Gavin.

'Providing I get the normal lump sum I would have got and the details are acceptable, I'll go. But this is merely a provisional indication of my commitment. If the fine print is unacceptable, I reserve the right to change my mind.'

'Of course, Harold. I'm not asking you to agree to a contract that hasn't been drawn up yet. But I will go ahead, then, and I'll try and get a good deal for you.'

'Thank you, Gavin. And you might advise personnel that I'll be getting my union to check it out too.'

'Absolutely.'

'What about the timing of this?' said Harold.

'Well, my reading of the situation is sooner rather than later. I mean, I think you could have a full two months if you wanted it, from the signing of the agreement. We might be able to get it done sooner if you were happy. However, I understand you have a couple of research papers currently submitted to the academic journals?'

'Well, yes. I have to make some revisions to one and the other is currently under review.'

'Yes, I see. How can I put this, Harold? The university would be very pleased to have those publications on its list of current research outputs before you go. I think that would strengthen my hand enormously in terms of getting an early-retirement deal for you.'

Harold laughed. 'Squeeze the last drop of blood out of the stone, hey, Gavin?'

'Oh, Harold! Come on now, you will always have your little joke.'

'Well, apart from squaring off these research papers, I shall need to get some alternative survival strategies in place, you know.'

'Sure, Harold. Well, look, I don't think you have much left by way of teaching right now. I can turn a blind eye if you need to ease out and take a bit of unofficial time off, you know. As far as I am concerned you will be sorting out the requirements of the journal editors on those remaining two papers. You can forget your other duties. And you'll have saved me a very difficult decision by doing this, Harold.'

'Will you be handling the paper work and stuff?'

'I shall to begin with. But once those publications are solid, I think you will probably be better off dealing direct with personnel, Harold. They'll be in touch with you when they are ready to give you a date. But if there is anything I can do to help or expedite things, just give me a call. And best of luck, old man.'

'See you, Gavin.'

Harold walked back to his office, slightly stunned. The deed was done, for better or for worse. He wandered across the quadrangle in the direction of his office but peeled off at the cafeteria by the river for another coffee. He was standing in the queue to pay when he caught sight of Trevor at a table by the window. He put down the right money for the woman on the till and sauntered over to Trevor.

'Hi Trev,' he said

'Harold, my old mate! Sit yourself down.'

Harold settled himself into a chair by the window and looked out at the river.

'So, how are things?'

'Bloody hell, Trev! Where do you want me to fucking start, mate?'

'Not so good, huh?'

'Could be worse, Trev, could be worse. The thing with Veronica has calmed down a bit and it looks like we are into some sort of trial separation. She's going to tell Emma that I'm shacking up with you, by the way.'

'I shall endeavour to be non-committal without actually lying if I run into Emma, if that's what you want.'

'Well, I don't think that bit is going to work, but for the time being it'll keep her happy, I suppose.'

'Right,' said Trevor.

'The thing is, Trev, I've just had a session with the lovely Gavin.'

'Oh, dear. That doesn't sound too good, Harold. What happened?'

'It was all a bit predictable. He made me an offer I couldn't really refuse. Looks like he's going to try and get an early-retirement deal for me from personnel. The message underneath was that if I didn't play ball I'd probably get the bullet anyway, so I might as well go quietly. But he wants me to stay on board to do the revisions to the two research papers I have coming out. The bastards want my outputs accredited to the university.'

'I guess you could fight it, you know?' said Trevor.

'Nah. Haven't got the energy, mate. I think I've had it with this place anyway. I think I'll be able to come back and pick up some casual teaching, though, so if you have anything for me, let me know. I've got to sort things out financially.'

'Funny you should mention that. I was talking to the delectable Prof Picton about some possible staffing problems only yesterday.'

'And what did your boss lady have to say to you?'

'Well, she thinks we are going to be pushed to cover some of the psych stuff on our media and communications course. Could be a bit there for you, Harold.'

'OK. Well, keep me posted. Everything's up in the air right now.' Harold finished his cup of coffee and made to get up. 'I'll be in touch, Trev. Need to have a pint sometime.'

'Give me a call and we can pop down to the Cracked Bell. Take it easy, mate.' Trevor waved goodbye to Harold.


Harold collected his bag from his room and left for Julia's house. He let himself in with the key Julia had given him and started whistling to himself.

'Harold, is that you?' Julia's voice greeted him from the sitting room and he went to investigate.

'I thought you were going to be out all day.'

'Cancellation, my darling. Papers to read. Might as well do that here. How are you? How did things go?'

Harold sat down beside Julia and told her about his chat with Veronica and his interview with Gavin. She listened sympathetically.

'Basically, you got what you wanted from Veronica and what has happened at the university is pretty much what you thought would happen anyway.'

'That's right', said Harold. 'Mind you, I was feeling rather depressed by it all, the other day, in the supermarket.'

'But then you met me, and I became your fairy godmother!' Julia turned round on the settee next to him and jabbed her fingers into his ribs, like greased lightning. Harold started laughing.

'Julia, will you stop tickling me. This is serious stuff I'm talking about. Can we have a little gravitas about the house?'

'No, Harold, we can't. I'm not going to let you get all serious and mopey. You can do that when you go round to Veronica's.' She kissed Harold lightly on the cheek and put her arm around Harold's shoulders. 'What on earth drew you to her in the first place, Harold?'

'Well, hard as this might be to comprehend, it was Veronica who trained her sights on me.'

Julia smacked Harold on the thigh. 'I told you I will not have you talking yourself down in this house, Harold. I do not find it at all surprising that Veronica found you attractive. But why did you find her attractive?'

'She had a great pair of tits and her buttocks were very curvy, too.'

Julia raised her eyebrows in mock horror. 'So, you were very P-C back then? Hey, Harold?'

'Oh, well, of course I would never, back then, have dared put into words a sentence packing such a potently sexist punch as that, but you did ask.'

'Do you like my tits, Harold?'

'I love your tits, Julia.'

'And do you like my bottom, Harold?'

'I worship your bottom, Julia.'

'Excellent. Well, see to it that you continue to do so. I am here to be worshipped, Harold. I need that from you, and I expect it on a continual and daily basis.'

'Wow! I don't think I will find that at all difficult, Julia, but I might need lots of practice.'

Julia laughed. 'Harold, you can have as much practice as you want!'

Harold sat beside Julia, gazing contentedly at the cleavage revealed by her low-cut dress.

'Right now, though, I want you to make me a cup of tea and one for yourself, too, if you like.'

'Fair enough,' said Harold. He trundled off towards the kitchen to make the tea. He actually felt happy.

# Chapter 4

The weeks passed and Harold began to settle into his new life. One morning he had come to Anthea's clinic to write up some case notes for her. He climbed the stairs, easing the burden on his legs by heaving rhythmically on the wooden banister. He had become susceptible to sciatica over the past few years and he felt a familiar twinge of pain run through his bum and down his right leg as he hauled his body onwards and upwards to the therapeutic penthouse. He made a mental note to speak to Julia about her penchant for sexual acrobatics when he got home this evening; he was getting past all that yogic grunting. He shuffled into Anthea's clinic and waved to Mavis, her secretary.

'Hello, Mavis. I think I need to go and lie down after climbing those bloody stairs!'

'I know what you mean, Harold. I'll tell Anth you're here.'

Harold nodded and unlocked his consulting room. The first thing he did was to lie down on the couch that Anthea had provided for the benefit of his clients. He was just thinking about the possibility of nodding off for an early morning nap, when there was a cheerful rap on the door. Anthea sashayed across the floor and perched on the edge of the couch.

'Har-rold. Darling! Would you be a sweetie and see someone for me this morning? I've gone and double-booked myself,' she said.

'I guess I could. I was going to write up those notes for you but they can wait, can't they?' he enquired.

'Oh, yes. Don't worry about them, my darling. I want you to see a Mrs Cunningham; she's a contact I've made from one of my talks at the Fenwell Health Club.'

'It costs an arm and a leg to join that place. I thought about going there when I moved in with Julia but I gave up the idea when I saw the tariff,' Harold said.

'From a hasty perusal of her designer labels, Mrs Cunningham did not appear to be short of money, as far as I could see. She hasn't been to a counsellor before, so she is just coming in to see how she gets on. But if she likes us, she'll probably sign up for the 10-session package at our special rate. So do your best, Harold.'

'Am I not a journeyman of the unconscious?' joked Harold.

'Harold. I'm running a business and I can't pretend that side of things doesn't matter. I'm not asking you to do anything dishonest but I don't want you to sell yourself short. If you think she is getting something out of the session, make sure she knows she can have the full treatment package at our concessionary rate.' Anthea showed a trace of impatience.

'OK. I get the picture. No problem,' said Harold.

Anthea left the room and Harold decided that he probably had time for a quick cup of coffee. He stood at the window and watched the people bustling along the street below, while he sipped his coffee. A red sports car turned into the car park and eased into a bay. The exhaust made a seriously expensive farting noise as the driver killed the engine. Harold made a wager with himself that this would be the affluent Mrs Cunningham. A woman got out and walked towards the entrance of the building. She was wearing pale blue jeans and a pink mohair sweater that left her midrift exposed. Her skin was tan. Harold speculated that she would have achieved her tan on a recent holiday somewhere exotic like the Caribbean. She was by no means fat but, there again, she certainly wasn't coming to him as an anorexic. The word that sprang into Harold's mind was *voluptuous'*. She had not yet crossed his threshold and yet he had already built up an image of who she was and what she was going to be like as a person, merely on the basis of a handful of stereotyped assumptions. He resolved to set all this to one side, like the good counsellor he ought to be. He heard voices in reception. His door opened and the pink sweater eased through the gap.

'Mrs Cunningham? I'm Dr Hake but you can call me Harold, providing you feel comfortable with that.' Harold extended his hand in greeting.

'Hello. Yes, thank you, Harold.' She put her hand in his, making no attempt to squeeze or grasp it. 'I'm Dianne,' she said.

'Do sit down. I'm afraid Anthea is a great one for couches but you don't have to lie on it!' Harold laughed as he indicated where she should sit.

'Oh, I think I should rather like to do that,' she said, as she made herself comfortable. She had a pretty face and wore lipstick to match the colour of her jumper. Her blonde hair looked like it had been cut with an expensive pair of scissors. Altogether, she was definitely a girlie girl, probably in her late twenties. In fact Harold thought that she was the antithesis of Veronica.

'Anthea tells me that you would like to work on your tendency to engage in midnight snacking and that sort of thing. Is that right, Dianne?' Harold enquired.

'Yes, I know I could get down to a size smaller if I could only stop doing that. I'm very good when it comes to eating my main meals, and then I go and blow it by snacking, uncontrollably sometimes,' she said.

'Dianne, before we start it is helpful for me to get a feel for the background picture. Are we talking bulimia nervosa here? Or do you just overindulge from time to time and regret it afterwards?' he said.

'Right. No, fortunately I don't do puking. I have to tell you, Harold, I'm glad I don't because one of my old school-friends got into that and it is not nice, as I am sure you are aware.'

'Indeed not. Well, Diane, that is very helpful for me to know. It means we don't have to worry about anything like that and we can focus on the temptation and snacking episodes in a simple and straightforward fashion.'

'Yes. So how will we do this? How does it work? I mean, I've never been for counselling before. I guess I've got a vague idea,' she said.

'At the moment I'm just setting things up with you. We haven't started counselling proper. It is necessary for us to negotiate roughly what it is that we think might be best for you. Then when we have done the preliminaries, I'll take you through a short session this morning. If you like it and want to take it further, then we will make a series of weekly appointments, perhaps about ten, and each one will last about fifty minutes.' Harold paused for her to respond.

'I remember Anthea explained this at her talk at the health club,' she said.

'Right. There are a range of possibilities open to us and one way of looking at that is for me to sketch out the sorts of roles I might adopt as your counsellor,' Harold said.

'That sounds rather theatrical,' she said.

'Absolutely. When you come for your session with me here, things will be a little different from the way they are in everyday life. Our sessions will sit outside the stream of your normal events. Think of it as an episode shrouded in confidentiality, set apart, with its own conventions and procedures,' Harold said. 'I could be a rather strict parent or teacher figure for you, setting up a series of goals and rules, arranging rewards for good behaviour and even setting up some punishments for any instances of transgression.'

'That sounds a bit scary,' she said.

'On the other hand, I could sit here and listen to you talk. I could be a sounding board, merely reflecting back to you your own thoughts and ideas. In this way, you would find your own solutions.'

'I don't think that would work. I'd just talk for hours and nothing would change.' Diane dismissed Harold's offering of Rogerian, non-directive therapy. Basic behaviour modification had already been ruled out. Harold thought he would cast the Rational Emotive Behavioural Counselling bait to see if he could get a bite.

'Perhaps you need me to challenge your thoughts and ideas more. It sounds to me as though you may be stuck in some highly irrational behaviour patterns. Perhaps your habitual ways of thinking about your body and about food could do with a fundamental make-over.' Harold had adopted this term recently, especially when talking to young women. He secretly preferred the analogy between psychologist and beautician to that between psychologist and doctor. In fact, Harold's favourite inspirational model was that of hairdresser. He had been sorely tempted on more than one occasion to start a therapy session with the enquiry: '*Are you going out tonight, then?*' Harold waited for Diane's reply.

'I don't like the sound of that. I think I'd end up bursting into tears all the time,' she replied.

'One possibility would be hypnotherapy. It would be appropriate if we focussed primarily on the midnight snacking and the trips to the fridge,' Harold said.

'That sounds interesting,' said Diane, 'My friend had that for cigarette smoking.'

'Right. In that case we shall proceed along those lines.' Harold felt that in the end one had to stop chewing over strategy at the meta-level and get on with it.

'I'll go and let Mavis know what we are doing so she knows what's what.'

Harold was very meticulous about these things and he would never embark on such therapeutic adventures were there no Mavis hovering in the vicinity. He felt that what he most wanted, but could not realistically expect to have in this modern age, was a chaperone. Then everyone could relax. No risk of malpractice, enticed or not. In the absence of such old-fashioned conventions, he made do with Mavis in the reception area and trusted in the thinness of the partition walls to facilitate impartial auditory observation. Having done all he could to set his mind at rest, he turned his attention to Diane. 'I want you to lie out on the couch with your head on the arm, as if you were about to take a nap,' he said. Diane swung her shapely legs up and shuffled her fleshy bottom into a comfortable position.

'Is that ok?' she asked.

'That's just fine,' Harold intoned. He took a pencil wand from his pocket. It had a tiny red light at its tip. 'I want you to look at this red light and relax. Just follow it with your eyes and listen to the sound of my voice. You are feeling very relaxed. I want you to follow the light.' Harold moved the beam of the light just above her eyes and watched them as they swung to the left and to the right again, repetitively following the movement of his arm. His own voice began to change as it moved more comfortably into his rich bass register and he, too, relaxed. 'You are starting to feel tired and sleepy, tired and sleepy. Listen only to the sound of my voice. Breathe slowly and deeply, slowly and deeply. Relax, relax.'

Although it was technically true that Harold could see Diane's gorgeous breasts rise and fall beneath him, more or less at his command, this was a fact that barely registered in his consciousness. He had tried to explain this sort of thing to Trevor time and time again but he just would not believe him. Having said that, Harold did not come across as the cold, distant scientist. He threw himself into his therapeutic entanglements with great energy on some occasions.

'Your eyelids are feeling heavy, heavy and tired. They are closing now, closing slowly. You feel warm and comfortable.' Harold could chunter on like this for ages. He never hurried; he could take as long as his client needed. Harold was best at being a 'nice' counsellor, although he could do Mr Nasty if push came to shove. The slightly pudgy Dianne allowed her eyelids to close.

'You are falling backwards in space and time, floating away, feeling so relaxed, so tired, so comfortable. Tired and sleepy.' Harold always camped this bit up slightly, especially when he drawled that tiny word '_so_'. Diane seemed to be falling away into her own world. Harold went through a few more hurdles along the hypnotic highway. She let her arm float up on imaginary balloons, she allowed her elbow to become so set she couldn't bend it and she became unable to pronounce her name when asked to do so. Harold rubbed his hands together and went in for the kill.

'I want you to imagine that you are going downstairs in the middle of the night. You are moving towards the kitchen. And when you are standing in front of the fridge your right-hand index finger will give me a signal.' Harold watched her hand. Sure enough, her finger twitched. 'You want to open the fridge and have a most delicious snack, don't you? Move your finger if you do want that cream cake.' Harold noticed that her finger twitched with negligible delay. He didn't know exactly where she was but he knew she was gagging for it. 'I want you to notice this moment. You are by the fridge and you want to open the door. Signal with your finger if you do want that.' An immediate and somewhat urgent response was communicated. 'Dianne, when you grasp the fridge door and pull it open just a fraction, you will find that you are consumed with the uncontrollable desire to pass wind. Now, as you go to open the fridge wider, you smell the pungency of your own odour. This makes you push the fridge door closed again and the smell vanishes. If you have the smallest desire to open it again, the image of your friends and family holding their noses watching you standing guiltily at the fridge immediately floods your mind. And you will then return quietly to the bedroom, like a good girl, without having eaten a morcel of food.' Harold looked at Diane and wondered if this would be enough to do the trick. He decided to get on with the business. 'Now, listen to me carefully. Unless there is some sort of genuine emergency, you will not go down to the fridge in the middle of the night: not for a naughty snack, not for a nice snack, not even for a piece of smoked salmon. For if you do, you know what will happen.'

When Harold had started on his induction, he hadn't a clue what he was going to say to her. However, he felt moderately pleased with his improvisation. He began to bring her out of the trance. He thought to himself that it might just work and if it didn't he was pretty sure that no major harm would have been done. He suddenly noticed that he was rambling on, unnecessarily about her not being able to recall the details of what she had heard, at a conscious level. He reminded himself that he had a client before him and that he was not giving a seminar at the university. He started to bring her back to the land of the living. 'I shall count from one to ten, and as I count from one to ten you will begin to feel awake and refreshed. You will feel very pleasant, as if you have had a wonderful sleep.' And so it went on until Diane woke up and stretched like a contented cat on the couch.

'Hi. What were you saying, Dr Hake? I think I dropped off a bit there,' said Diane. Harold went through his debriefing bollocks. She seemed very happy. He steered her towards Mavis who did all the cheque-extraction stuff. As far as he was concerned he was done. He was even in time to have lunch with Anthea. Harold felt good.

Harold and Anthea sat in the open, at a table overlooking the river. They had gone to the Dog and Duck for a pub lunch. Harold had scampi and chips, while Anthea wrestled a very large cheese sandwich into her ample mouth.

'So, how's it going with you and Veronica?' she spoke with her mouth full.

'It's mainly communication via the lawyers, I'm afraid,' said Harold.

'Are you into a legal battle or something?' she asked.

'No, not really. I think it will all get sorted fairly amicably. I just meant that we are not really having anything to do with one another. It's all notes through the post, businesslike emails, and tense phone calls. I think because Veronica was so violent the time she kicked me out, she is almost bending over backwards to be very formal and correct about things,' said Harold.

'Maybe there is a bucketload of aggression still seething under the surface, just waiting to come out. You must be careful, darling,' Anthea said.

'Could be. I hope it doesn't erupt again; I had a dreadful black eye last time.'

'What about the highly delightful Emma? How is she taking it all?' Anthea had met Harold's daughter the previous summer.

'She seems to be holding up well. She's left home now and she is very wrapped up in a relationship with a boyfriend at university. I think they are madly in love. His parents are separated and, as far as I can gather, that's worked out not too badly. So it could be a lot worse,' he replied.

'She's still based at Veronica's?'

'She's still got a roomful of stuff there but she and George, her boyfriend, have recently found a new flat and so she is moving most of her things out of Veronica's place, anyway.'

'Right.' Anthea looked at the river. She shifted her body, as if to draw the topic to a close. They both sat in a comfortable silence. Some gulls were squawking overhead. The pub was close to the mouth of the river; there was a smell of salt in the air.

'So, how are you, Anth?' Harold turned to look at his friend. She squirmed slightly under his gaze.

'I don't know, darling. I'm ok. No man about the place right now.' She provided him with her best nervous giggle at that point. 'Wouldn't mind a nice love affair.' Anthea sighed and took another bite from her cheese sandwich. 'Quite apart from that, my main problem is that I seem to waste so much time. I can never make my mind up about things and then when I do, I just procrastinate and dither about.' She laughed defensively at her own admission.

'You need someone to take control of you,' said Harold.

'Don't you think that would be a retrograde step, given the advances of feminism over the past century, Harold?' She said this with a trace of sarcasm in her voice.

'Personally, I don't see that sort of thing as a gender issue,' said Harold.

'Well, you wouldn't, would you; you're a man,' she replied.

'That's irrelevant. Julia tells me what to do all the time. It's great, I don't have to think about things,' he replied.

'From what little you've told me, that's more of a sex thing,' she said.

'I don't deny it. But it could still work if there was no sex,' he said. Anthea looked puzzled.

'I don't see how,' she said.

'Do you want to try it? Perhaps after you have finished work? For an hour or two this evening, maybe?' Harold was being so reasonable he was making it difficult for her to refuse.

'I've finished work for the day, now,' she replied. 'No more appointments for me until tomorrow, my darling boy.' She seemed to enjoy rubbing this in, since Harold knew that she was aware he had to go back to the clinic after lunch.

'Free time!' he exclaimed with a mischievous smile on his face. 'We could try it this afternoon. And then review how things are going by phone and extend the project through the evening, if you feel happy to do that. What do you think?' Harold awaited her reply, expectantly. Anthea screwed her face up, sucking in her breath to help her make up her mind.

'Okaay,' she drawled cautiously, 'what do I have to do?'

'You have to start by giving me up to three alternatives that you might do this afternoon. In other words we are going to address the issue of what you will do with your free time.' He sat back in his seat, munching his scampi, looking pleased with himself.

'Well, there you are, darling. That's exactly my problem. I don't know what I'm going to do with myself. I could go home and do some domestic stuff: laundry, tidy the garden, bring my accounts up to date.' She looked up at the sky, possibly for inspiration.

'We can lump those together as one alternative. Go on,' said Harold.

'I could go to the Cineplex and watch a film. I always think watching a movie in the afternoon is so naughty, don't you darling?'

Harold refused to be drawn into conversation on that topic. 'Anything else?' he said.

'If you absolutely must know, I ought to go and see my great aunt at the nursing home, sometime over this coming week. I haven't been for ages,' she said.

'Fine. This afternoon you will go to the cinema. I want you to sit in a row half-way down the theatre, somewhere near the centre on the right.' Harold clapped his hands and rubbed them together as he said this. He appeared positively gleeful.

'That's very precise,' she said.

'And you must buy a small tub of vanilla ice cream, in the foyer, to take in and eat as you watch the advertisements before the film starts,' he added.

'Really?' She looked puzzled.

'Yes, there is no more to be said. I want you to send me an SMS text message when you have bought your ice cream, before you go into the auditorium, and then another one afterwards when you get home to tell me it all went according to plan,' Harold said.

'Ok, darling, I think I can do that,' she said.

'Oh, you must. That's very important. You have to do exactly as I say, else the whole thing will fall apart and the deal will be off,' he said.

'This feels very odd. You mean I just go off to the cinema now?' she asked.

'Yes. You've done with your sandwich. Drink up and go. You can leave me here to watch the river while I finish up my scampi,' he said.

'And that's it?' she asked, uncertainly.

'Yes; but remember, if all goes well, I want the option to control your evening, too. That will be my bonus for the successful launch of our new relationship. I'll phone you after I get your second text message.' Harold spoke quickly, without smiling. 'Off you go.' He dismissed her with a nod.

'Text you later, then. Bye, darling.' Anthea drummed her fingers nervously as she got up and left the table. She waved as she drove out of the car park.

Harold sat watching a gull that was perched on the mast of a small fishing boat and thought about Anthea. It was strange how easily he had found it to issue his commands to her when so much of his time was spent obeying the orders Julia issued to him. He felt no conflict in this; perhaps he had multiple personalities. He hoped that Anthea would enjoy passing to him control over some of the more mundane aspects of her quotidian life. He saw this as helping a friend. He was convinced that he could make her life less stressful in this regard. Harold got up and walked over to his car. He had to get back to the clinic for one more session. It was a weekly assertiveness training and confidence boosting session for a handful of clients who had enrolled with Anthea at the suggestion of their GP. Today they were due to talk about how they got on with their 'homework' tasks that they had agreed to attempt, last week.

Harold briefly poked his head around the office door to let Mavis know he was about to start, and then walked across to the small-group room. Only two of the four clients had turned up so far. He greeted them and suggested they press ahead with the session, given that they had no idea when or if the others would turn up. He took a seat and beamed at the young woman on his left and the slightly older man sitting in the chair opposite from him.

'I'd like to check out with you how things went with homework assignments this week,' Harold said. Homework consisted in tasks that the clients would agree to do, or things they would work on, over the coming week. Although the term was borrowed from the schoolroom, Harold found that people could relate to it and usually did what was required.

'Mary?'

'Yup, the old bitch came round on Tuesday.' Mary was trying to stand up to her mother-in-law.

'Good. I'm looking forward to hearing all about it,' Harold said. 'Richard?'

'Er.. Yeah.. sort of. I mean I dint do very well. In fact I were crap. You know?'

'That's fine, Richard, don't worry. We'll try and see what went wrong.' Richard was trying to stand up to the people he worked with, especially his boss.

A mobile phone beeped. Harold suddenly realised that it was his.

'Sorry, everyone. Shall we all check that our mobiles are turned off? My fault this time.' Harold smiled sheepishly at the others and, dexterously, managed to take a secret peek at the message on the screen before he switched it off.

*Vanilla tub purchased. About 2 take seat, as instructed. This is fun. c u l8r. Love Anth :-)* Harold smiled.

'Mary, would you like to tell us how you got on?'

'Right. Well. She come in, see, and right off I can see she's got a bit of a strop on. "*This place is a bloody tip*," she says, "*Why don't you get rid of some of them toys*." It's just that I've still got my daughter's tricycle in the hallway, cos there ain't nowhere else to put the bloody thing. And anyway, you never know, I might get lucky and 'ave another. Just because she's a fuckin' dried up prune don't mean my lovin' days are over.'

Richard looked down at the carpet when she said this and seemed decidedly embarrassed. Harold wondered whether Mary would ever get to the point. He was feeling tired. He frequently experienced an energy dip after lunch and today was no exception. He yearned for a quick nap and wished he had not had a pub lunch. He forced himself to concentrate upon the matter in hand.

'Are you telling us about the tricycle incident, Mary, or was it something else that you wanted to share with us this afternoon?' prompted Harold.

'Nah. Well, I'm gettin' to it, Harold, I'm gettin' to it. Now, where was I? See what you've gone and done? You put me off my bleedin' stroke, Harold, that's what you done.'

'She came in and she was in a mood,' Harold said, helpfully.

'Yeah. Right. First thing she's pilin' stuff up off the table and takin' plates into the kitchen and that,' Mary said.

'Right,' said Harold, throwing in a double head-nod as a token of encouragement and a step towards the establishment of good rapport.

'Cos the kitchen's a fuckin' tip. What d'ya expect if I just got home from work,' said Mary.

'Quite so,' said Harold. He hadn't a clue where this was going and didn't feel in control of the situation. He decided to let it run for a bit longer. He imagined Anthea, sat in the cinema eating her ice cream. Indeed, as Mary droned on about her domestic idyll Harold found that in his daydream he had draped his arm over Anthea's shoulders and she was feeding him little spoonfuls of her ice-cream.

'... and this is it, Harold, she's sayin' if I was a good wife, I'd iron her Freddie's shirts for him.' She shrugged in mock horror, as she said this, and paused for effect.

'My Mum irons my shirts,' Richard offered, tentatively.

'Well, that's as may be, Dicky-boy, but I ain't Freddie's fuckin' mother, am I?' said Mary. Richard wilted as she rounded on him; he looked as though he would have preferred to be a coffee table rather than a human being, at that point.

'I think what we need to focus on is how you dealt with this, Mary. Now, last week we were talking about how you usually ended up crying and that often resulted in you giving in to her. You were going to try to keep calm and to keep repeating what you wanted. We called it the 'broken record' technique' Harold said.

'Except we've all got cds now,' volunteered Richard. Harold had found it difficult to grasp the fact that Richard had never possessed either turntable or vinyl records. Harold had introduced the technique to them off the top of his head last week when the session had gone flat and ran out of steam. He had remembered it from some assertiveness workshops he had attended back in the 1970s. He had forgotten that technology had moved on. He would have to talk to Trevor about this. They could have fun inventing a new name for it over a couple of pints in the pub. Harold longed for a pint. He was getting bored.

'Go on, Mary,' said Harold.

'So, I says to her, "*Cynthia, I am not ironing his friggin' shirts,*" and she looks a bit huffy at that. "*And why not? May I ask?*" She's gettin' real riled now. I can see she's gonna start shoutin' soon. So I said, "*It doesn't matter why not. I'm not ironin' Freddie's shirts and that's all there is to it.*" I told her, Harold, just like you said.' She smiled triumphantly at Harold.

'Well done, Mary. Jolly good,' Harold slipped her a long slow head-nod at this point. 'And were you tempted to be drawn into an argument with her?' Harold asked.

'Bloody right I was. I mean, I had some good ammo there, Harold. For starters, I ain't got time. Then what was I doin' goin' to the trouble of buying him easy-care shirts in the first place? I mean, I'm not stupid,' she said.

'Indeed not, Mary. But I think she would have just dragged you into other areas where maybe she felt she could browbeat you. I mean, she could have had a go at you for watching TV or something if you said you hadn't the time,' Harold said, 'but how did it end?'

'I kept on repeatin' that I wasn't goin' to do it and she just said "*Well, if that's how you feel, then. But I'd have thought you would have wanted him to look nice.*" And then I thought I'd just leave it at that. But, and I really surprised myself here, Harold, I then told her I'd brought a spare chocolate cake home from work and she could have it if she wanted it.' Mary leaned towards Harold. 'You remember I told you I worked at the baker's shop, Harold?'

'Yes, indeed, Mary. A mighty temptation for those of us who are prone to put on weight, I should say.'

'Yeah, whaddever, Harold.' Mary rolled her eyes. 'Anyway, she opened the fridge and said she liked the look of it. Then she more or less left me alone for the rest of the evening. Even said my new skirt showed me bum off nicely.'

Harold's eyes drifted to Mary's skirt. He couldn't see her bottom, given that she was sitting in the chair, but he did seem to recall that she had the sort of buttocks that were well-disposed to being shown off to good effect by a skilfully designed skirt. He surreptitiously checked his watch and thought to himself that he had better move things along.

'Good. That seems to have gone well, Mary.' He beamed at her. 'Richard, would you like to tell us how you got on this week?' Harold waited. Getting Richard to start talking was a task equivalent in magnitude to teeth extraction but once he got going he was usually ok. Harold always waited patiently and Mary had now learned not to jump in and fill the silence as the existential void stretched out to infinity. While Richard moved on to the protracted throat-clearing rituals that indicated a sentence might be in the offing, Harold thought ahead to how he would fill out the latter part of the session. He was inclined to try a bit of role-play. Truth be told, he was having some difficulty getting into this session. He would be glad when it was time to go. He knew it was his fault. The clients were fine but he wasn't in the mood. At such times he had to slip firmly into the role of the counsellor and switch on the automatic pilot: it was called being professional. He would hear Richard's story and he would be helpfully constructive in his advice. He would try to enable Richard to withstand the pressures of his dreary workplace. In part, he would do this because that is what he was being paid to do. But if he allowed himself to be swallowed into the moment, he could also convince himself that he had a vocation; that he did it because essentially he was a healer of the human psyche. Of course, he kept very quiet about that; it was not the sort of thing he would admit to Trevor in the pub. With a heave of will he kept himself awake until, with some relief, he found that the session was over.

Harold locked up his room and wandered down the corridor to Mavis' office.

'That's me done for today, Mavis. I'm off home now.'

'Alright for some, Harold.'

'Well, Anth isn't in this afternoon. Why don't you treat yourself to an early night?'

'Oooh! Do you think I could? Do you think Anthea would mind?'

'Mavis, think of all the times you stay late to help out when she's got a rush on. I'm sure she won't mind at all.'

'Well, thank you Harold. I might just do that.'

Harold smiled. 'Bye for now, Mavis.' He found his car and drove back to Fenwell.

## Chapter 5

Harold was in Julia's kitchen, preparing a bastardisation of *coq au vin* for supper, when Anthea's second text message came through:

*Gr8 film. Goin home now. What next Oh Trainer of Mundane Events?*

Harold sent a reply text:

*Shall phone u within the hour. Meanwhile, txt me listing 2 possibilities 4 yr dinner. HH xxx*

Turning his attention to the evening meal, Harold took packets of chicken breasts, thighs and drumsticks out of the fridge. He felt a little guilty about doing this because it was an expensive way to buy chicken; he knew he should have bought a whole one and quartered it but he was sometimes lazy in that regard. He heated up some oil and butter in a large, heavy casserole and tipped in the chicken portions to brown. He also threw in some garlic, button onions and a couple of diced rashers of streaky bacon. Once the chicken appeared to be sealed, he poured in a ladle of warmed brandy, and ignited it. He held his breath as he watched the flames flicker over the meat until they died down. Fortunately, they did not trigger the fire alarm. This was just as well, since he would not have known how to turn it off or reset it if they had. The smell in the kitchen was improving by the minute and it had him salivating like the proverbial Pavlovian dog.

Harold's phone bleeped. Another message had come in from Anthea:

*Mushroom curry; corn on the cob: which one?*

Anthea was a vegetarian. He replied:

*Mushroom curry. Serve in soup plate. Eat with fork only in left hand; put r.h. under bum and sit on it while eating. HH xxx*

Harold didn't see why he shouldn't have some fun while he was about it. He went on to send a second text message:

*Digital photo of yr messy face, prior to cleaning up, 2 b emailed 2 me afterwards :-) HH xxx*

He removed the chicken portions and the onions with a slotted spoon, setting them aside for the time being to rest in a large mound on a plate. Another bleep announced the reply back from Anthea:

Harold smiled; she had not refused, only complained. He opened a bottle of cheap burgundy, added a spoonful of flour to the juices in the pan and, after a while, started to slowly blend in the wine. He never bothered to use additional chicken stock but to compensate he added a little water and threw in a couple of bay leaves with a sprig of thyme. He got the boozy liquid on the boil and left it to reduce somewhat. Meanwhile, he called Anthea.

'Hello. Anthea Partington,' she said.

'Hello, Anth. What are the possibilities for this evening?' said Harold.

'I've still got laundry, garden, and accounts to do sometime. And I suppose I could visit my aunt but that would take two hours, darling, and it would have to be between about 7.00 p.m. and 9.00 p.m.,' she said.

'Here's what you do,' said Harold. 'It's still quite early. When you've finished your meal and taken the photo, set the timer on your watch for 30 minutes and do half an hour in the garden. Then come indoors and get tidied up and changed. Go visit your aunt and then email the messy photo to me when you come back. Then you can have some free time to potter.'

'What about my accounts and laundry?' asked Anthea.

'No time for them tonight. Forget them. We shall get round to that sort of thing tomorrow,' he said.

'Harold, darling, is this going to continue?' she asked.

'Only if you want it to do so,' replied Harold. It was important to him that she regarded her agentic submission as consensual.

'OK,' she replied, 'put like that, I think I might. Although I can't quite understand why I do.'

'Don't worry about it. I want you to send a brief text message to update me on progress as the evening unfolds,' said Harold.

'I will. Can we speak later, on the phone?' Anthea enquired.

'I can't promise anything. It depends what's happening here. Julia has a guest coming over for the evening,' said Harold.

'Right. Well, I shall see you in the morning anyway,' said Anthea.

'Yes, but you can always text me if you need to speak to me. I'll reply as soon as I can.' Harold wanted to reassure his charge that she would not be completely cut off from all communication and support.

'I'd better get back to chopping my mushrooms. Bye!' said Anthea.

'Bye. Have fun.' Harold put the mobile back into his pocket. He turned off the heat beneath the casserole and then put the chicken and onions back into the thickened liquid. He placed the lid on the casserole and left it; it was ready to go in the oven as soon as Julia arrived home. Meanwhile he made a side salad and prepared some dressing. As he finished this he heard the key turn in the front door.

'Do come in, Penny,' said Julia, 'Are you there, Harold?'

'Yes, just coming,' Harold called, as he walked out of the kitchen.

'What a delicious smell,' said Penny Charlton.

'This is my man about the house, Harold,' said Julia, by way of introduction.

'Hello, Harold.' Penny smiled at Harold. He felt as though she was looking him over, checking him out. He was sure Julia had talked to her about him. Perhaps Penny knew some of the more embarrassing details. He felt his face colouring and turned back to the kitchen.

'Come in and sit down, Penny. Harold, we'll have a G&T, I think.' She said this as she invited Penny to share the settee in the sitting room. Harold went over to the drinks cabinet and pulled out the bottle of Bombay Sapphire; he sliced some lemon and made three G&Ts. He gave one glass to Penny, one to Julia and, then, lifting his own he said,

'Cheers'.

Julia waved her hand at Harold in disapproval.

'No, Harold, I don't want you to have one just yet. You must concentrate on the cooking. Maybe I'll let you have a glass of wine with the meal, if you're a good boy. Now, run along. I have some business to discuss with Penny.'

Julia looked away from Harold when she had finished speaking and turned her attention to Penny. Penny sat impassively, as she might have done had she been witness to a mother scolding a naughty child.

For Harold, this was another defining moment. It was a good opportunity to walk away, if he wanted to do so. However, if he did not, then he would have travelled one further step along the path. He was not entirely sure where this path was leading but he was convinced that he was moving beyond the point of no return. Part of him was seething with indignation at the way Julia had treated him. His immediate thought was: '*How dare she?*' However, in a trice resentment gave way to feelings of rebellion: '*I've a good mind to tell her to fuck off and then get the hell out of here.*' What he actually said was, 'I'm sorry, Julia.' The words came out rather stiffly as he rushed out of the room to hide his embarrassment.

'Harold!' Julia called after him, 'Come back here.'

Since Harold had been intent on dealing with his humiliation in the privacy of the kitchen, he was dismayed to find that he had been summoned, once more, to the sitting room. He felt little control over what was happening to him. He turned back. Julia stood up and walked across to meet him. She kissed him on the cheek and gave him a cuddle.

'You'll get used to things, Harold. It's just a bit strange at first,' she said.

'Will I?' asked Harold, a little tearfully.

'Of course you will,' she said. 'Everything's going to turn out just fine.'

'Is it?' Harold had slipped into bi-syllabic sentence mode.

'Yes it will. But you must relax and stop worrying. Stop resisting; accept your fate and you will start to feel much better.' Julia stroked Harold's face. 'Now, run along and cook us a wonderful dinner.' She patted his bottom as he turned to leave. He heard Penny talking to Julia as he walked back to the kitchen:

'Do you want me to go? We can talk business another time if it's not convenient,' said Penny.

'Oh, no. Not unless you want to. Harold will have to get used to doing what he's told in front of my friends,' said Julia. Harold paused before going into the kitchen; he could not stop himself from eavesdropping.

'I hadn't realised that you were so firmly into the D/s lifestyle with Harold,' said Penny.

'I don't think we are in a conventionally stereotypical BDSM scene here, Penny. It is more as though I am bringing together, into a distinctive package or framework, a number of roles that Harold might come to occupy while he is living here with me in my house,' said Julia. 'In a way, you could think of it as if I am providing him with a new persona, given that the old one has become obsolete owing to his redundancy and the breakdown of his marriage. It is early days, but I think it could be good for him.'

'I don't quite follow you, Julia. It sounds interesting. Could you say a little more?' asked Penny.

'He is a paying guest who can't pay. So he is earning his keep by being my domestic help. He is carrying out the old-fashioned roles of cook, butler and lady's maid, all rolled into one. Apart from that I'm having sex with him when I feel like it, for good measure. Mind you, I find him to be an interesting person to be with and so I am hoping that he will also double up as my household and travelling companion, too'

Harold heard Penny burst into laughter at this point. He went into the kitchen and closed the door quietly behind him. At least he knew where he stood now. He had always been interested in obedience, control, action and social roles but hitherto it had been from an academic standpoint. Now he was getting some fascinating real-life practical experience. He felt that he could only play his part with Julia if he could establish and maintain control over Anthea; he needed to experience both sides of the coin. He worried about whether Julia would be happy for him to do this. He would have to ask her, in due course. The dinner was cooking itself. He went into Julia's dining room to lay the table. He set three places but he acknowledged to himself that he would be prepared to eat separately, in the kitchen, were Julia to ask him to do so. He would not make a fuss this time; he was starting to accept his lot.

A bleep from Harold's phone indicated that another text message had arrived for him. He inspected the content: 'Just about to eat my dinner. I hate u darling. Anth xxx.' Harold felt pleased that he was not alone in his plight.

'Harold!' Julia called.

'Coming!' said Harold. He went into the sitting room.

'Penny and I want our dinner now. Is it ready?' said Julia.

'Yes, I can serve within five minutes,' said Harold.

'Good. We have a little more business to attend to so you can serve us in the dining room. You will eat in the kitchen. I may let you come and have coffee with us later. You can pour yourself one glass of red wine and then leave the bottle with us,' said Julia.

'Fine. I think I've got that,' said Harold. He stopped briefly, in the dining room, to remove the third place that he had earlier set and retreated to the kitchen where he started to plate up the *coq au vin* and dress the salad. He served himself a portion and then took everything through to the dining room where Julia and Penny were now seated.

'Thank you Harold,' said Julia. 'I'll tell you when you can come and sit with us.'

Harold went back to the kitchen and started to eat his own meal. He felt relieved not to have to sit with Julia and Penny. He switched on the radio and listened to the news. The chicken tasted wonderful in the sauce.

When he had finished, Harold washed up his own plate and cutlery. He drank the last dregs of wine from his glass and then rinsed it out. Left to his own devices, he would have been half way through the bottle by now. Strangely, he was pleased that he wasn't. The experience of having a clear head at the end of the meal was a fairly novel one for him.

'Harold,' called Julia, 'you can clear away our things and bring in some coffee.'

It didn't take him long to sort everything out. After he had poured the coffee for Julia and Penny he sat with them at the table.

'Julia tells me you are looking for freelance work,' said Penny.

'That's right,' said Harold.

'I may have something for you,' said Penny. 'It's not what you would call a run-of-the-mill project, though.'

'Sounds interesting,' said Harold. 'What is it?'

'I think Julia has explained to you that I sometimes get commissions from a firm of lawyers who handle trusts and bequests, that sort of thing,' said Penny.

'Yes, she mentioned something about vegetables,' said Harold.

'Quite so. Well, I have a client who is trying to execute the wishes of a wealthy deceased widow of a highly successful market gardener,' said Penny.

'Go on,' said Harold.

'There are some very straightforward things like a bequest to establish a sanctuary for cats, and so forth,' she said.

'Can't help with that,' said Harold.

'No, I did not suppose you could!' Penny smiled. 'Anyway, she has then left money for research into genetic modification for the improvement of edible brassicas,' she said.

'Making Brussels sprouts taste like smoked salmon? That sort of thing?' asked Harold.

'Don't be cheeky, Harold!' snapped Julia, a smile playing on her lips.

'Those monies have now been placed with a horticultural research institute,' continued Penny, ignoring Harold's interjection. 'There remains one final thing to be done.'

'What's that?' asked Harold.

'There has to be an action research project commissioned to improve the image of brassicas, such as Brussels sprouts, in the public's eye. This could involve an examination of existing attitudes and the development of a public awareness campaign, possibly involving television advertising, that will effect a change upon the prevailing, negative attitudes.' Penny Charlton paused and looked expectantly at Harold.

'You mean you want me to do some questionnaire design, focus groups, that sort of thing?' said Harold.

'That's precisely what we want, Harold,' said Penny.

'But I couldn't handle the advertising campaign. That would be beyond my area of expertise,' said Harold.

'Yes, I understand that. You won't have to. The project will be given to Julia. She will subcontract the attitude research to you. It's up to her whether she brings you in as a consultant in the design phase of the advertising campaign or not,' said Penny.

Harold asked a few technical questions and raised the issue of money. When he heard what he would be paid by way of a consultancy fee and that all his additional expenses would be charged to the account separately, he nearly fell off his chair.

'I'll be in touch through Julia, then,' said Penny.

'Yes, fine,' said Harold.

'You can clear away these dinner things and then go upstairs and wait for me, Harold,' said Julia, 'I have to give Penny some papers before she goes but I won't be long.'

Harold made his way upstairs. He felt that several more threads connecting him to his previous existence had been cut that evening. Sooner or later he would have to admit that he was becoming a different person. Harold switched on his laptop and checked his email. Anthea had sent him a photo of herself, liberally splashed with curry sauce. She was pulling a face at him that screamed *'I hate you'*, except that if she really did she would never have taken the photo or pulled the face. He sent her a brief reply:

*Anth, lovely pic. Let's meet for coffee tomorrow. I think we should discuss the long-term extension of this project, don't you? I should be at the clinic sometime mid-morning. xxx*

As he was saving the picture of Anth to his hard drive he heard Julia, downstairs, saying goodbye to Penny. He turned off his computer. He wasn't sure what to do. He had no intention of going out, since the evening was wearing on and he felt a little tired. He took off his clothes and slipped into a pair of blue and white striped cotton pyjama bottoms. They were a definite improvement on the pink baby doll number that Julia had given him on his first night at her house. Harold was about to pick up a novel to read when his mobile bleeped to announce the arrival of a text message:

*I want 2 c u Harold; now in my room. Julia*

Harold loved the absurdity of receiving text messages from Julia when they were both within the confines of the house. He walked across to Julia's room and knocked on her door.

'Come in, Harold,' said Julia. She was wearing a white robe and appeared to be packing.

'Are you going somewhere?' asked Harold.

'Yes, I have to go down to London for a meeting tomorrow,' she said. 'I hope to be back by the evening but I'm taking an overnight bag just in case I have to stay in a hotel.'

'Anything interesting?' asked Harold.

'I'm not sure about interesting,' she said as she put a set of purple lace panties into the bag, 'it's about the problems of marketing electric cars.'

'I suppose it might have its own challenges,' said Harold.

'Let's drop the subject, Harold. I want to talk to you about something else.' She zipped her bag shut, as she said this.

'What do you want to talk about?' said Harold.

'I think it is about time we had a chat about you and me and how things are going. That sort of thing.'

'You're not about to kick me out, are you?' asked Harold.

'No! Don't be silly, Harold,' she said, 'You didn't really think I was going to do that did you? Look at me!' She made him turn to face her; he blanched momentarily as she held his gaze.

'No, I didn't,' he said. He sighed. He was trying not to think about how much he had come to like her over the past few weeks. Truth be told, he half-suspected that he was falling in love with her. The idea that this state of affairs might be reciprocated was a notion he could not afford to entertain. He felt very vulnerable still, this close to the dissolution of his marriage with Veronica.

'Do you know one of the things I most like about you living in this house?' she said.

'Being able to ravish my body without regard for the laws of physics?' said Harold, hopefully.

Julia laughingly elbowed him in the ribs. 'Don't be daft,' she said. 'No. I like it when you play your guitar in your bedroom and sing. If I'm sitting in the kitchen or somewhere, I always open the door so that I can hear you better.'

'Do you really?' Harold was genuinely surprised by this. He had become so used to Veronica making derogatory remarks every time he picked up his guitar, that hearing someone say they liked his songs made him feel almost light-headed. 'I'm glad about that because I really like to sing. I always have done.'

'You've got a lovely voice, Harold,' she said, 'Mind you, some of the songs you write are a bit off-the-wall.'

'I don't deny it,' said Harold, smiling at Julia.

'Anyway, I've got a bone to pick with you, Harold.' Julia squared her shoulders and clipped back her hair more tightly.

'What about?' said Harold, apprehensively.

'I think you know what about,' she said, cupping his face in her hands.

'I don't! Honestly,' said Harold, uttering a white lie.

'So, you think I was pleased about the little scene you made tonight? And all because you weren't allowed to have a G&T?' she said.

'I didn't exactly make a scene,' said Harold.

'Perhaps not. But you came very near to stamping your foot,' she said, 'and that won't do.'

Harold could not deny this. He sat quietly. He would have liked to have got up and run to his room but he didn't. He stayed: unmoving and sullen. He wasn't stupid. He knew that what Julia was talking about was both trivial and serious at the same time. Any sane person could dismiss his situation as preposterous. He was a grown man and he should not be letting Julia dictate when and where he can or cannot have a drink. Or should he? This was the crux of the matter. They were evolving a relationship at the point where the abnormal or the deviant met the predictably conventional. They had not joined a bondage club and they did not meet with like-minded couples for sessions involving reciprocal spanking. They had purchased neither whips nor restraining devices. Yet it would not be difficult for them to obtain the necessary apparatus to support extreme fetishistic and sadomasochistic activities, either from internet sources or easily accessible high street sex shops. In one sense, Harold thought that it would be much easier if they did join a BDSM dungeon club; he was aware of two or three within the region. However, that did not seem to be wholly appropriate for them. Somehow their dominance and submission had to be ordered within the humdrum activities of their mundane vanilla existence.

'It's difficult not to let normal behaviour creep into what looks like a normal situation,' said Harold.

'I know. Except we don't have a 'normal' situation, do we?' Julia replied.

'No, we don't. Although it's not that abnormal, either.'

'I like that,' said Julia. 'It's kind of slippery.'

'I think I would call it fuzzy,' Harold said.

There was a lot about this situation that Harold liked and he didn't care if other people might think him a trifle odd or even pervy on that account. After all, a certain calculated eccentricity was woven into the fabric of his self-concept and had become thoroughly ingrained over the years.

'Fuzzy or not, it's what we've got,' she said.

'Yes, it is. I find it hard to admit to myself that I am doing what I am doing, sometimes. I think the fact that Penny was here unnerved me. I mean, for most of the time nobody else is here to see what we do. It felt that she was witnessing not just the fact that I cooked for you but that you had control over me at a very fundamental level,' Harold said.

'I know. It is all about control, Harold. When you think about it, the more insignificant the act that you do for me, the less likely can there be any reason for doing it other than the fact that I have told you to do it. So pointless, trivial actions enable you to demonstrate your obedience to me,' she said. 'Strangely, it is the quotidian stuff that reveals the asymmetrical dynamic of our relationship better than anything else.'

'Put like that, I have to agree,' said Harold. 'Only we haven't really talked about it quite as explicitly as this before. It has always been left slightly below the surface,' he said.

'That's right, Harold. I go along with that, but we may have to be more explicit from now on. We are not choosing the conventional way of conducting our relationship. We can't take a set of societal rules from off the peg; we have to work it out for ourselves. It is a bespoke relationship, and we are the tailors, so to speak,' she said.

'And you think we can do that?' he asked.

'Oh, I know we can. We are two imaginative and intelligent people, even if our taste in sexual relationships is mildly deviant.' She smiled when she said this.

'It isn't compared to what a lot of people are up to nowadays. You only have to look at some of the alternative lifestyle sites on the internet to realise that we are rank amateurs in that domain,' replied Harold.

'Quite possibly. But I don't want to become ensnared in a formal group. We would then become caught up with their sets of rules. It would be a bit like joining a church or a religious cult,' she said.

'So what are we going to do?' Harold asked.

'What are we going to do?' Julia mimicked him and then burst out laughing. She caught him completely off balance and wrestled him over her knee. 'I'm going to spank your bottom, Harold,' she said.

'No, please, help. Anything but that.' Despite the mutual giggling, Harold's pyjamas were pulled down and Julia's hand did land crisply on his buttocks.

'Ouch!' wailed Harold.

'Keep still! It'll be worse if you wriggle about,' she said, as she brought her hand down again and again. At first Harold merely shrieked and protested as part of the game. Now it was starting to hurt and the situation was complicated by the fact that between each slap Julia had begun to allow her hand to stroke his buttocks. He felt her fingers wander down between his legs. She started to fondle his balls and stroke his penis. He was becoming very aroused.

'I think you like me doing this, Harold. There is certainly something stirring down there,' she said. 'Are you going to be a good boy in future, Harold?' she rubbed his reddened bottom as she said this.

'Yes, Julia. Anything you say, Julia. Can we get into bed now?' Harold asked. He had pressing biological needs to satisfy; his self-esteem and status as a person could be put on the back burner, under the circumstances.

'Alright, Harold. You can get into bed with me now,' she said. They clambered beneath the duvet. Julia was sat up slightly against the pillows. She cradled Harold's head to her bosom.

'I feel very close to you Harold,' she said.

'I think I might be falling in love with you, Julia,' said Harold. He was trembling slightly.

'I'm glad about that, Harold,' she said, 'I think we are good for each other. We go well together in all sorts of ways.'

'Do you think that?' he said, 'I thought you might really be a bit fed up with me.'

'No, Harold. I think I've always wanted something like this but I just couldn't find the right person to do it with,' she said.

'So, do you think I'm the right person?' said Harold.

'Harold, you're fishing for compliments,' she said.

'I think I need the odd one or two. It hasn't been great lately,' he said.

'Come on. Don't feel sorry for yourself. You've got me to boss you about now. It'll be just fine.' Julia slid down the bed slightly and Harold moved to kiss her. A lot of hugging and stroking and ear-nibbling went on, during the course of which Harold's penis found its way into Julia's incredibly moist vagina.

'I want you to be on top tonight, Harold, and be very gentle.' This was the last thing Julia said to Harold before she lost the power of speech. Her vocalisations became more uninhibited, as Harold's humming grunts became more melodious. When she bit his lip savagely, he took it as permission to abandon 'gentle'. It wasn't long before they exploded towards their separate, although not simultaneous, orgasms. Harold noticed that there was a lot of post-climactic kissing and stroking going on. He felt that this was a true indicator of their emotional progress. But, inevitably, the moment was broken by the necessities of hygiene and trips to the bathroom.

'By the way, Penny's coming round first thing in the morning to give you the paperwork on the *Brassica* brief. Will you be here? If not, you'd better phone her,' said Julia.

'I'm not going to the clinic until later in the morning. That'll be ok,' replied Harold.

'Good. You know I'm off early for the train,' she said.

'Yes, you mentioned it. Electric cars,' he said.

'I'll leave you in bed. Pity Penny is coming or you could have slept in a bit.'

'Good heavens. You are getting a bit generous there, Julia,' said Harold.

'I have to look after you. I can give you days off and little treats from time to time, if I want to.' She smiled at him.

'Julia?'

'Yes?'

'I started sorting out Anthea's day-to-day activities, this afternoon. She didn't know whether to go to the cinema or go to visit her aunt and I told her to do the cinema. That sort of thing.' Harold paused.

'Go on,' said Julia.

'Well, is it ok if I do that for her. I mean, sort of take control,' he asked.

'Yes, I think that would be ok, Harold, so long as there is no sex involved,' she replied.

'No, we're mates. I'm just sorting her out as a friend and colleague.'

'Keep me informed of your progress. You'll do that?'

'Sure. I'll mention that to Anth tomorrow. I want to get it sorted out a bit more formally with her,' he said.

'Right,' said Julia. 'Harold, I'm going to sleep now.' She kissed him on the cheek and snuggled down. He felt her breath upon his face. For the first time since Veronica had kicked him out, he began to think that happiness was not a total impossibility.

## Chapter 6

'Penny, come in.' Harold ushered Penny into the house and closed the front door. 'Julia has already left for London.'

'Yes, I thought she might. She did say she was going early. I assume she told you I was bringing the Brassica brief to you?'

Harold looked at Penny, trying to do so without appearing to stare. She was wearing a black pinstripe jacket over a starched white shirt. Her pencil skirt was dark grey, as were her tights. Her high-heeled shoes were elegantly strappy.

'Yes, I was expecting you,' said Harold.

He paid more attention to her face than he had done last evening. Her eyes were brown and very deep; her cheek-bones pronounced. She had a lean body and quick, efficient movements.

'Good. There's not a lot to be said about the matter, actually. It's all a bit odd, if you ask me,' said Penny, flashing a micro-smile in his direction. Harold settled Penny onto the settee in the sitting room and then offered to make tea or coffee.

'A cup of tea would be wonderful,' said Penny. When Harold brought the tea in, Penny opened her briefcase and pulled out a folder.

'The benefactor established a society called SABRE, before she died,' Penny said. She raised her eyebrows at Harold, inviting him to share in her disbelief.

'Whatever does that stand for?' His question was laced with a touch of incredulity. He could not stop himself from trying to provide Penny with whatever response he thought she wanted; he had always been a pushover in front of a beautiful woman.

'Society for the Advancement of Brassica Research & Enlightenment,' she said.

'You're joking!' said Harold, taking the opportunity to cement his position.

'I'm afraid not. I told you it was all a bit weird. Do you know much about brassicas?'

As she asked this question, she turned towards Harold and rested her hand momentarily upon his knee. He began to panic. He was being inconsistent. He had only recently acknowledged that he was falling in love with Julia and yet he did not appear to be doing much to stop Penny flirting with him. He was sure that that was what she was doing.

'No. I know very little about brassicas,' said Harold, trying to deepen the register of his voice in order to sound more professional. He also turned up the dial for received pronunciation in the way that middle-class English people can do when under pressure. He felt that this would lend an air of formality to the situation. Penny smiled at him.

'Apart from the obvious Brussels sprouts, the category of brassicas includes cauliflower and cabbage, as well as the two root vegetables: turnip and swede.'

'I'm surprised that turnip and swede are in the category.'

'Me too,' Penny agreed.

Harold felt the hand upon his thigh, this time a little more firmly.

'And I expect you know that mustard and rape are, too?' She looked him in the eye when she pronounced 'rape'.

'What is it you want me to do?' asked Harold.

Penny started leafing through her papers. 'I'll jot something down for you, Harold'. She patted her jacket pockets. 'Have you got a pen I could borrow? I seem to have come out without one.'

'No problem. I'll get one from upstairs,' said Harold. As soon as he reached his room he shut the door and dialled Julia on his mobile phone. She answered immediately and he got straight to the point of his call.

'Julia, I don't know what to do. Penny's being very flirty with me.' He sounded wretched.

'Calm down, Harold. You don't have to go along with it. Why are you telling me, anyway?' asked Julia.

'I don't know. I think I feel guilty,' said Harold.

'Sounds like an insurance policy to me. You tell me all about it on the phone, then you can go downstairs and let Penny give you a blow job and you don't have to worry because you have already alerted me. Is that it?' Harold was taken aback by Julia's response.

'No! Well, I don't think so. Oh, maybe. I don't know.' Harold was starting to wail.

'Harold, don't be so neurotic. Penny's always flirty. She won't do anything, I bet you,' said Julia.

'How do you know?' asked Harold.

'I just don't think she will. Why don't you flirt back a bit and see what happens,' she said.

'I can't believe you said that to me,' said Harold, 'Veronica would have killed me if she thought I was flirting with someone else.'

'I'm not Veronica, Harold. I know you won't do anything serious. I trust you,' she said.

'Do you?' said Harold.

'Yes, I do. So give her a bit of her own medicine. She's only playing with you. She's like a cat with a mouse when it comes to men like you,' Julia said.

'I'd better get back. She's waiting downstairs,' he said.

'Go to it, Harold. And I want you to give me a full report when I get home.' Julia's phone went dead. Harold grabbed a pen and went back downstairs.

'Harold! Did you have to go out and buy me one?' said Penny, smiling.

'No, sorry about the delay. Only Julia phoned me on my mobile.' He lied about the fact that it was he who had initiated the call, and walked over to give her the pen. He sat down beside her on the settee. She wrote several bullet points down on the pad, tore off the sheet and handed it to Harold.

'There, I have written down the main points for you, Harold'.

She slipped her hand onto his thigh again and very slowly began to squeeze it, almost imperceptibly. Harold responded with a display of excess gratitude.

'Oh, that will be incredibly helpful! Thank you so much, Penny.' As he said this he slipped his hand around her shoulders and hugged her, drawing her over to lean firmly into his body. He felt her withdraw her hand from his thigh. She shifted her posture, restoring their previous distance, and adopted a pose that indicated that she was about to be serious. Harold smiled to himself, while acknowledging the correctness of Julia's prediction. He retracted his arm and leaned away from her, placing his shoulders more squarely into his corner of the settee.

'The problem with this assignment is that the instructions are rather vague. As far as I can make out from the papers relating to SABRE, you must conduct some survey work to assess the attitudes of the general public towards brassicas, with regard to their culinary use and taste. Then, partly based upon your data, Julia will be asked to co-ordinate an advertising campaign that will be targeted on one geographical region and the results will be compared with those obtained from a similar region that is equivalent in most respects but has not been subjected to the campaign,' she said.

'Sounds like you want a straightforward comparison with a control group,' said Harold.

'Yes, that's the idea,' she replied.

'So, I suppose you want a couple of questionnaire assessments for each region group: one before the campaign and one after?' said Harold.

'If you think that is what is necessary, that will be fine,' she said.

'I'll sort something out along those lines, then.'

Although Harold thought the idea was a bit ridiculous, he kept his consultancy fee firmly to the forefront of his mind.

'Does SABRE still exist, even though the founder member is now deceased?' asked Harold.

'Yes, it does,' Penny replied. 'She established a membership of about 100 before she died and money has been set aside for occasional meetings. Often the gatherings are arranged around the fringes of horticultural events or flower shows,' she said.

'Absolutely amazing,' said Harold.

'I think you would need to submit the audiotape and transcript of any focus group or interviews or whatever, as evidence that you had complied with the requirements. And we shall also require a copy of your analysis of the questionnaire data.'

'Sounds straightforward enough' said Harold. 'What do I do about the money side of things?'

'We can pay any expenses you incur as they arise. You must keep receipts. However, your fee will only be paid when the job is finished,' Penny said.

'The sooner I start the better,' said Harold. 'It would be good if I could knock together a focus group more or less straightaway.'

'I have a contact, locally, who can put together things like that at very short notice. She keeps a list of names and contact numbers and they form a panel. A lot of them are single parents who have flexible working hours and need the money. How many do you want?'

'I could get away with five or six, at the pilot stage, I think. After all, it's not exactly rocket science, is it?' he said. She pulled out her mobile phone.

'I'll call my contact. When could you do it?' she asked.

'I've got the afternoon free, if that's not too soon. Other than that it could be Friday morning,' he said.

'I'll try for this afternoon. We'll be paying them a good fee. She should be able to sort something out for us. Where shall I tell her to send them?' she said.

'Anthea's clinic at 2.00 this afternoon or it had better be 10.00 if it's Friday morning,' he said. 'You know where the clinic is, don't you?'

Penny nodded. Harold went upstairs to pack a few items into his briefcase while Penny was on the phone. When Harold came back, Penny was in the process of hanging up. She turned to Harold.

'The organiser of the panel is called Angela and I've given her your mobile number. She'll call you later this morning to say if it's going to be this afternoon or Friday. She thinks this afternoon will probably be OK.'

Harold thanked Penny for sorting things out for him. He escorted her to the door, putting his arm around the small of her waist. She resisted slightly but he drew her closer and kissed her on the cheek. He felt her place her hand firmly on his chest and push to extricate herself from his grasp. She did smile at him, though, as she did this.

'Gotta go, Harold. Keep in touch. Call me to tell me how you are getting on,' she said.

'Will do, Penny.' He shut the door and took a few moments to tidy up before driving downtown. He phoned Anthea and arranged to meet her for coffee in a cafe by the river, not far from the clinic.

'Har-rold.' Anthea moved into her greetings ritual. Harold used all his skill to speed it up but she seemed determined not to be shortchanged in this regard. He gave in and allowed time to be suspended for the duration of their hug.

'Anth! Good to see you,' said Harold.

'I'll get the coffee. Usual?'

'Yes, please.'

While Anthea went to the self-service counter, Harold found them a seat by the window where they could watch the river go by. A large crane was unloading containers from the hold of a ship moored on the opposite bank. Harold thought of it as a gratuitous piece of performance art. He could imagine someone writing up a project proposal and submitting it to a funding council: '*Maritime caesarean at ship's birth*'. He would develop an argument for construing the containers as babies, the cranes as doctors, and the tugs as midwives. He supposed that the artist could make a minimal contribution by painting the containers or something of that nature. And a special viewing platform could be built on this side of the river. A bunch of aesthetically-tuned spectators could easily transform this mercantile activity into artistic performance, with minimal (if not minimalist) disruption. Anthea returned with the coffee.

'That was horrid of you to make me take a photo like that, last night,' she said.

'Yes, it was, wasn't it.' He laughed; Anthea giggled.

'Seriously, Harold, I sort of enjoyed our little game, apart from eating my dinner,' she said.

'Do you want to carry on?' he asked. She sat quietly, watching a cormorant perch on a buoy that was bobbing gently in the river. Harold waited patiently for her reply.

'Yes.' She was unsmiling when she said this and looked at him. 'Do you think that's odd?'

'Not at all, Anth, although many people would think so, of course,' he replied.

'I guess they would,' said Anthea.

'But it's not really any of their business, is it?' said Harold.

'No, that's true,' she agreed.

'Julia does much the same for me. You do know that?' Harold asked.

'Yes, you hinted that she did and I suppose I guessed that was how things were from the occasional remarks you've made. But will this work? Can you be one thing to Julia and another to me?'

'I think so. It feels perfectly ok so far. To be honest, we won't know until we try. It sounds as though you want to try,' said Harold.

'Yes, why not? There is nothing to lose, really,' she said.

'You can think of it as a real-life experiment. If it works, then that's just fine. However, you can walk away from it at any time. You just have to tell me you want to stop,' he said.

'Put like that, it sounds harmless enough,' she said.

'Indeed. Think of something simple, something easy that we can focus on for a start. Just to see how things go,' said Harold.

'You mean something I can't make my mind up about?' said Anthea.

'Yes, that's right. Think through your day, perhaps. Maybe something will stand out. So, you get out of bed. Then what...'

'Get out of bed, take a shower, open the wardrobe, and that's it, Harold.' She smiled excitedly at him: 'I can never decide what to wear.'

'Your first task, then, is to email me an inventory of your clothes. It needn't be absolutely everything you own. But I want a selection under all major categories,' he said.

'What do you mean, darling: shoes, tops, trousers, skirts, sweaters, and so on?' she said.

'That's right. And don't forget your underwear, Anth,' he said.

'Might have known you would have wanted to know about that,' she giggled.

'Absolutely. I shall then email you with instructions as to what you should wear. I shall probably give you some optional slots. Don't want to reduce your opportunity to dither completely,' he added.

'I shall go through my things tonight. I've been meaning to have a clear-out for months. I ought to be getting back now, though. I have a client coming, in about twenty minutes.'

'Right. I have to check with Mavis to see if Penny has fixed up a focus group for me this afternoon'.

'Oh, yes. What's that about?' she said.

'Brassicas. Don't ask!' They made their way out of the café, back to the clinic.

'Hello, Mavis!' Harold said, when they arrived.

'Message for you, Harold. Four people will be coming at 2.00 p.m.'

'OK. And that's from Penny Charlton?' he enquired.

'The person who phoned was Angela, on Penny Charlton's behalf,' she said. Harold went to his office and busied himself with some light paperwork. He then popped out to the newsagents' shop to get a paper, When he came back, Mavis motioned him into her office.

'Harold, there's only three of them turned up,' she said.

'I told Penny I ought to have six or seven.'

'Well, this Angela woman told me to expect four but only three are here.' Mavis shrugged her shoulders.

'Damn. That's cutting it a bit fine.' Harold wondered if he could get away with presenting a session with three people as a pilot study for the questionnaire rather than dressing it up as a focus group. The last thing he wanted was to waste time sorting out a second group and he couldn't very well turn this lot away now, not after they had made the effort to come. He decided that he would cut corners and make do.

'I'll take what I've got. Can you phone Angela back and tell her about the no-shows. Tell her to assume I don't want any more unless I get back to her,' Harold said.

'Right, I'll do that now. I've put the visitors in the room you use for the group work,' she said.

Harold nodded and made his way down the corridor to meet the group.

'Good afternoon. Thank you for coming at such short notice.' Harold beamed round the room. He was not entirely sure how best to introduce his topic. Given that he found it difficult to take things seriously, he could hardly blame them if they did too.

'I am conducting this session on behalf of my client who requires some market research information concerning brassicas.' The man with the crew-cut hair squared his shoulders and leaned forwards slightly.

'If you will pardon the interruption, Dr. Hake, I shall need to be brought up to speed on brassicas. Is it something to do with vegetables?'

Harold glanced down at the list of names Mavis had scrawled on the front of his folder in pencil, as he turned to answer the question.

'Yes, indeed, Mr. ... Copplestone.'

'Please call me James, that will be fine.'

'Then James it is. And, likewise, I hope you will all feel comfortable with addressing me as Harold.'

The two women nodded. Harold made a bet with himself that the one wearing a green sweater stretched taught across a rather splendid pair of breasts would be Tracy; the stick insect with a string of pearls around her neck would have to be Victoria.

'All will be revealed shortly, James. I just need to ask you to sign this attendance sheet, otherwise your fees will not get processed in the office.' He handed the sheet Mavis had given him to the green sweater. A smile flickered over his face as he watched her sign in the box against Tracy White's name. He took the form from her and handed it to the stick insect.

'If I could have yours, too, Victoria. Then perhaps you could pass it over to James for me.'

'Yes, Dr. Hake. Oh! I mean Harold. I forgot!' Victoria giggled and blushed a little. Harold found her girlishness rather endearing.

'Were you at that margarine tasting, last month?' Tracy asked Victoria.

'Yes, I was. I thought I recognised you,' replied Victoria.

'You women should get organised. I got myself booked onto a discussion about tourism in Scotland, and we had a freebie whiskey tasting,' said James.

'Alright for some! How did you manage that, you lucky sod?' Tracy flashed her eyes at James. At this point Harold cleared his throat noisily in an attempt to regain control of the situation.

'I think we should make a start. I'll just turn on this recorder. Are you all happy with that?' All three nodded their assent. This confirmed to Harold that they were veterans at this sort of caper.

'As I said a moment ago, we are here to talk about brassicas.'

'I'm with James on this one, Harold. I haven't a clue what they are.' Tracy smiled at James. At the edge of his peripheral vision, Harold noted a surreptitious wink from James in Tracy's direction.

'Brassicas are a family of vegetables. Although they do include some root vegetables, we are going to focus on the greens today. So, we can think about cabbage and Brussels sprouts, possibly cauliflower. That is what we mean by brassicas.'

'That sounds a bit on the dull side, Harold,' said James. The women nodded in agreement.

'Are we going to talk about this for the full hour?' asked Victoria.

'That's the idea. Didn't Angela tell you?' Harold inquired.

'Not really. She just said it was a focus group about food or something,' said James.

'That's right!' said Tracy. 'I hate cabbage.'

'Maybe that's as good a place as any to start. Tell us why you hate cabbage, Tracy,' said Harold. He glanced at his watch and noted the time, thinking that he could let the negative stuff run on for ten or fifteen minutes.

'School dinners,' said Tracy.

'I always found the colour of cabbage so unappealing,' added Victoria.

'In what way?' prompted Harold.

'Either it lay in a pale, almost translucent lump of yellowish glumph or it had the intense green of a pile of seaweed,' Victoria replied.

'I hated that green stuff,' agreed Tracy.

'Not a nice apple green like your sweater, Tracy,' said Victoria.

'So, you are not too keen on the colour. How about you?' said Harold, turning to James.

'As far as I am concerned, cabbage is green. End of story,' replied James. 'However, get me onto the smell of the stuff and we could be here all day!'

'I can remember that smell on a Sunday morning at my gran's house,' said Victoria.

'Didn't Kris Kristopherson do a song about that?' asked James, innocently.

'Yeah! Like I wrote '*A hard day's night*' for the *Beatles*,' said Tracy.

'I can hear him singing it in my head now. *Sunday morning, stinking on down.* Yes?' James smirked.

'You've got it all wrong, James. You are thinking of the hit by *Prefab Sprouts*,' countered Tracy.

Harold began to worry that things were getting completely out of control. He didn't like the idea of this exchange appearing in the transcript of the proceedings but no transcript meant no fee. He attempted to bring the group back to order.

'Does anybody have a good word to say about cabbage?'

'I rather like it shredded in salads,' said Victoria.

'I quite like nibbling it in the kitchen if it's that white cabbage,' said Tracy.

'Right. The sort that comes in a tightly wound ball?' replied Victoria.

James yawned and looked out of the window. Harold decided to move things on.

'What about sprouts? Would anybody like to share their thoughts on sprouts?' asked Harold.

'Christmas dinner. That's alright,' said Victoria.

'Yes. Wouldn't be Christmas without them, would it?' replied Tracy.

Harold began to doodle on his notepad. His squiggles began to look a bit like a father Christmas. He became so bored, he hardly noticed what was being said as the women rambled on about the best way to cook turkeys and roast potatoes. He was brought back into the here and now when James mentioned his name.

'I think Harold's drifted off into another world, Tracy,' said James. Harold put down his pencil and shuffled his papers together. He glanced at his watch and figured he could just about get away with an early finish.

'I think I have all that I need. We can call a halt to the proceedings, if you are agreeable. I shall tell the office to make sure you are credited with the full hour in terms of your fees, of course.' This triggered a speedy exit for all three of the participants. The sound of their goodbyes echoed down the corridor as he switched off his digital recorder. After he cleared the paperwork with Mavis, he put a call through to Trevor to see if he fancied a late afternoon pint. The upshot of this found him sitting in the corner of the bar at the Cracked Bell, half an hour later. He savoured the first sip of his pint and had no sooner licked the froth from his lips when his friend arrived. Trevor waved, ordered a pint, and then ambled over to Harold's table. He settled himself into the opposite seat.

'How did it go, mate?' asked Trevor.

'Bloody Brussels sprouts, you mean?'

'What else?' said Trevor.

'I nearly fell to sleep at one point,' said Harold.

'I can imagine. Still, did you get anything useful?'

'Bugger all, mate.'

'Well, what did you expect? I'll introduce you to the amazing Prof. Picton. Maybe we can sort out that teaching I mentioned the other week.'

'I wish you would. Picton's your boss, Felicity, right?'

'The very same. Want another pint?'

'Thought you'd never ask.' Trevor went to the bar for the pints.

'What are you going to do for Penny, then?' inquired Trevor, as he put the full pints down on the table.

'I dunno. It's a bit tricky. I have to submit stuff before I can get my hands on the fee.'

'That sounds fair enough, though, Harold.'

'I guess so. The trouble is that only three people turned up, and what they talked about did not amount to very much. There should have been six of them. What I ended up with hardly counts as a focus group.'

'You've still got some questionnaire stuff to do.'

'Yes, I do. I'll have to cobble together something quite soon.' Harold grimaced.

'So what on earth will you do for that?'

'Oh, I dunno. *"Brussels sprouts make you fart. - AGREE/DISAGREE"*   Something like that, I suppose.'

'What happens if you think farting is good when you are on your own at home, but bad if you happen to be in bed with someone?' asked Trevor.

'You're buggered,' said Harold.

'What about "*Coming out as a Brussels sprouts eater will increase my sex appeal*"? That might hot it up a bit,' offered Trevor.

'I don't think I will even bother to write that one down on the back of my beer mat,' said Harold.

'Do you really have to do all this stuff, Harold? Can't you just take it easy and get into your retirement?'

'The thing is, Trev, there is no way Veronica is going to subsidize me. I have to take whatever I can get to improve the cash flow. I've got to build up these sorts of contacts.'

'So this redundancy business is really going to have an impact on your day-to-day life?' asked Trevor.

'It looks that way, mate.'

'Still, it can't be all bad, Harold. Someone was telling me this Penny person is rather gorgeous.'

'She's very attractive. And I'll tell you something else: she's a bit flirty!'

'Really! So, what's she been up to?'

'She put her hand on my knee this morning. Anyway, Trev, are you not going out with What's-Her-Face anymore?' asked Harold.

'Nope. She gave me the elbow. Fucking bitch!' Despite his choice of words, Trevor did not seem particularly bothered about this.

'I think you and Anth might make a nice pair,' said Harold.

'Oh, yes. I can just see me chanting mantras, covered in massage oil. She's all incense, brown rice and sandals, is that one. Not exactly my cup of tea, Harold.'

'Well, probably not your cup of herbal infusion, to be more accurate.'

'I've gotta go, Harold. I can't do this afternoon drinking thing anymore. If I had another pint now, I'd be here till closing time.'

'Could be a worse fate than that, Trev. Sure I can't tempt you?'

'No thanks, mate. I'm off. Look after yourself.'

After Trevor left the pub, Harold finished his pint and headed for Julia's house. When he got home, he half-heartedly made a start on the design for the questionnaire. However, his eyes began to droop and he ended up taking an afternoon nap, instead. He awoke feeling refreshed and glad that he had not had the third pint during the session in the pub. He made himself a ham sandwich with plenty of English mustard and washed it down with a glass of milk. Finally, he turned his attention to the question of Brussels sprouts. He was half-way into his sixth draft question when his mobile phone rang.

'Harold Hake.'

'It's Veronica, Harold.'

'Oh. What can I do for you, Veronica?'

'It's Emma. She is coming home this weekend.'

'Is she bringing the boyfriend?'

'No, she is just coming herself. She arrives Saturday lunchtime. She will stay overnight then she is off again by train early Sunday afternoon. She says she needs to get some papers and stuff from home.'

'So, do you think I should come round?'

'Well, yes. I mean it is what we agreed Harold. I'll make up the bed in the spare room for you.'

'And you don't think Emma will think that's a bit strange?'

'I'll tell her you haven't been sleeping well and it was disturbing me. I don't know. I'll make something bloody up!'

'I'll come over mid-afternoon, in time for a cup of tea.'

'You'd better bring your guitar over or it will seem a bit odd, not hearing your bloody voice droning out all over the house with those bloody songs you insist on singing all the bloody time.'

'Veronica, I am not going to get into any musical arguments with you. We are way past that. I shall come in order to slow the apparent pace of disengagement for Emma's sake.'

'What do you mean by that?'

'I mean, I think it will be ok for Emma to get a hint that things are not totally rosy between us, on this visit. Then when we divorce, after she graduates, it will not come as a complete bombshell.'

'That sounds a bit on the Machiavellian side for you, Harold!'

'I shall only come, though, if you give me your word that you will be moderately civil to me while I am there.'

'I suppose so, providing you don't expect me to laugh at your stupid jokes.'

'I would not even expect you to get them. Goodbye, Veronica. I shall see you on Saturday afternoon.'


When Julia got home from work, Harold poured her a gin and tonic and sat down for a chat with her in the sitting room.

'I got a call from Veronica today.'

'Oh, and what was that about?' asked Julia.

Harold then explained that he would be away overnight at the weekend, and would see his daughter, briefly.

'In that case, I will probably go for a sleep-over with Penny. We have some business to discuss and then we can share a bottle of wine and watch a chick-flick DVD. Lovely!'

Harold laughed. 'I would be happy to watch a chick-flick with you any time, Julia.'

'Oh, how interesting. So, are you are bit of a girlie boy at heart, Harold?'

'I don't like violent, tense, aggressive films. I have always preferred romcoms.'

'It's alright, Harold. Your secret is safe with me.' Julia laughed.

When Saturday arrived, Harold shoved a few bits and pieces into his backpack, put his guitar into its case, and drove across the city to his old house. He used his key to open the door, since he figured Emma would regard it as weird were he to ring the bell. He quickly went through the hall and straight upstairs to the spare room, where he unpacked his things and took his guitar out of the case. He went down stairs and found Veronica in the kitchen.

'Hi! Have you heard anything from Emma?'

'She's on her way. The train got in and she said she would get the bus. I told her you had just popped out or you could have picked her up in the car. She seemed ok about that.'

'Right. So, we put on the *Happy Families* face, I guess,' said Harold.

'Well, we can do our best. It's for Emma, Harold, not for me.'

'I know. I shall behave myself.'

The bell rang and Veronica answered the door. Emma struggled out of her large backpack and leaned into her mother's hug.

'Hi, Mum.' She looked over Veronica's shoulder and trilled her fingers at Harold. 'Hi, Dad.'

'Come on in. I'll put the kettle on,' said Veronica.

Harold grabbed the backpack. 'I'll put this up in your room, Emma.' He lifted it off the floor. 'This weighs a ton! I thought you were coming to get stuff not to deposit more clutter.'

'Don't go on at me when I've just got in the door, Dad. I'll sort things out later, anyway. I might put some of that stuff out for recycling.'

The kettle boiled and they all took mugs of tea into the sitting room. Emma sat on the sofa with Harold, while Veronica took one of the armchairs. Emma leaned over and gave her dad a peck on the cheek.

'Missed you Dad. How are you coping with redundancy?'

'Oh, not too badly, you know. And I am thinking of it as an early retirement. It feels better when you look at it like that.'

'My Dad - retired! It makes me feel quite old.' She laughed.

'We are all getting a bit older, including you, Emma. You will be finished at university soon.'

'I know. How scary is that!'

'What about your boyfriend, Emma. Is this his last year, too?' asked Veronica.

'Mum, he's called George. I've told you that hundreds of times.'

'Yes, but we haven't met him yet. When are you going to bring him to see us?'

'I don't know. Soon. It has been difficult for him. His Dad was in hospital and he has been going home to visit him and help his Mum out and that.'

'So it's quite serious, then. Your relationship with George?' asked Harold.

'Dad, we have been sharing a flat most of this year!'

'Oh, I know. I just wondered whether the sound of wedding bells might be in the air.'

'Look, we don't even know where we will be working. Who knows, we might get jobs at opposite ends of the country. Anyway, can we talk about something else, please.'

'Have you got any photos to show us?' asked Veronica.

'Oh, yes. I've got loads on my tablet. I'll go and get it. I think I'll just wash my hands and face while I'm about it'

'OK, pet. No hurry,' said Veronica.

Harold and Veronica sat in silence, sipping their mugs of tea while Emma moved around upstairs. Eventually she returned, carrying her tablet.

'So, what's with the spare room. You usually have a lot of old junk in there.'

'Ah! Well, your father has had a bit of trouble with his sciatica. He's been having some sleepless nights and that has disturbed me. I need a good night's rest because school just gets more and more hectic, nowadays. So he has been sleeping in the spare room for a while. Just until the school term is over.'

'Oh, ok. So do you want to have a look at my pics?'

Veronica came to sit on the arm of the settee so she could look over Emma's shoulder.

'Most of these are from the time when me and George went up to Scotland for a long weekend.'

'I remember you said something about that in one of your emails,' said Harold.

'One of George's friends has an aunt who rents out a little cottage up near Loch Lomond and we went up with him and his girlfriend.'

Harold and Veronica looked at the photos. Occasionally, Harold made the odd comment. Veronica then collected the mugs and took them out to the kitchen.

'What do you want to do this evening? Did you want to go out for a meal?' asked Harold.

'I'm not sure. I might phone Alison and see if she wants to meet up for a quick drink a bit later. We could get a take-out. I fancy some Chinese.'

'That would be easy enough to arrange.' Harold smiled.

'I think I will go and do a bit of unpacking now.'

'OK. See you in a little while,' said Harold.

Veronica switched on the TV and began channel hopping. Harold leafed through the paper. The phone started to ring. Harold commenced the complex physiological series of integrated balancing acts across a range of unstable equilibria that allowed him to get up from the settee and pick up the receiver.

'Harold Hake.' He turned to project his voice in the direction of the partly open door. 'Emma, it's for you,' he shouted.

'I'll take it up here, Dad.' Harold trundled up the stairs and passed the phone to Emma. He then returned to the sitting room and sat down.

'What's the bet she'll be off out for the evening with her friends?'

'Well, you can't blame her for that, and it'll make things a bit easier for us,' replied Veronica.

'If she does, I'll probably pop out for a pint with Trevor.'

'Suits me. I've got some TV I want to watch, anyway.'

The sound of footsteps on the stairs heralded Emma's entrance.

'The gang's going to meet up for a pizza. I'm just going to get ready and then I'm going round to Daisy's house and we'll go into the city and have a drink together before we meet up with everyone else.'

'OK. Well, have fun!' Harold nodded and gave Emma a smile.

'It reminds me of how I was when I used to go home for a weekend visit. My mum hardly saw anything of me.' Harold said to Veronica. He then dialled Trevor's number on the phone.

'Trevor, it's Harold.... Yes, Emma's here but she is off out. I suppose you couldn't be tempted by a pint at the Cracked Bell? ... Oh, excellent. I'll see you soon, then.'

In no time at all Emma was back downstairs. She hurriedly said her goodbyes and slammed the front door shut as she went out.

Harold turned to Veronica. 'I think I'll be off, too. I'll be back by eleven. That should be well before Emma gets in. In fact I am pretty sure I'll be in bed before then.'

'Well, you can rest assured I won't be pining for you, Harold,' said Veronica, acidly.

Harold bought himself a pint of beer and settled onto a comfortable bench seat in the corner alcove. He glanced out of the window and watched a few of the passers-by. Then he pulled out the paperback he was reading from his coat pocket. He had chosen the book partly for its size, massively preferring ease of pocketing to quality of writing when deciding on what to read. He had more or less finished the current chapter when Trevor turned up. He went to the bar and bought his friend a pint.

'So, has Emma arrived?'

'Yes, she has. Well, she dumped her stuff, got changed and buggered off out again to see her friend Daisy. Then they are going to meet up with a bunch of their old school friends and have a pizza. So, it sounds like a night out for her. I'm not really surprised, but we won't be seeing much of her.'

'How is *Happy Families* going?' Trevor asked.

'Well, the way things have turned out, we might just get away with it. I mean, there is not going to be any time for chat today and so no opportunity for me and Veronica to give the game away, as it were. And if I know Emma, she will have a stonking hangover tomorrow morning and won't be in the mood for an in-depth chat with her ageing parents!'

'So, I suppose that is good news, on balance?'

'Yes, I guess so. In the sense that no news is good news, in this context.'

'You don't sound so sure?'

'No, I'm not sure that I like it. I can see the sense of the strategy but I don't like deceiving Emma.'

'Well, I doubt if she tells you everything about her boyfriends and so forth,' replied Trevor.

'No, indeed. I'm sure she doesn't. And we are not really ready to speak to her about our impending divorce. We are still some way away from that point.'

'So, Veronica isn't pressing for a speedy resolution?'

'No. I was rather surprised about that. She seems really keen to keep things pending until Emma gets her degree and gets settled down into some kind of career.'

'And are you alright with that?'

'I suppose so. I mean things seem to be working out quite well between Julia and me.' Harold gave Trevor a wink and a grin.

'Dirty old sod!' Trevor chuckled and took a swig of his beer.

'I think I would have preferred to tell Emma about Julia. I would like them to meet at some point.'

'But you said Veronica was adamant that they should not?'

'That's right. But I don't think she has the right to enforce that decision.'

'Well, given the damage she inflicted on you the last time you got into a fight with her, I should invest in some protective head gear.'

Harold laughed. 'Maybe I'll enrol in some kick-boxing classes.'

Trevor hooted derisively. 'The only thing you will be kicking any time soon is the bucket, my old mate!'

'Thanks, friend. I don't need to be reminded of that, truism that it undoubtedly is.'

Harold pumped Trevor for the latest university gossip. He listened attentively and laughed at the appropriate moments. There were one or two things that he didn't understand fully. New initiatives for which he was no longer briefed. No university papers were circulated to him any more. Eventually, they parted and bid each other farewell. On his way back home he reflected how quickly he was slipping out of the loop. In a few more years, he would no longer know all the staff, as people left and were replaced by new faces. He called out as he let himself in the house. Veronica, sat glued to the TV, ignored him. He went upstairs and settled in for the night. At some point he became aware of the front door slamming as Emma got back from her night of revelry.

Harold had set the alarm on his watch and this is what woke him on Sunday morning. He had kept some bathroom basics at Veronica's so he freshened himself up and got dressed. He went downstairs and put some coffee on to brew. It was not long before Veronica joined him in the kitchen, as he was munching some toast and marmalade.

'Emma got back late, then?'

'I think so. She wasn't home when I got back and you were watching TV, anyway.'

'I went to bed after my programme finished.'

'She won't have much time, by the time she's slept off whatever it was she got up to last night,' said Harold.

'Maybe that is not such a bad thing. We don't really want to get into any stuff on this visit, do we.' Veronica stated this as a fact, not a question.

Harold shrugged his shoulders and took another bite of toast. 'I'll go and get a Sunday paper.'

'Better pick up a carton of milk while you're at it. We are a bit short.'

'Will do.' Harold went out to the corner shop. He returned a few minutes later, put the milk in the fridge and dumped the paper on the kitchen table. Veronica flicked throught the various sections and lifted out the colour supplement. Harold took the news section. They sat in silence, reading.

'I've got a couple of things to prepare for lessons tomorow at school. I think I'll go and get started on that.' Varonica went to the room at the back of the house that Harold used to use as a study. She had taken this over for herself as an area where she could dump project materials and piles of stuff to mark. Eventually Emma came down, carrying her back pack which she put in the hall, near to the front door.

'Hello, my dear. How are you feeling this morning?' asked Harold.

'A bit grotty, truth be told. You know - night out with the girls!'

'Ah! Paying for your pleasure.' Harold smiled, knowingly.

'Look, I've picked up the books and notes that I needed for my exam revision. I think I'll get a slightly earlier train back.'

'Well, it has been brief, but delightful to see you again, Emma, as always,' Harold said.

Emma smiled. 'Nice of you to say so, Dad. I don't suppose you could give me a lift to the station, could you? Only my back pack is quite heavy with the books and that.'

'Yes, of course. Did you want to go now?'

'Well, I think I could catch that train if we left more or less straightaway. I can get a snack on the train.'

'I'll take your bag out to the car. You had better say goodbye to your mother.'

Harold stowed the backpack in the boot of his car. Emma got into the passenger seat beside him. Veronica stood on the step to wave her off. Harold pulled away from the kerb and headed for the station.

'Dad, that stuff about you having sciatica. It didn't sound very convincing. I mean, you haven't been hobbling about much or groaning and moaning the way you like to, at the first opportunity.'

'Me? Groan and moan! I never heard of anything so ridiculous.'

'Come on, Dad. Be serious. What's happening?'

'Well, your mother and I haven't been getting on quite as well as we might, just lately.'

'Oh. Are you going to be alright?'

'I expect so. I don't think there is anything for you to worry about. It will probably blow over. You need to concentrate on your exams. Don't worry about us.'

'If you say so.' Emma frowned.

'Here we are, and I think I can see a nice little parking space at the dropping off point,' Harold said. He parked the car and opened up the boot. He helped Emma get her arms into the backpack and gave her a hug. They said their farewells. Harold drove back to Varonica's house.

'I'm just going to pick up a couple of things I need, then I'm off.'

'Did she get her train?' asked Veronica.

'I would imagine so. We got there with ten minutes to spare,' Harold replied.

'OK. I have to get this lesson plan finished. Bye Harold.' Veronica disappeared into her study room. Harold got his stuff and let himself out. He drove back to Julia's house. As he let himself in the front door, he suddenly realised that this was where his home was now. He was surprised that a feeling as fundamental as that could alter so categorically in such a short space of time.

## Chapter 7

All morning Harold worked on the Brassica project. By mid-afternoon he decided to pop round to Penny's house to talk over what he had completed so far. Although it was a fair distance, he chose to walk. Many of the houses he passed in Fenwell boasted closed-circuit TV cameras and burglar alarms. The hedges were clipped, the lawns were mowed, and the borders appeared to be devoid of weeds. Harold felt sure that, in the main, this was the handiwork of professional gardeners: a truck pulls up, the lad unloads the mower while the boss goes to work with pruning-shears and hoe. From time to time Harold passed a house with a more eccentric profusion of planting; he assumed this to be attributable to the idiosyncrasy of a green-fingered owner.

Harold found Penny Charlton's house and walked past the shiny black BMW parked in the drive. He rang the door-bell.

'Harold, come in,' said Penny, standing aside from the open door.

'Thanks. How are you?' He asked the question more from nervousness than out of genuine curiosity.

'I'm fine.' Penny led the way through the tastefully decorated hallway to her sitting room. 'You're quick off the mark. I didn't expect anything quite so soon.'

'It's just a first draft, I'm afraid, and the focus group wasn't brilliant.'

'That's OK. What was wrong with the group?'

'Maybe I rushed it. Only three people turned up and I didn't get too much out of them,' Harold said.

'Let's see how it goes. If necessary you can scrap the one you did today and hold another one later next week.'

'That would be alright? I mean you will have to pay the three who did turn up today.'

'Let me worry about the expenses, Harold. You just do your market research thing.' She put her hand to his cheek as she said this. Harold had a sinking feeling. She was wearing a chocolate and blue striped rugby shirt and he felt the cotton sleeve brush against his jaw. She was smiling as if to reassure him. Her eyes seemed to be saying that he had no need to feel anxious. She had a generous mouth, and her lips parted to reveal white, even teeth that sparkled as she spoke.

Harold smiled back at Penny. His world had been turned upside down. He supposed that things would settle eventually but there was no guarantee whatsoever that he would end up with a replica of the situation he was in before he got that bloody letter from the university. There would be no Veronica. He could not afford to buy another house. Perhaps he was being too hard on himself. Maybe all he could do was to try to live fully within the present moment and take what happened to him with good grace. He had begun to abandon any attempt to be able to predict the future course of his life. How could he think that he was beginning to fall in love with Julia when here he was feeling flustered and excited by the penetrating presence of Penny Charlton? There again, why not? Why could he not serve Julia to the best of his ability while coming also before Penny when she called for him? When Harold made love to Julia he betrayed Veronica's trust. Yet at that point he was still shackled to Veronica by the expectation of monogamy. His behaviour amounted to a transgression for which Veronica could have extracted a retribution. But she could only mete out a punishment and she could only exact her revenge if she continued to hold him in the bonds of monogamy. By casting him out violently, with hate and vitriol, she effectively cut him loose. He was no longer bound; he was a free man. It was as though he had been transported to a new life-world with an entirely different psychological and social landscape. He was lost and confused. That was what was so comforting about his relationship with Julia; he had traded some of his freedom for security and discipline. Harold was used to living in bad faith. He could not possibly cope with the full force of an existentialist's freedom. Julia protected him from the harshness of being alive; she shielded him from the constant barrage of quotidian choice. At least he could limp from one day to the next under her protective aura. Now, looking into Penny's dark brown eyes, he felt no protection. He felt exposed and raw. He was uncomfortably alive. He couldn't go back and he didn't know how to go forward. His games with Julia and Anthea helped to dampen the anxiety that springs from becoming entangled with more than one person at once, not that his relationship with Anthea was sexual. The roles they adopted provided little more than a protective shell within which to hide away from the slings and arrows of fortune. Harold knew he was in a bad way when he had to shore up his thought processes with Shakespearean tropes. He began to tremble slightly.

'Harold, are you alright?' Penny asked.

'I don't really know whether I am or not, to be honest.'

'We don't have to talk about the stupid questionnaire, Harold. It isn't important and it will wait until another time.' She said this not without a degree of tenderness and that caught Harold by surprise.

'I'm sorry Penny.' By this time Harold was sniffing, if not actually crying. He felt that, at any moment, he would be overcome with waves of uncontrollable emotion. He stoically tried to stop it happening.

'This isn't very professional of me, is it? I'm supposed to be starting my new career as a freelance consultant and here I am falling apart. Perhaps I'd better go.' He snuffled through his apology.

'You'll do no such thing, Harold.' Penny sat beside him and gave him a cuddle. This calmed Harold slightly.

'Thank you, Penny. You are so kind.' He stayed still, hugging Penny for comfort.

'I know that you split up from your wife earlier this summer. Maybe this is all part of the reaction.'

'I guess so.' Harold began to regain his self-composure.

'I'll go and make us both a cup of tea. OK?' Harold nodded.

Penny briefly returned to put a small box of tissues on the coffee table before vanishing into the kitchen to make the tea. Harold felt foolish. He took a tissue and blew his nose. He dabbed the moisture from his eyes. At least he had stopped short of breaking down into a flood of tears, and he was thankful for that. He began to calm down. He had no urge to impress Penny; she would have to take him as he was. Penny returned with the mugs of tea.

'Here you are, Harold. Get some tea down you.'

'This has turned out differently to what I thought might happen,' said Harold.

'And what did you think would happen, Harold?' she said.

'I guess I thought we would flirt and maybe fool around a little. I mean, I thought the signals were there when you came round to see me. Julia said you were a flirt and that I ought to flirt back. I lied, by the way. She didn't phone me. I phoned her. I panicked.'

'I know, Harold, I talked to Julia later in the day. I am a bit of a flirt. I know about your relationship with Julia but I felt sure she wouldn't mind. I thought it might be fun to lead you on a bit,' she said.

'Well, precisely a bit of fun was what was in my mind when I came round here, if I am honest. But fun it isn't. I'm sorry.'

'Stop apologising. So, what brought all that on, do you think?'

'When your hand touched my cheek, it felt tender. And when I looked into your eyes, it felt good. It wasn't like before. You seem really nice. You're meant to be this shallow, hard-assed business type who drives a BMW and I'm supposed to despise you and feel vaguely superior in an intellectual, non-materialist fashion.'

'Jesus! You really are a little shit, Harold. I'm not as bad as that. I just work in the hostile world of business. It's not all cosy libraries and tutorials, Harold. It's not like your world.'

'Yes. Anyway, the university isn't my world anymore.'

'I know.'

'Would you have taken me to bed? If I hadn't had an attack of the tearful trembles? What would you have done to me?'

'I wouldn't have let you make love to me because I would want to be sure that was alright with Julia. But I'm quite sure that Julia would be very relaxed if I told her I'd snogged you.'

'Do you think that snogging is an essentially adolescent activity?'

'Not at all. People often snog at office parties,' she said.

Harold's mind went back to Veronica and the geography teacher. He felt that there had been nothing terribly wrong with that. However, what he had done with Julia, the day Veronica kicked him out, was an entirely different matter. He brought his mind back to the conversation in hand, and shifted himself into seminar tutor mode.

'Do you think it is the exchange of bodily fluids that is the key factor?' he asked.

'Whatever do you mean?' replied Penny.

'With snogging it's just saliva. With fucking we are talking semen.'

'But that's not true if the man uses a condom. Is it? Anyway, Harold, stop it. Enough!' And with that, she leaned over and kissed him on the mouth. 'Now, are you satisfied? We have kissed. It was nice. But that's all we are going to do,' said Penny.

'That was great. We don't get to do it again, then?'

'We might do it again sometime, Harold, but not now.'

The doorbell chimed. Penny got up. 'I'll be right back,' she said.

'Hi! I'm on my way home from the station and I've brought you a present from London.' It was Julia.

'That's sweet of you. Come on in,' said Penny.

'It's not much. A packet of green tea from that shop in Neil's Yard. You know? Near Covent Garden?'

'Well, thank you. I shall enjoy that. Harold's here.'

'Is he? I hope he's been behaving himself!' said Julia. 'I can give him a lift home if you like.'

'I thought you went by train.'

'Yes, I did. But I put the car in the long-stay park by the station,' said Julia.

'Right. Now, Harold had a bit of a turn earlier on. He got a bit upset and weepy.'

Harold cringed slightly when Penny gave him away. He had been able to hear every word of the conversation, given that the two women were stood merely a few paces down the hall from where he was sitting.

'Has he? I wonder what that's all about,' said Julia.

'You'd better come in and ask him,' replied Penny. They both entered the sitting room and stood looking at Harold. Julia came across the room and sat down on one side of him.

'What's up, Harold? Are you OK?' she said.

'I think so,' he replied. He let Julia take his hand in hers. Penny came over and sat down on the other side. She took hold of his remaining hand. He felt very strange.

'I gave him a kiss just before you came, in fact, and he seems to be a bit better now.' Penny spoke across Harold, directly to Julia and then turned to him.

'Isn't that right, Harold?' said Penny.

'Guess so,' he replied, sullenly.

Julia inspected his face. 'He does look a bit peaky,' she said.

'Yes, he does. Perhaps he could do with an early night,' Penny replied.

They continued in this vein for a few more minutes talking about Harold but seldom to him. He felt invisible. The thing that shocked him was that he did nothing to challenge the situation. He let their talk wash over him. With every turn in their conversational flow he became increasingly distant from the status of adulthood. They were regressing him to childhood and there was no need for him to do a thing. As they effectively stripped him of his powers, they simultaneously eased his burden of responsibility. It occurred to him that this was what he needed: to be divested of his old duties, obligations and liabilities. He intuited that this was how he could become anaesthetised against the pain of choice that had been forced upon him in his new, chaotic, shattered life-world. Loss of stature and a diminution in terms of personhood was a small price to pay. He squeezed both their hands and stilled their conversation. Turning to Julia, he said:

'Can we go home now?'

'Yes, Harold, we can.' They all rose, one by one. Julia and Penny said their goodbyes. Then Penny turned to Harold and gave him a hug. She kissed him lightly on the cheek. This was not the kiss that she had given him earlier. This kiss belonged to the ritual of leave-taking; the other one could easily have taken its place as the opening gambit in love-making. As Julia bundled Harold into the car, he wondered if there might be a treatise lurking somewhere in all this, if only he could unravel it. Julia put her foot down on the accelerator and the car screeched off in the direction of home.

Harold took a shower and emerged with unexpected fragrance; Julia's shower gel did not come from a discount shop. He took his time getting dressed, picking a nice shirt to go with his mustard needle chord trousers. He was going to Craig Melcheter's retirement party. At home, Harold had been given the equivalent of a free-time pass by Julia, so when he was dressed he went downstairs and poured himself a gin and tonic. He phoned for a taxi and, by the time he had drunk the G & T, the taxi had arrived.

Harold paid off the cab and walked into the pub. He could see his mate Trevor, propping up the bar next to Graham Antrobus.

'Harold! Just in time. I'm getting a round in. What do you want?' Graham asked Harold.

'Make mine a pint of bitter, please, Graham,' said Harold, moving over to the bar. Graham bought the drinks and Harold took his pint off the tray. 'How are things, Graham?' asked Harold.

'Not too bad at the moment, Harold. How about you?'

'I'm on the same ticket as Craig, mate. Getting pushed out on a retirement deal.'

'So, did they send security round to escort you off the premises within the hour?'

'No, nothing like that. There is some research they need me to sort out before they get rid of me, and so they are going a bit slow with the paperwork. My guess is that it will be a couple of months before they release the guillotine.'

'Oh, they want your journal articles for the university research profile. Is that it?'

'Yes, that's right. There are some minor modifications that I have to do for the journal editors and only I can do them. So, basically, I'm getting paid for another couple of months while I sort that out, but I have been relieved of all my other duties, including teaching.'

'Could be worse, Harold, but it is a bit of a bummer though,' said Graham.

Harold turned to Trevor. 'Do you think this is going to be a heavy session?'

'Shouldn't be surprised, Harold. Folks are feeling very fed up and pissed off. This is going to be more like a wake than a retirement party, if you ask me.'

'Has anyone spoken to Craig yet?' said Harold.

'No, we only got here a few minutes before you,' Graham and Trevor chorused.

'Let's go and see him. He looks a bit forlorn, over there,' said Graham.

'Well, you're his mate. Lead on, Graham,' said Trevor.

They wandered across the room and sat down at Craig's table at one of the open plan booths scattered around the edges of the room.

'How does it feel to be retired, then?' asked Graham.

'I don't know. It hasn't really sunk in yet. To be honest, I feel a bit numb,' said Craig.

'What are you going to do with yourself?' asked Trevor.

'I haven't really thought about that. Sit at home and read some novels, I guess.'

'Sounds good to me. I wouldn't mind a bit of that!' said Trevor. 'Mind you, you should get yourself out and about a bit. It doesn't do to mope around the house too much.'

Craig sighed. 'No, I guess not.' He then straightened his posture and, as he looked around at all three, stood up from his chair. 'You'll have to excuse me for a moment. I have to check with the barman that they remembered to include a few veggie alternatives with the buffet we are having later.' Craig walked over to the bar.

Graham turned to Trevor. 'Go easy with that stuff about moping at home, Trev. You do know that his wife died last year?'

'Oh, shit! Yes, I forgot. Still, he should get himself out and about. That's all I said.'

Harold nodded and looked around the room. He had been to so many of these farewell parties over the years. He thought that he would enjoy this one, but now he was there he was starting to feel depressed. Trevor and Graham were moaning about the new rules for the university timetable that were, apparently, supposed to come into force next term. A shapely blonde eased herself into the booth and sat down beside Trevor. She leaned into him, put her arm around his shoulders and kissed him on the cheek.

'Hello, Trev. It's lovely to see you here. How's it going?'

'Not too bad, Millie.'

Graham nodded to her and raised an arm in her direction, by way of greeting.

'Hi, Graham,' Millie responded. Trevor touched Millie's arm, narrowly avoiding her right breast.

'Do you know my mate Harold?' A puzzled frown swept across Harold's face as he attempted to speedily sort through the *Women-I-Have-Slept-With* category in his long-term memory.

'Hello, Harold. Still singing about fish 'n' chips, I suppose?'

Harold generated an indulgent guffaw, offset by a few rapid head nods. This information allowed him to place her within the audience of an amateur live music club he used to run on a weekly basis at this very pub, back in the 1980s. His creaky mental arithmetic did the sums. It must have been about thirty years ago. On this basis he estimated her current age to be around the 50 mark. She had aged very well; she was looking good.

'I mourn the fact that fish 'n' chips are no longer wrapped in newspaper, Millie. So I am moving on to Brassicas - or should that be Brassicae?'

'If you start talking Latin, Harold, you are going to turn me on. So, be careful!' she said.

'Caesar ad sum jam forte. Brutus ad sum tu. Caesar sic in omnibus, Brutus dedit tu.' Harold sat back with a self-satisfied grin.

'What the hell does that mean, Harold?' asked Trevor.

'Bugger-all, mate; a bit of meaningless doggerel. Not unlike my lectures on Monday mornings used to be, come to think of it.' His grin transmogrified to a rueful smile. Millie got up and moved around to the other side of the curved bench seat, to sit next to Harold. She snuggled slightly.

'Doesn't matter what it means, Harold, it's doing it for me.'

Everyone broke into laughter.

'Looks like they've got a band on tonight,' said Harold.

'Snakeskin. They're bloody good. Have you heard them, Harold?' she asked.

'No, I haven't. But I will take your word for it, providing they play nothing post 1980.'

'Harold! I grew up in the '80s. That's my adolescence you are talking about,' she said.

Harold let his gaze drop pointedly in the direction of Millie's breasts.

'Well, I can see that, biologically speaking, that was an entirely successful event, Millie.'

'Harold, I shall take that as a compliment, even if it is coming from a dirty old sod like you!'

'Drink up folks! I'll get another round in.' Trevor seemed intent on pushing the group's alcohol consumption to the maximum, irrespective of any danger to livers. They all supplied him with requests and empty glasses. He went to the bar. A sporadic thumping of drums, crashing of cymbals, and twanging of guitar strings indicated that the band were getting ready for their first set. This preamble differed from the sound of a classical orchestra tuning to the note of A, inasmuch as it came across more as a sequence of disconnected random riffs. The lead singer, who also played bass guitar, approached the microphone. No spring chicken, his jowls quivered as he kicked off with the inevitable 'One, two, three, four...' Within the space of a couple of bars it became clear that this band was going to be tightly driven by some powerful drumming. Harold relaxed. Millie leaned over and shouted something into his left ear; he could not make out a single word. Modern technology no longer needed a powerful Marshall stack to render conversation impossible. On this occasion, all that seemed to be required were a couple of sophisticated speaker units mounted like single flowers on spindly stems. Harold glanced over to the bar. Craig Melcheter was propping it up, tapping his foot to the beat in a somewhat desultory fashion. He did not look happy but Harold decided that there was nothing he could do about that, under the circumstances. It would have been pointless to drift over to him and attempt to start up a conversation. He used a visit to the men's room as an excuse to get some privacy. Once locked into a stall, he took out his mobile phone and sent an SMS text to Julia.

*Am bored. Getting depressed at this party. What shall I do?*
Almost immediately the reply came back:
*Wait there. I shall come and get you - 10 mins max.*

Harold took a pee and then went back to his seat in the bar.

'That pint's going down a bit slow, Harold. Drink up old man. It's your round next,' said Trevor.

'Look, I'll get you a round in but I have got to go soon. Something has cropped up.'

'Oh, Harold! Just as we are getting started,' said Graham.

' I know. It's just that one of Julia's friends is a lawyer and she might be able to give me a bit of freebie advice about this situation with Veronica,' replied Harold. He felt that the white lie was plausible and provided him with an easy way out.

'Sounds a bit boring to me, Harold,' said Trevor.

Harold asked them what they wanted to drink and fetched the order from the bar. He then made his farewells, and waited outside the pub entrance for Julia. It was not long before he heard the sound of her expensive exhaust system, as she rounded the corner and pulled up beside the pub. Harold hopped in and Julia drove off at speed.

'So, I give you a free evening and you can't handle it,' said Julia.

'I don't know what happened. Suddenly, it all seemed so stale. I felt that I no longer belonged.'

'Literally, that is in the process of becoming the case, Harold.'

'Yes, but I didn't expect to feel it quite so soon.'

'You have been cut adrift from the two major domains of your life-world. You are no longer living with Veronica and you are more or less done with your old job.'

'I can't see the way through all this. One might expect a rite of passage, but passage implies movement from one situation to another. I can see what I am leaving but not where I am headed.'

'We have talked about this, you know, Harold. Maybe not exactly in these terms. But your coming to live with me as my paying guest opens up a new vista for you.'

'You are so beautiful, so energetic, and so powerful. I find it difficult to accept that I am the desired focus of your attention, let alone love.'

'I know you do, Harold. But you mustn't worry about that. I have told you before, that is my responsibility. You just have to trust me.'

Harold sighed and lapsed into silence for the remainder of the journey home. Once inside they watched the evening news before going up to bed; Julia had an early start in the morning.

The next morning, after Julia had left for work, Harold mulled over the way he felt distanced from his old university colleagues. He decided to make the trip down to the campus to explore his feelings in a little more depth. He therefore drove to the car park and wandered about the buildings on the campus. He soon became listless. He slipped into the back of the large hall which was used for plays and concerts, as well as some lectures. The choral society and the university orchestra were in rehearsal. He could see the head of music wielding his baton in a most animated fashion. It sounded like Handel, possibly the Messiah. The conductor was taking them through the piece without interruption. Harold felt that it could be a final rehearsal. As the chorus swelled into a glorious crescendo, his thoughts turned to Julia. He visualised her standing giant-like before him down the hall just in front of the orchestra. In his imagination, her head and shoulders filled out the space beneath the beams of the roof; her hair brushed against the rafters. He visualised her wearing a pair of leather boots, standing tall, with her legs apart and her hands on her hips. It occurred to him that she existed in this form only in his head. A smile played over his lips as he contemplated the privacy and secrecy afforded to him in thought. There was something sacrilegious about what he was doing which rendered the Messiah into a work of titillation. With some reluctance he got up and slipped out of the door, back into the bustle of students streaming from one class to another. He looked at his watch: it was eleven o'clock precisely. He watched some of the stragglers running to catch the start of their lectures. Although not physically moribund, he was well past running for a train or a bus. Being a university teacher provided a constant reminder to him of how old he was getting as the students, like policemen, looked younger and younger each year. Harold sauntered over to

Trevor's office but he was nowhere to be seen. He ambled down the corridor and stuck his head round the secretary's door.

'Hi, Maureen. Is Trevor about?'

'I think he is in a Board of Studies meeting, Harold.'

'Any idea when that will be over?'

'God knows. The dean ordered a sandwich lunch, so my guess is they will work through. I should think it will be mid to late afternoon.'

'OK. Thanks.'

'Any message, Harold?'

'No, I'll probably phone him later.'

'OK. Bye for now.'

Harold walked over to the car park and drove back to Julia's house. He was surprised to find that her car was in the driveway. He let himself in.

'Hello! Julia, are you home?'

'In the sitting room, Harold,' replied Julia.

Harold went through, kissed Julia on the cheek and sat down in one of the easy chairs. 'I thought you were in Sheffield today,' he said.

'Cancelled. To be honest, I'm not disappointed. What have you been up to?'

'Nothing much. I went down to the campus. Listened to a classical music rehearsal for a while, then looked for Trevor but he was at a meeting.'

'Oh. You sound a bit down.'

'I seem to have no energy or enthusiasm lately. I don't know what it is.'

'Do you think you might be depressed?'

'Not in a debilitating clinical way. But I certainly have the blues. Or more than my share of it.'

'It's the same as yesterday, isn't it. You went to the retirement party and then you just had to leave.'

'Yes, I suppose so. I felt so aimless today at the university.'

'Well, in a sense, that is not surprising. I mean, you have nothing to aim for. There are no plans that you have to work towards, apart from that little bit of part-time teaching Trevor fixed up for you.'

'I had a fantasy about you while I was listening to the music.'

'Oh, what was that about?'

'I imagined you were a giant, standing in the hall. You were as high as the ceiling.'

'I rather like being thought of as an Amazon woman.'

Harold smiled.

'You are bored and fed up. And that is going to be a problem for us if it goes on much longer,' said Julia.

Harold nodded. 'I don't know what to do about it.'

'What are you doing tomorrow?'

'I'm supposed to be going to a guitar show with Trevor.'

'So that should be fun for you.'

'Yes, we usually have a good time at these events.'

'OK. Well, let's hope that will shake you out of your depression. If not, we shall have to think more deeply about it.'

Harold nodded.

'Now, Harold, I have to leave early in the morning tomorrow for a meeting, so I shall probably be out of the house before you are awake.'

'Oh, right. Fair enough.'

'So I think I shall get an early night,' said Julia. She came over to Harold and kissed him briefly on the lips. 'You can sleep in your room. Don't stay up too late, though.'

Harold nodded. 'I might just read a bit more of my library book.'

'Whatever! Goodnight, Harold.'

'Goodnight, Julia.'

It was not long before Harold pottered off to bed, too.


Harold woke up the next morning to a stillness that pervaded the house. He slowly realised that Julia must have already left to catch her train. He fumbled for his spectacles and checked his watch. He was ahead of the alarm which he duly disarmed. He hurried through his early morning ablutions. After a quick swig of tea and a bite of toast he got into his car and drove round to Trevor's house. His friend was waiting for him and waved through the curtains. Harold did not bother to park properly; he sat in the car with the engine idling. He glanced in the rearview mirror from time to time to see if any cars were approaching, since he was blocking his side of the road. Fortunately, Trevor soon emerged. He was carrying a guitar case and pointed in the direction of the luggage boot. Harold wound the window down a fraction.

'It's open, Trev.'

Trevor opened the boot, stowed the guitar, and then clambered into the passenger seat. Harold took the main road out of the city, going south. They were going to a guitar show at a nearby conference hall. The event took place about once a year in their region and they were both regular attendees.

'What's with the guitar, Trev?' asked Harold.

'I've been thinking of getting rid of this one. You never know, I might be able to shift it today.'

Conversation ebbed and flowed around the theme of guitars in general; it was not long before they pulled into the gravel field that served as a car park at the venue. They joined the end of an orderly queue and shuffled along at a reasonably steady pace. At the entrance they each parted with a ten pound note and in exchange had the back of their hands inked with a pass-out stamp. It was clear from the outset that the security for the event was modelled on that of a music gig.

In the main hall they were greeted by serried ranks of guitars standing to attention along the length of long trestle tables. Had the tables been covered with white linen and laid for dinner, they would not have been out of place at a wedding feast. As it was, capos and plectra stood in for cruets and condiments, while ukuleles and mandolins served as manqué floral displays. The two friends trudged up and down the aisles. They paused at the stall for peculiar mandolins constructed with bodies made from cigar boxes and oilcans. The leather-faced stallholder was demonstrating with a blues tune played on what appeared to be a three-stringed instrument made from a car hubcap and a banjo fretboard.

'He looks bored out of his mind,' Harold whispered to Trevor.

'We've seen him before. He was here last year,' replied Harold.

'And the year before that.'

'I bet he does the summer festivals, too.'

'I think I'd go mad if I had to do that all day,' said Trevor. They moved on.

Trevor turned to inspect something on one of the tables and caught Harold's coat sleeve to bring him back.

'Look at this! It's an electric ukulele,' said Trevor.

'A Fender, too,' said Harold with a note of surprise in his voice.

'Looks like it,' said Trevor.

The stallholder came out from behind and offered to take the instrument off its stand, so that Trevor could play it. Trevor sat down upon a handy stool and plonked about for a bit. Amplified, with the sound sweetened a little through an effects pedal, the instrument appeared to have good tone and depth. Trevor began the process of haggling for a price by describing the electric guitar he had brought to the show. The trader seemed happy to explore the idea of part-exchange and so they told him they would go and get the guitar and be back within the hour. They picked up the guitar from Harold's car and brought it back into the show. The security guard tied a stamped label onto the guitar case and wrote the letters 'PV' across it. They walked through and made their way back to the trader's stall.

'Why has he put PV on the label?' asked Harold.

'I guess that is because the guitar is a Peavey,' said Trevor.

'Oh, neat. There must be a name for that sort of thing. I mean, it is not an acronym.'

'Maybe musicians like to do that. I mean, think of FX,' said Trevor.

'What do you mean?' said Harold.

'Well, FX is short for effects.'

Harold blushed slightly, as he realised he had displayed his ignorance. 'I'd still like to know what you call it, though.'

They arrived back at the stall and caught the trader's attention. Trevor opened up his guitar and the trader cast an expert eye over the body and checked the neck for warping. He then started to dwell on hypothetical difficulties he might encounter in shifting it. This told Trevor that the trader was happy with the guitar in principle. In fact, it amounted to the trader's first step in talking down the price he would allow on the exchange. Trevor cut in.

'Will you do a straight swap?'

The trader paused for a second and then nodded. Within a couple of minutes he had boxed up the ukulele and handed it to Trevor. Harold and Trevor moved off down the aisle.

'I think you could probably have got some cash out of him, if you had pressed,' said Harold.

'Yeah. You are probably right. But I didn't really want the hassle. A swap was good enough for me.'

'Shall we get some coffee?' asked Harold.

'Good idea,' replied Trevor.

They made their way upstairs to the cafeteria. They each bought a coffee and a cheese sandwich, then found a table on the balcony overlooking the main hall.

'Have you realised that this place is full to capacity and they are nearly all men?' asked Harold. Trevor leaned over the balcony a little and swept his eyes across the sea of folk.

'You are right, Harold. I can only see a handful of women.' Harold nodded.

'I'll tell you something else,' said Trevor.

'What's that?'

'A significant proportion of the heads down there are either balding or covered in grey hair.'

'Guitar-mad lads of the 1960s grown old,' said Harold.

'That's right. It is strange that this should be such a cohort-specific phenomenon, though,' said Trevor.

'I don't understand it. It makes me feel as though I am a bit of a has-been,' said Harold.

'Nah! Don't worry about it, mate.' Trevor sipped his coffee and munched his cheese sandwich.

'I must say that I quite like the way some of the greybeards have got their long hair tied back in a ponytail,' said Harold.

'Didn't you used to do that?' said Trevor, smiling.

'Not since I was a postgrad student,' said Harold.

'You should give it a go. Why don't you? Let it all grow out and see what happens.'

Harold laughed. 'Well, I suppose I could do that if I wanted to. I mean, it is not as though I am in a responsible full-time job anymore.'

'I bet your Julia would be up for it,' said Trevor.

'You might even be right there, Trev. Maybe I'll ask her when I get home.' The two friends chuckled.

When they had finished their snacks they went back downstairs and found the performance area where the equipment demonstrations were held. They could hear some fancy guitar work going on as they entered the studio theatre and found seats. The poster outside indicated that the pro generating the noise was a brilliant shredder, there to put a range of amplifiers through their paces. Harold reminded himself that this had more to do with hemi-demi-semi-quavers than small pieces of paper. After about ten minutes, Trevor looked at Harold.

'What do you think?' he mouthed, since lip reading was the only possibility at the time. Harold looked pointedly in the direction of the exit door; they both got up and shuffled to the end of the row of seats and swiftly departed. Once outside the hall, Harold turned to Trevor.

'He demonstrated great skill and dexterity as a shredder, but I could have done with half the decibels,' said Harold.

'The thing is, he switched on a full backing track with drums, bass guitar and rhythm guitar. So, really, he was doing the equivalent of lead guitar karaoke!' said Trevor.

'Exactly!' said Harold.

They both touched their hands to their mouth as if stifling a yawn, and then burst into laughter. In the perfect timing that only old friends can achieve they then chorused 'Boring!' and headed for the car park. Harold dropped Trevor at his home and then drove back to Julia's house. He made himself a cup of tea and watched some TV.

# Chapter 8

Harold was conscious of a bell ringing in close proximity. As the volume swelled, he became aware that it was his alarm clock. His arm responded as if to a Pavlovian stimulus. He reached out and pummelled the clock into silence. Grunting, he lifted himself out of bed and attended to his early morning ablutions. He then made himself a cup of coffee and pottered into Julia's back garden. He fetched a sun lounger from the shed and made himself a makeshift coffee table from an upturned storage box. As he inhaled the aroma of the freshly brewed coffee he had what could be described as a minor olfactory orgasm. In his mind he coined the term '*olfactogasm*' and took a long swig. He toyed with the idea of writing a spoof scientific paper and chuckled as he dreamed up an appropriate title: *The caffeine-induced olfactogasm and its relation to gastro-porn addiction*.

Harold acknowledged that he was fed up. He gave himself his usual lecture: he was not starving; he had no terminal illness; he was not being tortured in some war-torn hellhole the other side of the world. This did not have the effect of snapping him out of it. If anything it increased his feeling of guilt. Indeed, he figured that guilt generally multiplied the magnitude of his 'fedupitude' by a factor of at least two.

He stretched out and listened to a birdcall coming to him from the bushes on his left. It sounded like a robin, not so much a peep as a Morse code dash. He vacillated about whether to go into the city. Above him, a propeller-driven aircraft droned lazily in the sky. He began to be attracted by the idea of a full day of inaction. He wondered what Julia would think about that. He opened the library book that he had picked up more or less at random from the supermarket shelves a couple of days ago and settled down to read. The novel he was reading was set in the heart of the English countryside. The village life, so depicted, was more or less a fantasy of the rural idyll, although Harold had to acknowledge that it felt as though it probably was written by somebody who regularly pulled on a pair of cowpat-encrusted Wellington boots. There was certainly enough descriptive detail to allow the suspension of disbelief to kick in strongly. Harold almost caught a whiff of virtual pigshit as he turned the pages. He took a final swig of coffee and put the book down. After some deliberation, he decided that he would make the journey into the city and return the new toaster he had bought for Julia's kitchen (the old one had sadly expired the previous week).

He found the shop near the main square. It looked as though it really wanted to be an old-fashioned department store but, sadly, it had been blighted by a nudge towards modernisation. A row of supermarket-style check-out tills ran parallel to the wall containing the entrance and exit doors. To get to the 'returns' desk he had to ascend an escalator. As always, this took him back to his schooldays, travelling across London on the Tube when he was *en route* to and from his boarding school. He presented the toaster which he had neatly re-packaged. He was glad he had not broken up the cardboard box for recycling, since things seemed to go more smoothly if the item looked more or less the same as when the purchase was made. He fished in his back pocket and produced the slightly rumpled receipt.

'Hello! Are you the *'returns'* person?' he asked the woman behind the desk.

'Yes. Just a minute. I will clear a space.' The assistant tossed a couple of items into a cart that was standing behind her.

'How can I help you?'

'I've brought this toaster back. Basically, the toast fails to pop up before the bread starts to burn.'

'I see. So, do you want a replacement or a refund?'

'I want a refund, please.'

The assistant unpacked the toaster and started poking at her computer screen with a stylus.

'I need a few details for the customer complaint form that I have to do,' she said.

'OK,' said Harold. He gave his name and Julia's postcode.

'Would you say it was unsafe or dangerous?' enquired the assistant.

Harold's mind began to wander. He was tempted to launch into a philosophical analysis of the concept of danger, with reference to domestic toasters, but decided to postpone this to a future conversation that he might have about it with Trevor, in the pub.

'Let's say unsafe,' said Harold.

The assistant poked her screen a few more times before handing Harold his cash refund. She dismissed him with a smile. He left the store and wandered into the central mall where he found a coffee shop. He noted that this would be his second cup that morning. His Americano was good; he assumed the beans to be Arabica, possibly Columbian in origin. Harold was perfectly aware that he would be hopeless in a blind tasting but sometimes he liked to pretend he was, in theory, capable of exuding the confidence of a connoisseur.

Once settled unobtrusively at a small table he glanced around to observe his fellow caffeine addicts. There were about ten other people sitting either in the booths or on stools at the shelf by the window. He wished he had brought a sketchbook and pencil with him since they all seemed to have a distinctive line to their faces. He resolved that, one day, he really would overcome his anxiety about sketching in public.

As he sipped his coffee he felt himself sinking further into his depression. There was no rhyme or reason for this, as far as he could see. He wondered whether it was because he was now separated from Veronica, but if he was honest he had to admit that that brought him a sense of relief rather than anything else. There was not a single bone in his body that longed to be back with her; he was glad that he had escaped. He lacked the self-confidence to believe fully that Julia really wanted him, just the way he was. Yet she seldom complained about his weight or his lack of physical fitness. She laughed at his jokes and his humorous quips. She never seemed bored by his sometimes tortuously rambling anecdotes. In the end, he managed to persuade himself that Julia could not really be the cause of his negative mood. He finished his coffee and accepted that the source of his blues remained a mystery. He left the coffee shop and made his way back to the car park. Harold shoved his ticket into the machine and paid for his parking. Amazingly, today, he had remembered where he had left his car and was able to walk directly to the bay. At the exit another machine ate his ticket; the barrier snaked upwards in response. He edged his way into the traffic flow which, for a change, seemed to be relatively light and sprightly. He drove around aimlessly for a while. He even entered the main university car park at one point, only to complete a full circuit before continuing out of the exit gate. He drove a few miles up the coast road, pulled into his favourite clifftop car park and positioned the car so that he could watch the waves breaking on the shore. He didn't bother to switch off the engine. In fact, even before a couple of cormorants on the rocks beneath had settled their territorial dispute, he found himself reversing out and rejoining the road.

In the privacy of his own car he once more gave himself a piece of his own mind. Before long he was swearing like a trooper. His voice grew louder and louder, eventually drowning out the noise from the engine. As he reached the climax of his crescendo he beat his hands upon the steering wheel, inadvertently sounding the alarm. This brought him back to his senses. He furtively glanced around and checked his mirrors; fortunately, no other cars were nearby. He felt a little sheepish, and set a course back home to Julia's house.

Harold parked behind Julia's car in the drive, since she was away on business. He made a mental note to move it later on before she got back. He let himself into the front door and was surprised to hear some music playing. It seemed to be coming from upstairs. He wondered if he had left the bedside radio turned on, since he was sometimes careless in that regard. He pondered this for a moment but he could not recall having listened to the wireless before he went out. He quietly ascended the carpeted stairs. The music was loud but there were other noises, too. Perhaps a woman crying out, maybe in pain? He began to feel nervous. He wondered whether there might be an intruder in the house, yet he felt that a burglar would hardly hang about listening to the radio!

Once he reached the landing it became obvious that the music was coming from Julia's room. The door was shut. He speculated as to whether she might have returned home early from her trip. He stood still, hesitating in something of a cowardly funk. Eventually, he felt that he had to act. He grabbed the handle and threw open the door, with considerable flourish.

The scene that greeted him stopped him in his tracks. Lying naked on the bed, with bodies entwined, and writhing, lay Julia and Penny Charlton. He wanted to close the door quietly and creep away downstairs. Perhaps he could pretend to himself that it had never happened. However, his feet would not move; he could not take his eyes off the copulating female flesh before his eyes.

Penny had her back towards him. Julia moved her head to the side and looked at him over Penny's shoulder. She smiled and then, speaking into Penny's ear in a loud whisper, she said

'Harold's come to see us. I think he wants to watch.'

Penny turned over onto her side so that she, too, could look at Harold.

'Hello, Harold. Does this excite you? Why don't you sit on the chair over there. You will be more comfortable and you can have a ringside seat.' The women laughed a little and adjusted their embrace so that it was more open towards Harold.

'I didn't know. I had no idea. I feel as though I have made a dreadful fool of myself. I should go,' said Harold.

'Don't be silly, Harold. There's nothing to get upset about,' replied Julia.

Penny shifted her body slightly and turned to Julia.

'Never mind Harold, Julia, I want some more of what you were doing to me just now. Can we get on with it?'

Once more limbs coiled and undulated in curvaceous abandon. Harold realised that Julia and Penny were ignoring him, and in doing so had paradoxically forced him into the role of *voyeur*. Part of him wanted to watch but he did not know how to stay and enjoy it. His upbringing had saddled him with a prudish sense of guilt with regard to this sort of thing, and at that moment he felt exceedingly weighted down by it. He decided that the only thing to do was to go and make a cup of tea. He closed the door and went downstairs, to the sound of the sexual cacophony which had recommenced with transcendent gusto.

The kettle boiled and Harold made his tea. He took it into the sitting room and turned on the TV. He switched to the news channel and caught up with what was happening in the world. This took his mind off Julia and Penny. By the time the news anchor handed over to the weathergirl, things were much quieter in the house. Harold picked up his novel and started to read it in a desultory fashion. After a while he found that his eyes were closing from time to time, and it wasn't long before he had fallen into a nap.

Harold, dead to the world for a couple of hours, nevertheless woke up still feeling tired. He was stiff and his mouth was dry. He swilled some of the cold tea from the mug he had put down on the coffee table, earlier. He made himself a bite to eat, and then went out to the back garden. The evening was getting late. Harold went over to the sun lounger which he had forgotten to put away earlier. He settled back and listened to the silence. He noticed the faint sound of what might have been traffic noise from the motorway. There was an absence of birdsong.

As the light began to fade, the colourful garden metamorphosed into a black and white version of itself. This reminded him of his school science lessons about the different functions of the rod and cone receptors in the eye. The clouds stood out dark against the pale blue of the sky, those closest to the horizon being tinged with a hint of orange. A bat swooped towards him, only to veer away to its right. Over by the garage, the waste bins began to take on the ominous shape of robotic sentinels. He felt completely alone, but not unpleasantly so. He was vaguely conscious of the sound of Julia and Penny's voices in the street outside. They seemed to be saying goodnight to one another. He heard Penny's car door slam and then the revving of her engine as she drove off. The back door opened; Julia strolled over to Harold. She swung her leg over the sun lounger and straddled him, easing her bottom onto his tummy, leaning above him with her hands pressing down against his shoulders.

'So, Harold, did that upset you? Me being in bed with Penny.'
'You know it did,' said Harold, crossly.
'Don't be so petulant, Harold.'
Harold looked away, pouting in the gathering darkness.

'Oh, Harold! You are so sweet when you go all sulky,' replied Julia.

'No, I'm not!' sulked Harold.

'Oh, yes you are, Harold.' Julia laughed, easily.

'I am not!'

Julia smiled down at Harold and caressed his cheek with her hand.

'You're behaving like a little boy, Harold, but that's all right.' She glanced around her garden. 'Do you like it out here?'

Harold begrudgingly looked over at the wide herbaceous border and nodded. 'Yes, it is a lovely place to be. I am quite fond of gardening, in a rather amateurish way. I used to look after the garden at my old house; Veronica hadn't a clue.'

'Well, Harold, to tell you the truth I don't have much of a clue, either. I know roughly what I want but I don't have the practical skills to get it there or to maintain it once it is there.'

'Yes, well, a garden is constantly changing anyway. The seasons, growth, death, that sort of thing.' Harold said this in a somewhat resigned fashion, as though he might be talking about his own life cycle. However, there was enough energy in his voice to suggest that he was being led successfully out of his resentful sulk by the Mistress of the house.

'Would you like to look after this garden for me, Harold? I used to have a wonderful old gent come in and tend it but he retired. I have had a succession of unreliable folk over the past couple of years. One of them was a bit shady; I didn't like him at all. And the youth who has been coming to me this summer has just been accepted for a job with the council parks department. So, the job is yours if you want it, my pet.' She bent down and kissed Harold on his forehead.

Harold gazed up into Julia's eyes. He felt helpless. He knew that he would just have to put up with her bisexuality. He would have to take on board the fact that Penny was Julia's lover. It didn't really matter if he felt a tad emasculated by it. *Que sera, sera*. He turned his attention to the question of the garden.

'What about the cost of things? Plants can be quite expensive and there is the issue of the upkeep and replacement of garden machinery. I couldn't afford any of that.'

'Oh, don't be such a silly boy, Harold. I will open up an account for you and you can use it for whatever you need in the garden. I can put in a good sum of money to get you started, then you can just let me know when you need it topped up. You will keep a proper record of your expenses and come to me with your *Garden Report* once a month.'

'I think I would quite like that. This is a much better garden than the one I had in my old house.'

Julia smiled down at Harold. 'Good, I'll set it up next week. Now, I think it is time to go indoors. It's getting chilly out here.'

'OK. I'll just put away this sun lounger.'

Julia levered herself up from Harold's lap and waited while Harold padlocked the garden shed. As he turned away from the door, he found her blocking his way. She enfolded him in an embrace.

'You are rather conventional, in an old-fashioned way, Harold. Maybe you need to loosen up a bit.'

'Loosen up? You mean my joints are a bit creaky?'

Julia laughed. 'Oh, no. I don't mind your creaky joints.' Her hands slid down his back; she then proceeded to grope handfuls of Harold's plenteous buttock cheeks. 'Do you find Penny sexy, Harold?'

Harold blushed and was glad that this fact was obscured from Julia by virtue of the night sky. 'I hadn't really thought about it. I suppose she is rather attractive. She has a nice body.'

Julia laughed. 'You are a hopeless liar, Harold. Of course you find her attractive. I have seen the way you look at her, especially her breasts.'

Harold wished that he could be swallowed up and hide in the shed but there was no escape from Julia, since he had padlocked the door.

'Why do you seem to delight in making me feel embarrassed and guilty and naughty and all that sort of thing?' asked Harold.

'Because it gives me a great deal of pleasure Harold. I love to see you squirm. I could never miss the opportunity to humiliate you a little, too. You are just delightful, Harold. And don't worry! I shall never hurt you in a nasty way. I have told you before, I am going to look after you.'

This broke through all Harold's resistance and he abandoned himself to Julia's embrace. 'You are a bit weird, Julia. You do know that!'

Julia laughed. 'Of course, Harold. And part of my job is to draw out a little more of your own weirdness. I know it is in there somewhere. My guess is that it has long been repressed, if that is not too Freudian a take on the state of affairs for you.'

Harold nodded. 'Maybe it is not. I mean weirdness to Veronica was like a red rag to a bull'.

'Well, you are free of her now. Maybe it is time to grow and explore some of the dormant facets of your being.'

'Like becoming your gardener, you mean?'

Julia laughed. 'No, Harold, not like that .' She stood smiling at Harold. 'I was thinking that I could loan you out to Penny from time to time. She could enjoy you as her toyboy. You would not have to get emotionally close. It could be pure sex.'

'I don't know that I could cope with that sort of thing!' said Harold.

'How can you know unless you try?'

'Well, there is an obvious truth in what you say, but it feels a tad radical to me.'

'Let's see if we can't change the way you think about this, Harold.'

'How do you mean?'

'Well, would you do it for me? Do it because I have asked you. So if you were to regard it as doing as you are told, you would no longer have responsibility. Guilt would be prised away from you. Another possibility would be for you to regard it as pleasing me. It would be like offering up to me a behavioural gift.'

'You mean like doing the dishes or shopping for your groceries?'

'Why not?'

'I suppose I could put her in a bubble bath and then dry her off with a fluffy towel. That is the dishwashing analogy, by the way.'

'There, you see, Harold. Your agile mind is working on the problem already. I don't want you to worry about it anymore, Harold. I'll talk to Penny; I'll take care of everything.'

The two of them went back into the house, arm-in-arm.

Over the course of the next couple of weeks, Julia established Harold's garden account and he began to order various plants and bits of machinery. It was no surprise, then, that he found he had an email informing him that one of his orders would be delivered later that morning. Sure enough, at around midday, there was a hammering upon the front door, punctuated by the repeated ringing of the doorbell. He got to the front door in time to see the parcel man writing out a note card about non-delivery.

'Ah! I was expecting this,' said Harold.

The deliveryman nodded. 'Right you are, mate. Just sign here.' He offered Harold an electronic pad and a wand with which to provide a digital signature. Once Harold had signed for the parcel, the delivery man pulled the barrow back onto its wheels.

'Where do you want this, mate?'

'Can you put it through that trellis gate there, please, by the garden shed?' replied Harold.

The guy nodded and set the large box down near to the shed door. He then departed swiftly, without another word. Harold had decided to purchase a lawn rake and scarifier when he saw how much money Julia had put into his garden account. Harold liked toys. He decided to unpack it straightaway. He opened up the shed and then bent down to pick up the box. It was heavy and the weight was unevenly distributed but he managed to get it off the ground. However, it slipped out of his hands just as he went through the shed door; it thudded onto the concrete floor. He hoped that there was plenty of polystyrene packing. He took hold of a sharp retractable knife and began to cut through the tape that sealed the parcel along its edge folds. With some difficulty, he managed to get the top flaps of the box open. Substantial, moulded polystyrene blocks protected the machinery within. He picked up what appeared to be the manual, a fairly hefty tome printed on off-white A5 paper, bound into something the size of a short novella. He decided to make a cup of tea before he did anything else.

Harold unfolded a deck chair and settled down to explore the manual, cup of tea by his side. The first thing he noticed was that it appeared to be printed in no less than fourteen different languages. Given that the machine was manufactured in Germany, it was no surprise that German was top of the batting order with English a close second. Harold noted that Dutch followed English and came before French, Spanish and Portuguese. Russian was way down the list. Tucked into the front cover resided a single loose sheet upon which there existed a fiendishly complicated diagram. This appeared between an engineering drawing and a set of instructions for assembly. On closer inspection Harold discovered that the various poorly drawn sketches of the metal and plastic fabrications were linked to numerical identification codes the size of telephone numbers. Harold exhaled wearily and took another swig of tea. On the front cover there was a diagram of the assembled beast: the combination lawn rake and scarifier. He turned to the index and found that the operating instructions for Great Britain were on page 13. Harold's immediate thought was that this was a singularly unlucky page number on which to attempt a deconstruction of the instructions to construct. Nevertheless, it was to page 13 that he turned.

The first page was devoted almost entirely to basic safety notes. Harold momentarily imagined that for each one there had probably been, at some point in the past, a nasty accident possibly involving a court case with claims for compensation. Speed-reading through a hefty list of bullet points, he noted that he should not use the machine were he to be under the influence of alcohol, drugs or medication. He felt slightly peeved that he didn't actually possess any drugs and wondered whether the manufacturers expected him to do so. There was a philosophical issue here. Were he to be in possession of a couple of king-size spliffs, he could then feel virtuous in his compliance with the manufacturers' exhortation, by NOT smoking them. As it was, he lacked the materials that might afford him the opportunity to show what a good citizen he was. Harold read on, in the forlorn hope that somewhere in the midst of all the prohibitions and stern warnings there might be a few hints as to how to put the bloody thing together. At last he found what he wanted: a section headed 'Assembly', written in bold type. When he examined it more closely, he assumed that it was a German engineer's idea of a joke.

*Assemble the machine in accordance with the illustrations (Figs A,B).*

That was the sum total of advice offered by the manual. He began to prod the various components and, with steely determination, cut away the plastic that covered some of the strangely shaped metal rods. As he wriggled the rods free of their packaging he managed to knock the manual off the bench table onto the floor. He bent down to pick it up and, to his joy, found a double page spread of diagrams at the beginning of the German section which had not been reproduced in the instructions for any of the other nationalities; they contained not only Figs A and B, but also Figs C, D, E, F, G, and H.

Figs. A and B contained simplified drawings of the assembled machine, together with several expanded sketches of what Harold took to be the tricky bits. Excitedly he unpacked the rest of the components. He moved all the cardboard, polythene and polystyrene to one end of the shed and laid everything out in an orderly fashion. He attempted to group all similar items together in piles and match the piles to the shapes depicted in Figs. A and B. He felt reasonably confident about most of the stuff but there were a couple of small stringy bits of plastic in a little bag that he could not find on the diagrams. He rummaged about and found an old saucer upon which to place these. He spotted a couple of marks on the diagrams that he had thought of as smudged ink blobs and thought that at a push they might be standing in as signifiers for the stringy bits. He rolled up his sleeves. Bit by bit he managed to assemble the various components, although each step seemed to be accompanied by a liberal dose of sub-vocal cussing. Once finished, he placed the scarifier next to the mower and dealt with the packaging. He felt in no state to carry out a testing at this point, his gumption having been drained by the stress of putting the damn thing together. He locked up the shed and pottered off into the house. He decided to take it easy for the rest of the day. Julia was away on business and so he caught up on some TV and made himself a sandwich from time to time. Feeling a tad tired from the stress of the lawn scarifier episode, he had an early night.

Next morning, Harold made himself a cup of tea and pottered off to his little room to check his emails, most of which looked extremely boring. He was about to delete the lot when he noticed one with a rather odd ID: '*smudger*'. Associations began to rattle along the corridors of his mind, down into the darker recesses of his boyhood past. Finally he was hit by a flash or recognition. *'Could it be Smudger Snelgrove? The Smudger Snelgrove who sat in the next desk to him in Form 3B at his boarding school?'*

Indeed it was, and the email had been languishing in his in-box for a week or more. The upshot was that there was to be an old boys reunion that very day. Harold, on the spur of the moment, decided to go. He quickly changed into something that passed for a business suit, found his old-boys association tie, scrawled a brief note to Julia, and took a cab to the rail station.

The journey was about an hour; Harold had treated himself and was now settled back in the relative luxury of a comfy first-class seat. The atmosphere in the compartment was quiet and tranquil, marked by an absence of howling brats. He glanced at his travelling companions. They, too, were dressed conservatively: a *balding* of middle-aged men (Harold was not sure if this was a legitimate collective noun but it seemed to him to be appropriate). The man in the seat opposite surveyed Harold over his open newspaper.

'Off to the Craggleden reunion, I presume?' He touched his own tie and then nodded meaningfully in the direction of Harold's.

'Ah, yes. You have spotted the tie, I see. And you?'

'Yes, me too. I haven't been to one of these things for a decade or more.'

Harold nodded. One by one the other men who were sitting in the nearby seats chipped in. It turned out that they were all Craggleden old boys, although only a couple of them had been at the school at the same time as Harold. It wasn't long before the reminiscences started.

'Do you remember old Whacker Green?' said the gent of extreme corpulence in the corner.

'Whacker Green? I'll say. Gave me the sorest bottom I ever had!' said the bald and gangly fellow, next to him.

Harold settled into the role of appreciative audience, contributing laughter and howls of derision in the appropriate places as one anecdote followed another. Eventually the train arrived at Craggleden station and they all bundled out. Looking about them, it soon became clear that a fair sprinkling of Craggleden old boys had also emerged from the other carriages. Greetings, slaps on backs, guffaws and associated indicators of forced bonhomie swirled and eddied around the ageing bodies drifting towards the exit. The consensus seemed to favour proceeding on foot down the avenue that led to the main entrance of the school, a walk of no more than ten minutes. Harold decoupled himself from his railway carriage cronies and fell in step with a man who looked as though he might have been a transmogrification of 'Twaggers' Judd. Harold chanced a conversational gambit based upon that hypothesis.

'Twaggers! How the devil are you?'

The said Twaggers turned his head towards Harold.

'Coddy? That's not you, is it?'

'It certainly is. Although I haven't been addressed as 'Coddy' for many a year. It is Harold, nowadays.'

Twaggers laughed. 'Yes, well, that goes for me too. I am Michael to my friends and family.'

Harold reflected on the derivation of his old nickname. He had no idea when it had started, but it must have been based on his last name, Hake. From there it would have been a short step to 'cod' and then on to the more familiar form of address, 'Coddy'. Harold and Twaggers turned into the main gate and walked up the drive towards the clock tower. The tower was not dissimilar, architecturally speaking, to Big Ben. As they turned off towards the cricket pitch, the half-hour chimed.

'I always found the school bell to be rather mournful,' said Harold.

'Yes. I seem to remember that it is E-flat in pitch,' replied Twaggers.

'Good heavens! I never knew that. Shall we go and see if there is anyone interesting watching the match?'

'We could do. Of course, we might end up with someone we don't want to see,' replied Twaggers. They left the path and climbed a small set of stone steps leading up to the level of the pitch.

'The sound of bat on ball brings back a few memories. Not that I was much of a cricketer,' said Harold.

'Yes, it does. I was more into swimming in the summer term,' said Twaggers.

'You were. A dab hand at water polo, if my memory serves me right.'

'I suppose I was rather good at it,' acknowledged Twaggers.

'Is that the Old Pig, standing by the practice nets over there?' asked Harold.

'I do believe it is. Worst French teacher I ever had. Let's give him a wide berth,' said Twaggers.

'I hated this place. God knows why I've come back again,' said Harold.

'Me too. I suppose it wasn't all bad, though,'

'Hallow'een was good fun,' said Harold.

'Do you remember the time they carried Brown's bed downstairs?'

'And left it in the quad.'

'With Brown still in it!'

'I do remember the story but I suppose it could have been apocryphal,' said Harold. Twaggers waved to somebody coming towards them.

'I'll just say a few words to Jones, here. I'll catch up with you a bit later, perhaps in the dining hall if you are heading over for some tea?'

Harold nodded and sauntered in the general direction of the refectory. Once or twice he paused to applaud as the old boys batsmen scored some runs. He ganced around at the spectators and saw nobody he knew, even though he seemed to have spent about an hour milling about. He caught sight of Twaggers who appeared to be talking to someone else dressed rather formally. When Twaggers noticed Harold, he left the conversation and caught up with him.

'Who was that you were talking to, in the morning suit?' asked Harold.

'That was Crock.'

'Oh, yes. I was never very close to him. I think he taught me a bit of organic chemistry at some point,' said Harold.

They made their way into the refectory hall and each picked up a small dish of strawberries and cream from one of the long tables at the side of the room. They were also handed a mug of hot tea by the maid who was dispensing it from an urn.

'I'm not sure how well school tea is going to go with strawberries and cream,' said Twaggers.

'Better than nothing, I suppose. Anyway, what did Crock have to say?'

'I said very little to him. I had to wait while he was talking to a guy from the year below me. I think he was called McTaggart.'

'Hmm. I can't remember a McTaggart,' said Harold.

'Well, anyway, he was talking to Crock in a very posh accent. I mean really posh. And I couldn't help hearing what he was saying,' said Twaggers.

Harold put his mug of tea down on a table so that he could eat his strawberries.

'Apparently McTaggart had gone into the army when he left school and he was now an officer in the guards.'

'Crock was heavily into playing at soldiers in the school cadet force. I remember that,' said Harold.

'That's right. Well, here was McTaggart who had done the real thing. He was speaking about people who he knew in the army who had served in the Falklands war and all sorts of stuff like that. And Crock was squirming. He really looked as though he wanted to get away from that conversation,' said Twaggers.

'Serve the bugger right. He was too stuck-up by half, was Crock,' said Harold.

They chomped their way through the strawberries and slurped their tea. Twaggers looked at his watch.

'I don't know about you, Harold, but I think I've more or less had my fill of this place.'

'Me too. I mean it has been nice to catch up with your good self but I haven't seen any of the crowd who I hung out with when I was here.'

'Same here. Are you going back to the station?' asked Twaggers.

'Yes. Might as well. Do you know how the trains are?'

'I think they are pretty frequent. If we go now, we should be in time to beat the evening rush hour.'

'That would suit me fine,' said Harold.

Harold and Twaggers said their farewells to a few of the people they had been chatting to where they were standing in the refectory and then they walked back to the station to catch their train. On the platform, they met up with a few more of the old boys and soon found themselves once more settled into a compartment together. Harold let the chat waft over him and allowed his eyes to gaze out onto the passing countryside. He looked up at the clouds. They were moving slowly: white and puffy shape-shifters. The clickety-clack of the wheels on the railway lines provided an accompaniment to the conversation going on around him. Yet, even as he became entranced by the rhythm of the train, the beating of the drums began to fade. A white noise, warm and comfortable, merged with the image of the clouds. Harold removed his spectacles and slipped them into the breast pocket of his jacket. The sky took on a fuzziness. It reminded him of being on the sports field at school, trying to play games without being able to see at all clearly. He seemed to be drifting. It was rather like being asleep, yet part of him seemed to have some degree of awareness. Harold felt the train slowing down. It seemed to be crawling along endlessly, at a snail's pace. Billows of steam appeared to have enveloped the carriage. Perhaps they were moving through fog, or an old-fashioned London smog. He thought he heard voices. Somebody seemed to be shaking his shoulder. He was vaguely aware of voices in the distance. He seemed to be lying down, floating along. The train had vanished. As he passed into unconsciousness, he vaguely heard the 'Nee-Nah' of a wailing siren in the distance.

Harold began to regain consciousness. He sensed that he was somewhere strange. He could hear footsteps in the distance. Maybe it was somebody pushing a trolley. He seemed to be lying in bed, propped up on some pillows. He decided to open his eyes a fraction. Blurred colour was what he got. He attempted to focus. Lemon yellow wall. White ceiling. He closed his eyes again. He needed a bit more energy to cope with lemon yellow! He felt his hands being clasped, left and right on different sides of the bed. This felt comfortable. There must be two people doing this, one on each side of the bed. He decided to investigate a little further. Once again, he forced his eyes to open.

'Harold! You are awake! How do you feel, darling?' Harold turned his head slightly. It was Julia, holding his right hand. She bent forward and kissed him. Harold attempted to speak, but found some difficulty in kick-starting his vocal chords. He cleared his throat.

'Julia!' That was all he could manage. That, and an attempt at a tiny smile. He slowly rotated his head left, in order to discover the identity of the other person. He saw Penny, smiling at him affectionately.

'Hello, Harold. You have had quite a long sleep, you know.'

'Penny. You are here! You must like me.' Penny laughed softly and bent over to kiss his other cheek.

'Of course I do, Harold. You are a darling.'

'So what's going on? Where am I?'

'You are in hospital. You had a bit of a funny turn on the train. I'm not sure I can allow you to go off gallivanting by yourself any more, you naughty boy.' Julia was smiling at Harold while she admonished him.

'Hmmm... I can remember being on the train. Then it all goes blank. I don't remember anything after that.'

'Well, don't worry about a thing, Harold. The doctors don't think anything disastrous has happened,' said Julia.

'Thank goodness for that!' said Harold.

'Just take it easy, Harold. I will go and tell the nurse you have woken up.' Julia left the room.

Harold began to relax. He flexed his toes and moved his legs around. He shrugged his shoulders and squeezed Penny's hands. He began to realize that his body was functioning more or less as it was supposed to do. Before long a nurse came back with Julia. The nurse smiled at Harold and then ran her eyes over the clip-board hanging at the foot of Harold's bed. She then turned to Julia and Penny.

'I have to run some checks on Harold now, and the doctor will be along to examine him a bit later. Maybe you should go to the canteen for a cup of coffee. I will come to the visitors' waiting area, and let you know when we are done. '

Harold was given a moderately superficial wash down. The nurse then allowed him to walk across the corridor to the bathroom. When he returned, the nurse told him to get dressed and then sit quietly in the chair by the bed. She said that the doctor would be along soon.

Harold felt OK, although he was reminded of the time he got concussion playing rugby on a hard clay pitch when he was at boarding school. *'Ah!'* thought Harold, *'that was how this all started. That bloody nuisance Smudger Snelgrove!'* He stared at the ceiling and started to get exceedingly bored. At last the doctor arrived. He put Harold through a brief examination and consulted the charts the nurse held for him. He told Harold that he had had an epileptic fit on the train and an ambulance had collected him at the next station. He explained to Harold that lots of people have just one fit, for no apparent reason, and it doesn't mean that he should think of himself as an epileptic. Indeed, he said that he thought it most unlikely that there would be a recurrence. Harold felt reassured by this. The doctor told the nurse to take him up to reception for discharge.

When they got to the reception area, they met up with Julia and Penny who rose to greet them. The nurse handed Julia a standard sheet of instructions about what Harold should and should not do, once home. She told her to make sure Harold complied with everything. She said that the hospital would phone to tell him when to come back for a follow-up examination. And so, off they went, and clambered into Julia's car.

'Harold, you have to stay at home and put your feet up for a bit for a day or two,' said Julia.

'Oh, how will that work out? Will you be alright, Julia?'

'Yes, I have cancelled all my non-crucial appointments and meetings. So I can be home to make sure you don't get up to any mischief.'

Harold chuckled.

'And I phoned the university and spoke to your friend Trevor. I explained that you were OK but had just been in hospital for a short spell. He seemed very concerned about you. I'm glad you have a good friend like that.'

'Trevor's a good mate,' agreed Harold.

'Anyway, I arranged to meet up with him during his lunch hour and I have given him a spare key. He is going to pop round from time to time. I just don't know how much time you will need for sleeping, so I thought it might be best if he can let himself in, on the days I have to be away.'

'Oh, that's very trusting of you.'

'Yes, well, if he is a good friend of yours, he can be a good friend of mine. Something like that. I just liked him, that's all. He seemed very straightforward.'

'Yes. Straight as a die.'


When they got home Julia took Harold upstairs and settled him in her big bed. It was not long before he was fast asleep. The next morning he woke up to find Julia lying in bed on his right-hand side. The pillows on his left looked crumpled and the duvet had been folded back slightly, as though somebody had just got out of the bed.

'You're awake, Harold! How do you feel this morning?'

'I feel good, thank you, Julia.'

'Excellent. Penny has just popped downstairs to make us a little breakfast in bed.'

'What? A fry up?'

'No, Harold. A little more continental, I feel.'

Harold tried not to let his disappointment show. At this point, Penny breezed in with a tray and dispensed mugs of coffee. They each had a small plate containing a warm croissant and a paper napkin. Harold took a surreptitious glance at Penny in her pink babydoll PJs. Julia lay back against her plumped pillows, her body draped in a black satin négligée. Harold was quietly sipping his coffee, when the doorbell chimed. The three of them paused, mid-croissant. Julia used her mobile phone, to speak over the intercom.

'Hello. Who is it?'

'It's Trevor. I thought I would just pop in to see how Harold is before I go to work.'

Julia replied, 'Let yourself in, Trevor. We are upstairs.'

As Harold heard the tramp of Trevor's feet upon the carpeted stairs, a smile crept over his face. The door opened and in walked Trevor. His jaw dropped as he took in the sight of Harold, flanked by Penny and Julia in their nightdresses.

'Bloody hell, Harold. So, you died and went to heaven? Yes?'

'It would appear so, Trevor, my old mate. It would appear so.'

Trevor grinned at Harold, winked, and then addressed Julia. 'Good morning to you, Ms. Rivers. I was just looking in on the patient on my way to work, as requested, but I can see he is being taken care of in no uncertain terms.'

Julia laughed. 'That's right, Trevor.' She leaned forwards slightly and glanced across to Penny. 'I don't think you have met my friend, Penny. Have you, Trevor?'

Penny put her plate of toast on the bedside table and leaned towards Trevor with outstretched hand. 'Penny Charlton. I'm pleased to meet you, Trevor.'

Trevor moved forward and grasped Penny's hand. It became obvious that, from his superior vantage point, Penny's delightful cleavage was freely available for him to gaze upon and this may have been the reason why he prolonged the handshake to the outer limits of polite social convention.

'Pleased to meet you, too, Penny. I'm Trevor Lamb.' Reluctantly Trevor let go of Penny's hand. As she leaned back onto the pillows, her breasts settled into a more modest mode of display and the faint blush that had appeared upon Trevor's face during the handshake begain to fade. He turned to Harold.

'So, just how ill are you, my old mate?'

'I don't think I'm ill, as such. I mean I don't have a fever or anything like that,' Harold replied.

'I guess what I want to know is whether or not you are under some kind of medical house arrest.'

Julia laughed. 'Honestly, Trevor, he'd be handcuffed to the bedpost if that were the case.'

'You want to be careful, Julia, you'll get Harold excited with talk like that,' replied Trevor.

'Chance would be a fine thing,' mumbled Harold.

## Chapter 9

Harold soon recovered from his epilepetic seizure. He quickly began to establish something of a routine for himself. He did some additional focus groups for the Brassica project, administered a half-decent questionnaire, and wrote up his report. He tarted up his findings with some delightful pie charts and a couple of graphs, to make the thing appear a tad more scientific than it was. The upshot of all this window dressing was that he got paid a huge consultancy fee which the delightful Penny Charlton presented to him over an extremely boosey lunch at a new Italian restaurant that had recently opened in the city. Penny promised to find him some more work if he was interested, and he said he was. Apart from his consultancy work, Harold was doing well in his role of counsellor/therapist at Anthea's clinic. In fact he and Mavis had become good pals by now. Harold did wonder sometimes whether that was partly due to the fact that he took it upon himself to give her an extra long lunch hour whenever he knew Anthea was out doing one of her highly lucrative stress talks for local business people. At home, he had slipped comfortably into the role of domestic slave and companion to the lovely Julia. He remained convinced that she could have found herself a toy boy whose tantric skills might have eclipsed his own, but she voiced no complaints on that score. Trevor's boss, Prof Picton, had begun to pass more and more casual teaching jobs to him, to fill in for sickness and holidays. The fact that he quite frequently knew almost bugger-all about the topics didn't seem to bother her unduly, since the students all seemed to love him. The practice of giving Maureen, the Prof's secretary, a cream cake to have with her morning coffee may well have resulted in his name being mentioned more frequently than any of his competitors whenever a teaching emergency loomed.

It was in the middle of a lazy, tranquil weekend that something of a bombshell hit Harold. Julia had a few days off, with no meetings or appointments; it was the university vacation, so Harold had no teaching to prepare. It was Sunday afternoon, and they were listening to some music on the sound system in the sitting room. There was a ring of the front door bell. Harold got up and answered it. A man in a slightly shabby suit and a trilby hat stood at the door. He held an identity card up for Harold to inspect.

'Mr. Hake?'

'Yes, that's me.'

'I'm Sergeant Craig. I wonder if I could have a word with you, Sir. Perhaps we could sit down?'

'Oh, er... Yes, come in.' Harold led the way into the kitchen. He heard Julia switch off the sound system.

'I'm afraid that there has been a road accident on the motorway, the Fenwell bypass. The person driving the car was a Mrs Veronica Hake, according to her registration details, and I believe you are her husband. Is that correct, Sir?'

'Yes, it is, officer. We are separated, but I am still married to her. What is wrong? Is it serious?'

'Well, Sir, she has been taken by ambulance to Fenwell General Hospital. I'm afraid I do not know any details as to her injuries, but she is in good hands. The ambulance crew were at the scene within minutes.'

'Oh, dear! I should go and see her. Where should I go?'

'The best thing would be to go to the desk at A&E, I think, Sir. Can you get there under your own steam?'

'Yes, yes. I'll go right away. Thank you for informing me, officer.'

The policeman drove off, leaving Harold in something of a daze. He went back into the sitting room.

'You heard that?'

'Yes, I did. Should I drive you down to the hospital?'

'Well, I don't think there is any sense in me taking my car down there. It is impossible to get a place in the visitors' car park, most days.'

'That's settled, then. I'll drive you, Harold. Make sure you have your mobile phone, then if there is anything you need you can call me and I will pick you up and ferry you about.'

'Oh, thank you, Julia. That will make things a lot easier. I mean, I don't think you should come in with me.'

'Oh, no. Of course not.'

Julia dropped Harold off at the A&E entrance. Harold queued for a moment at the reception desk and then explained that the police had advised him to come. The clerk interacted with her computer for a moment and then glanced up at Harold.

'If you could take a seat for a moment I will get somebody to come and attend to you, Mr Hake.' She moved to the back of the office and spoke to an older woman in a dark blue Sisters uniform. Harold had barely sat down before the Sister slipped out of the side door of the office and came across to speak with him. She asked him to follow her into a small consulting room down the corridor. It was there that Harold learned that Veronica had not survived the journey in the ambulance. Despite their best efforts, the paramedics had not been able to save her. She was dead on arrival. The nursing sister passed him over to an administrative assistant and, after a cup of coffee in the hospital cafeteria, he headed back down the long hospital corridors towards the exit and reception area. He phoned Julia; she picked him up and drove him home.

'Does Veronica have family you need to contact?' asked Julia.

'Her parents are both dead. She has a brother, living down south. I'll have to phone him. And I'll need to phone Emma, too.'

'Yes. Do you want to do that now? Might be best to get it over with?'

'I think I should, really.'

'I have some things to do upstairs. I will give you some family privacy and you can make your calls'

'Thank you, Julia.'

'Are you ok?'

'I'm not sure. I feel sort of blank. I expect I shall be hit by a wall of emotion at some point but right now I feel as though I am on automatic pilot. Going through the motions, as it were.' Julia nodded.

Harold made the phone calls. He suggested that Emma should give him a couple of days to sort out all the arrangements. To his surprise, she seemed to take the news philosophically. He promised to phone her to let her know when the funeral would be. He got through to his brother-in-law. The conversation was formal and stilted. Truth be told, they had never got on in the past and it seemed unlikely that they would now do so. He picked up a notebook and pencil and started to make a list of things to do. He needed to speak to the funeral directors and the local council first thing in the morning. He would have to go over to the house to pick up her driving licence and passport, and then make an appointment with her solicitor to see if she had made a will, unbeknown to him.

Julia looked in. 'How's it going, Harold?'

'It will be a busy day tomorrow. I still feel rather cold about it all. Still, that is useful, given that I am going to have to be efficient in terms of sorting out the arrangements.'

'What about Emma?'

'She was obviously surprised, but remained fairly calm, under the circumstances.'

'So, she wasn't too upset?'

'Veronica and Emma were not especially close, in my view.'

Julia nodded. 'Do you want a drink, Harold?'

'I don't think I will, Julia. I feel that I need a clear head to get through this. Maybe I'll have a proper drink after the funeral.'

'Yes. Will you sort something out for that?'

'I guess quite a few of her colleagues from the school will come to the funeral, so I might get something catered and set it up for afterwards.'

'Yes, that's a good idea. You don't want to have to worry about doing the food yourself, at a time like that.'

'No, I can't predict how I shall be. I'll have a word with the landlord at the Cracked Bell. He will probably let me use his functions room, if it is not booked up.'

'That's a good idea. You seem to be coping well.'

'I need to be on top of things. I can't allow myself to fall apart, in case Emma needs to lean on me, so to speak.'

'Yes. I'm sure you will be a great comfort to her, Harold.'


Harold slept fitfully but awoke with a determined set to his jaw. As the day progressed he completed his chores in the city and at the council offices. When he got back home, he spent some time on the phone finalising arrangements for the funeral and obtaining clarification from Veronica's solicitor and bank manager about formal business matters. The afternoon he devoted to tidying and cleaning the family home. He cleared out his own stuff from Emma's old room and made it comfortable for her to sleep in. He removed all obvious traces of Veronica from the double bedroom, putting some of her things into suitcases on top of the wardrobe, for attention at a later date. He made sure the fridge was stocked with some basic items so that there would be something for visitors, or for Emma when she came home. Once he was given a date and time by the funeral directors, he went down to the Cracked Bell and booked their upstairs functions room. He negotiated flexibility on numbers for a buffet reception, since he was unsure as to how many of Veronica's work colleagues from the school would attend. The pub landlord told him that this was the usual state of affairs and they could provide extra food from the kitchen once everyone had arrived, if that was necessary. Somehow, getting these details sorted out made Harold feel that he was doing something useful, and this provided him with his cover for not facing the full emotional impact of the situation. Indeed, he was holding that very much at arm's length; hourly, he gave thanks to the efficacy of repression, as a defence mechanism.

The funeral was scheduled for 2.15 p.m. on the Thursday. Harold had another, somewhat bland, telephone conversation with Emma who told him that she would travel down that morning and meet up with him at their home. Veronica's brother had made his own arrangements for his family to stay overnight at one of the budget hotels in the city.

And so it was that the cortege arrived at the crematorium. Quiet, restrained greetings were exchanged in the grounds around the corner from the main entrance, while they waited for the participants of the previous funeral to be disgorged. Timing was very tight at these places. Eventually they all filed in and sat on the wooden pews. Harold had arranged for a short basic Church of England service, since Veronica had been in the habit of going to church at christmas and easter. Privately, he had thought she was one of the most ungodly people he knew but he felt that it was her day and he should play the game. He was glad when, at last, the economy coffin moved through the screen on rollers, for her body to be cremated. The assembly piled out, with solemn faces, and adjourned to the Cracked Bell.

A couple of Emma's old school friends who had had many a sleep-over at the house had come along to the funeral. Harold was very glad of that and the way they seemed to be looking after Emma. Trevor sidled up to Harold.

'How are you doing, mate?'

'Not too bad, Trev. I hate funerals and when it's close to home it's the pits.'

'I guess you could treat this as a wake, and get drunk?'

'Trev, I can't really do that. It's like I'm the bloody event-planner and Master of Ceremonies, all mixed into one.'

Trevor nodded. 'Let me know if I can do anything to help.'

'There's a bunch of teachers from the school here. They've congregated over by the window, there.' Harold indicated with a sideways glance, and Trevor followed his gaze.

'Yes, I see them. Actually, I know one or two of them.'

'Do you think you could mingle with them a bit and put them at their ease. I think I need to make sure Veronica's relations are alright.'

'Sure thing, Harold.' Trevor moved over to join the group of teachers. Harold drifted over to the buffet bar and put a couple of sandwiches and a saussage role on his plate. As he moved away Emma came to join him.

'Who are those people Trevor is talking to, Dad?'

'Friends of your mother's from school.'

'Its strange to think she had a whole world there that we knew so little about.'

'Yes, she kept it pretty much to herself.'

'Why do you think she did that?'

'I don't know. She was a fairly private person. She seldom invited me to any of the social events they had. Being teachers, they were always doing fund-raisers of one kind or another.'

'Did she come to your things at the university?'

'Hardly ever. Actually, Emma, I should perhaps tell you that we had drifted apart rather. We were living somewhat separate existences, even though we were still maried.'

'Hence the spare room thing.'

'That's right.' Harold took a bite of his sandwich.

'You don't seem hugely upset, Dad, about Mum's death.'

'There has been a lot to think about and a lot to organise. I expect it will hit me later.'

'What's going to happen about the house?'

'Well, as you know, I have been pushed out to graze on an early retirement deal. It was either that or wait for redundancy. So, I lost my nice fat monthly pay cheque. I paid into a pension scheme at work for decades, so I do have considerably more than what I get from the state, but it is still a lot less than what I used to get when I was at work.'

'But you are managing?'

'Yes, I am. But I am not sure that I can manage the upkeep of our house for much longer.'

'So, you are thinking of selling it?'

'Look, Emma, I won't do anything in a hurry. I can keep it going until after you graduate, so you have your home base and somewhere to keep all your stuff. Once you get settled and get a job, I think it might be time to put it on the market.'

Emma stared at Harold lost in thought for a moment. 'Where will you live?'

'Oh, I hadn't really wanted to get into this right now but I suppose I should bring you up to speed on some things that have been happening.'

'What things? What's going on?' Emma sounded distracted.

'I did mention that your mother and I had been drifting apart, for quite a while actually.'

'Go on.'

'I hope this won't upset you, but I have been seeing another woman.'

'Dad!' Emma gasped. Then a smile played upon her lips. 'You old devil! What's her name?'

'She is called Julia. I have known her through work for quite some time but only by sitting on committees and that sort of thing. We have been together as friends more recently.'

'Do you mean friends or lovers?'

'You don't beat about the bush, do you?' Harold replied.

'Oh, come on Dad. You've come this far and we are at Mum's wake. You might as well spill the beans.'

'If you must know, we are lovers.'

'Are you going to let me meet her?'

'Of course. Your mother would not hear of it until after you had graduated. Now, things have changed. I know that Julia would very much like to meet you.'

'I assume she is not coming here?'

'No, we felt that would be most inappropriate. You said you would be staying a few more days. Maybe we could have something to eat together tomorrow. Would you be up for that?'

'Yes, I think so. I don't want to spend too much time in the house. Too many reminders.'

'We could go out for an Italian, then maybe go back to Julia's house for some coffee afterwards.'

'Alright. You can let me know about the arrangements tomorrow. I might go and sleep over with my friend Bernadette tonight. Speaking of which, I see she has just arrived. I'll go and see what she wants to drink.' Emma gave Harold a hug and went over to her friend.

Harold mingled with the guests, accepting their condolences with as much good grace and gravitas as he could muster. Eventually he came around to where Veronica's brother, Dale, was standing.

'Dale, if there is anything you want in terms of a personal keepsake I could take you over to the house when this has finished.' Dale stood, as if lost in thought for a moment.

'Nah! I don't think so Harold. I'm not the sentimental type.'

'Do you have the details of the solicitor? I think she made a will recently, so he will probably be in touch.'

'Oh, right. Yes, she sent me an email a while back. Said you were not exactly getting on together.'

'Well, water under the bridge, hey? Don't let's get into all that at her funeral.'

'Fair enough. I never thought you were the right one for her, Harold.'

'I think I guessed that, already, Dale. What about Emma? Will you keep in touch. I mean you are her uncle.'

'Yeah, well, I've never seen much of her. To be honest, I don't have much to say to her when I do see her. I post her a birthday card, if I remember. That's about it.'

'She has more or less left the nest now. She finishes university at the end of this academic year. I think I will leave it up to the two of you if you want to keep in touch or not.'

'I don't really think I'll be seeing much more of you, Harold.'

'No, I don't suppose you will.' Harold shrugged his shoulders and moved on. People were starting to leave; the room was thinning out. Emma confirmed that she was going to stay over at her friend's house. The landlord asked Harold if his staff could start clearing away the food. Trevor stayed until the end.

'That wasn't too bad, was it, Harold?'

'Could have been a lot worse, Trev. I half-expected Dale to get a bit nasty but he was ok.'

'Veronica's brother?'

'Yes. I doubt if I shall ever see him again.'

'Good riddance?'

'An apt turn of phrase, my old mate.' Harold smiled.

'What are you going to do now. You're not going back to the house, are you?'

'Nah. Don't think I could face it. I think I will go over to Julia's. She said she would wait in for me, in case I wanted to go over.'

'I think that sounds like a good idea.'

'I'll just go and tell the landlord that we are all done here.'

'OK, Harold. I'll be off, then.'

'Yeah. See you, Trev.' The old friends patted one another on the shoulder. This was not exactly a man-hug; they were always a bit 'lite' in that department. Harold signed off with the landlord, called a cab, and phoned Julia to let her know he was on his way.

Once back at Julia's house and seated in the sitting room with cups of tea, Julia looked over at Harold.

'So, are you going to give me a post-mortem, if that is not too close to a bad pun?'

'It was pretty grim, as these things tend to be. I mean, it went off ok. There were no gaffs, no outbursts, and no hysterical wailings. I felt a lot of the people there were somewhat dressed down, especially the younger teachers from Veronica's school. I always thought one wore black; dark suits for men and polished shoes.'

'You know, Harold, I'm not sure many blokes have that sort of clothing now, unless they work in an occupation that requires it and fewer places do nowadays. You can get by with 'smart-casual' for most occasions tainted with the brush of formality.'

Harold nodded. 'I think it makes for poorer theatre.'

'How do you mean?'

'A funeral is a formal ceremony that brings down the curtain on a life lived. It is the finale, the closing act. Of course, the churches were particularly good with this. They frequently provided brilliantly apt stage sets against which the drama could unfold. A crematorium is definitely low key, but that is true even if there is a service, like we had for Veronica. I suppose a Christian burial service is what I am talking about.'

'You can get humanist speakers. I'm not sure what one calls them. They are not priests, but they are aping that role. Perhaps they are equivalent to a Master of Ceremonies.' said Julia.

'I think an M/C might be more appropriate to the post-funereal piss-up.'

Julia giggled. 'You are dreadful, Harold.' She sipped her tea. 'Apart from all that, did you speak to your daughter or to Veronica's relatives?'

'Yes, I did. Emma is sleeping over with one of her girl friends. As for Veronica's brother, I doubt if I shall ever see or speak to him again. If there is a bequest, he will get that through communication with her solicitor.'

'So that gives you a clean break.'

'Yes, I think it does.'

'And the house?'

'I've told Emma that I shall have to sell it. I said I would keep it until after her graduation if she wants, but I really don't think she will want to spend any time back there now.'

'No. From what you have told me, it seems as though she is about to branch out into her own adult life space, as it were.'

'That's right. I did mention to her that I have been seeing you and asked her if she would meet you.'

'I would love to meet her, Harold.'

'I suggested maybe going out for an Italian meal together tomorrow evening, and then back here for some coffee afterwards. What do you think?'

'That would be lovely.'

'I'll phone Emma and see if I can sort it out.'

'OK. I need to phone Penny about a couple of work things. I'll go and do that upstairs and leave you to sort out the Italian.'

'So, maybe if I booked a table at Marcello's?'

'Sounds perfect to me.'

The dinner was arranged, as agreed.


Harold and Julia took a taxi to Marcello's and made themselves comfortable in the reception lounge. They were both sipping gin and tonics when Emma arrived. They got up and Harold made the introductions. He ordered a white wine from the bar for Emma. Before they had time to sit down, the waiter offered to take their drinks through to table. They followed him and sat down. Julia placed Emma opposite her father and sat down next to her. She turned to Emma.

'I love your outfit, Emma,' said Julia.

'Oh, I vascillated for ages. I felt I ought to keep to the black and grey spectrum out of respect for the memory of my mother, but I didn't want to look as though I had walked straight in from the funeral.'

'I totally understand. The pink silk scarf offsets the black dress perfectly.'

'Thank you.' Emma smiled at Julia, blushing slightly.

'What language are you two talking? I can't understand a word of it,' said Harold.

'Oh, Dad! I don't believe you. I've seen you looking at the women's fashion pages in the Sunday paper magazine section.'

Julia laughed. 'She's got your number, Harold.'

'Traitor!' replied Harold, grinning at Emma.

'It's alright, Julia. I never came across any hard evidence of him being a transvestite. Well, not while I was at home, at any rate.'

'Hmm... He is blushing a little. Do you think that is non-specific embarrassment or is it triggered by an interesting secret?'

'I don't think Dad's the type, do you Julia?'

'No, maybe not,' replied Julia.

'So what's the scoop? How did you two get together?' asked Emma.

'Bloody hell! You don't waste much time, do you Emm. Straight in for the jugular,' said Harold.

'Just curious, that's all, Dad.'

'You really want to know?' asked Julia.

'Yes, I think I do. It's not like I'm a kid any more.'

'Well, it all came from a coincidence. We had sometimes chatted at the university. I sit on one or two committees there and Harold was also a member of one of them. Then I bumped into Harold at the supermarket one day and he had just been served a notice saying that he would probably be made redundant.'

'Well, that doesn't sound like a recipe for romance,' said Emma.

'That's true. Harold had decided he would buy some wine and drown his sorrows that afternoon. So I told him he had better come round to my house to do it, or he would end up maudlin and depressed.'

'So that was purely an act of generosity, on your part?' enquired Emma.

'Well, Emma, I have to say that I have always found your father to be rather attractive, in a crumpled sort of way.' Emma hooted with laughter and choked a little on her wine.

'Dad! You old devil,' she said when she had recovered her composure.

'So, Emma, one thing led to another and your father and I became... Shall we say intimate, as the afternoon wore on. Admittedly we had both been drinking some wine and this might possibly have made us a little less prudent than we might otherwise have been.'

'Oh, Dad. Fancy you getting up to mischief. I knew I should never have left home.'

'This is very difficult for me. Can we order our food now?' said Harold.

The revelations were paused while they chose their dishes and the waiter took their order, returning to bring them a bottle of wine.

'So, go on. What happened then?' asked Emma.

'Look, Emm, I'm afraid your mother worked out what had happened. She actually kicked me out of the house. She was a bit violent towards me. I mean, she had every reason to be,' said Harold.

'Harold turned up at my house with a rather resplendent black eye. He had nowhere to go,' said Julia.

'Trev had some relatives staying over, so he couldn't put me up,' Harold explained to Emma.

'So Mum kicked you out, like for good?' asked Emma.

'Pretty much. She didn't want you to be upset so she told me to keep some of my stuff at home until you had graduated. I think she wanted to break it to you gently, once you were through university and had a job.'

Emma sat in silence. She looked pensive and picked at her food. 'Let me get this straight. You two have been living together for some time, now?' she asked.

'Yes, that's right, Emm,' said Harold.

'You didn't think about getting a flat or something, Dad?'

'I was about to lose my job, Emm. Money was going to be, and has become, very tight.'

'But I thought you just retired?'

'I was offered early retirement, if I wanted it. But if I didn't take it, I would have been made redundant.'

'Oh. So you just took him in?' Emma asked Julia.

'In a way,' said Julia.

'What do you mean?' asked Emma.

'Well, Harold wanted a roof over his head but he could not pay anything towards the household costs. Normally if somebody takes a room in someone's house, they pay rent.'

Emma nodded. 'But you two had become an item, as they say. So how did that work out in this arrangement?'

'Well, the one thing Harold does have a lot of, now that he is not teaching at the university, is time. I, on the other hand, am rather short of spare time. I am very busy with my work as a consultant,' said Julia.

'I still don't see what you are driving at,' said Emma.

'Your father agreed to look after the house in return for his bed and board, as it were. I pay all the household expenses and food bills and so forth. He keeps the house clean and tidy. He does all the kitchen stuff. He is the chief cook and bottle-washer!'

Emma smiled. 'You were always messing about in the kitchen at home, doing your foodie dishes, weren't you Dad.'

'That's right. You see it kind of worked out alright in the end,' said Harold.

'So, do you think Mum would have found somebody else, Dad?' asked Emma.

'I think she would, Emm. She was quite popular with her colleagues at the school. Maybe she would have teamed up with one of them,' Harold replied.

The main course arrived and the conversation broadened out to cover a wide range of topics from music to politics and the state of the planet. They decided against a pudding and caught a cab back to Julia's house for coffee.

'Harold, you do the coffee. I'm going to take Julia on a quick tour of the house.'

'OK. Will do,' replied Harold.
Harold pottered off to the kitchen. As he was boiling the kettle he listened to the two of them as they moved from room to room. There was a lot of what could only be described as 'girlie' giggling, interspersed with the occasional shriek of delight from Emma. They sounded as though they were getting along just fine and seemed to be enjoying one another's company. Harold smiled as he ground the beans. He took through the coffee things on a tray and let the cafetiere brew while he waited for Emma and Julia. Soon he heard footsteps on the stairs.

'Dad, this is a fantastic house!' exclaimed Emma.

'It is, indeed. I'm glad you like it,' said Harold.

'Dad, Julia said I could have a room of my own if I wanted. You know, when our house is sold.'

Harold glanced across at Julia, giving her an imperceptible wink.

'Would you like that, Emm?' asked Harold.

'You bet!' replied Emma, with no hesitation.

'Well, let's take things one step at a time. Maybe I should go ahead and put the house on the market straight away. These things always take a long time to get sorted out. I would be very surprised if we had to move out before your graduation,' said Harold.

'Whatever you think is best, Dad.'

They relaxed over coffee. Julia and Emma chatted about a couple of films they had seen recently. Eventually, Harold made a move to bring the evening to a close.

'I think we should get back to the house now, Emma.'

Emma glanced at her wrist watch. 'Oh, yes, is that the time. I have to get a train in the morning, Dad.'

'What time is that?' asked Harold.

'I think it is around 11.00.' replied Emma.

'At least it's not crack of dawn! I'll give you a lift down to the station.'

Harold phoned for a taxi to take them home. When it arrived they paused on the front porch to say their farewells.

'Thank you so much for the coffee, Julia, and for showing me around your lovely house,' said Emma.

'It was good to meet you, Emma. I'm sorry that it was on a sad occasion but, in my experience, people do move on and get stuck into their lives fairly swiftly once the funeral is over. It provides a degree of closure,' said Julia.

'Yes, I expect you are right,' replied Emma.

Julia hugged Emma when they said goodbye on the doorstep. Emma kissed Julia, lightly, on the cheek. The taxi driver honked his horn. Harold and Emma got in and they departed.

# Chapter 10

A couple of months had elapsed since Veronica's funeral. Harold was on edge about the sale of his house. He checked the morning post and found a letter from his solicitor. Hurriedly, he ripped open the envelope and started reading. Contracts had been exchanged, the house had been sold. As was his won't at such times, he put the kettle on for a cup of tea. Julia sauntered into the kitchen.

'You're looking pleased with yourself, Harold. What's up?'

'You are looking at the proud non-owner of a house!" He grinned.

'Really? That went well. There are usually so many hitches and delays in these matters.'

'I know. It could have dragged on until Christmas, at least.'

'Have you told Emma?'

'Give me a chance! I've only just opened the letter from the solitors.'

Julia smiled, 'I suppose it won't make a huge difference to her, if she is going to carry on living with the boy friend.'

Harold nodded. 'Yes, well, I guess that might depend on what happens with the job applications.'

'I think I'll sit and read the paper for a bit. Why don't you go and give her a call or Skype or something?'

'Yes, I think I might,' said Harold as he dumped his tea bag into the kitchen bin. He ambled off to his little room and phoned his daughter.

'Emma Hake.'

'Hi Emma.'

'Oh! Hi Dad. How are you, today?'

'I'm good, thanks Emm. The thing is, I got a letter from our solicitor, and the house is now sold.'

'Really?'

'Yup. We no longer own it.'

'Ah... It's a bit sad, though. Don't you think, Dad?'

'It is, Emm. But life goes on, as they say. It puts a closure onto the previous chapter. I think that must be especially so for you, having just graduated with Upper Second Class Honours, you wonderful girl.'

'Oh, Dad, lots of people get Upper Seconds.'

'I know. And they get them because they work very hard while they are at university.'

'Well, I sure did work hard.'

'Yes, you did.'

'I mean I did my share of partying, but I kept it under control; toned it down around exam time and stuff like that.'

'So, what is happening on the jobs front? Has George got anything yet.'

'Oh, God. Dad, he got offered this fantastic civil engineering job. He's going to be part of a team that's going to build a new motorway.'

'Well, that sounds terrific, Emm.'

'Dad...'

'Yes, Emm?'

'Well, it's just that...' Harold could hear his daughter sniffling at the other end of the phone.

'Are you alright, Emm?'

'Not really, Dad. It's George's job. It's in New Zealand.'

'Bloody hell! Well, what will you do? Will you go out there with him?'

'No, Dad. That's the thing. We split up. He wants to make a fresh start. He wants to be free to work all around the world. He says he will move on once he has completed the motorway contract in New Zealand.'

'Emm, I'm very sorry to hear this.'

'It's ok Dad. I completely misread him. I thought he wanted to settle down and have a family and stuff. He's ambitious. He just wants success, money and power. I don't know why I didn't see that before.'

'Maybe he kept it well hidden, Emm. I never twigged it, although I have to say that I didn't really have a chance to get to know him. You always wanted to stay up there in your flat.'

'I know, Dad.'

'Perhaps he regarded you as a sort of *trophy girlfriend*. You know, like a *trophy wife*.'

'Oh, Dad. Don't get into one of your analytic modes. I'm just sad.'

'And I've sold the old home, so you can't come back to that for some comfort. The place where you grew up no longer belongs to us. Maybe I should have kept it a bit longer, until you were properly settled.'

'Dad, what-ifs get you nowhere.'

'Indeed. I learned about that the hard way. Why don't you come back and live here until you get fixed up job-wise.'

'Actually, I did see an advert for a production assistant at the Hexington studios.'

'That would not be an impossible commute. There is a regular Metro service to Hexington.'

'How do you know that, Dad?'

'Oh, a guy I used to work with, Craig Melcheter, he was keen on walking. I can remember that he sometimes took a Metro there, instead of his car, if he wanted to have a drink after his ramble.'

'So was he one of your mates down the Cracked Bell?'

'He was, but he actually worked at the university, too.'

'Ok. Whatever. George and I are going to sell quite a bit of stuff to the people who are taking over the flat from us, so I haven't much to bring home.'

'Do you want me to drive over and pick you up sometime?'

'No, I'll be ok. I brought masses home at the end of term, and you took loads back for me after the graduation ceremony.'

'That's true. Well, I will tell the lovely Julia to expect your arrival sometime soon.'

'Ok, Dad. I love you.'

'I love you, too, Emm. Bye'

'Bye.'

Harold frowned and then took the remains of his mug of tea downstairs. He brought Julia up-to-date with the situation.

'Maybe it is a good thing that Emma found out about George's true colours, before she got in any deeper,' said Julia.

'Given that Emma said she was thinking of having kids with him, it would have been nasty if the split had come when they were toddlers or something.'

Julia nodded. 'Well, speaking for myself, I think it will be delightful to have Emma around the house. We must give her the space to grieve over her lost relationship but we must try to cheer her up, too.'

'Do you want to do my job?' asked Harold.

'Oh, Harold, what do you mean. Of course not.'

Harold chuckled. 'I didn't mean it was my job, and my job only, to cheer up Emm. I meant that the way you were talking, I might be forgiven for thinking you were a qualified counsellor!'

Julia laughed and threw a cushion at Harold. 'I might have made a good counsellor, Harold. You never know.'

'Actually, I think you would have been good. Providing you could have kept your bossy side under control.'

'Moi? I have a bossy side?'

'Don't make me laugh,' replied Harold.

Over the following weeks Harold increased his counselling hours with Anthea and picked up a few more teaching sessions, thanks to Trevor. He also got more interview work for Penny's market research projects, even though he found it extremely tedious. All in all, he was gradually carving out a niche for himself as a jobbing psychologist. Emma took up Julia's offer of a room and moved in with rather more clutter than she had led them to believe. Julia had some storage space in her basement and so that worked out well in the end.

Julia had just returned from an overnight conference in London. Harold put the kettle on for a cup of tea immediately he heard the key in the lock. They took their tea into the sitting room.

'How was it, then? Down in the smoke?' said Harold.

'Oh, Harold! Nobody calls it 'the smoke' nowadays.'

'Whatever.'

'It was...' Julia paused, searching for the right word. 'A bit boring, actually.'

'When I was an academic, I eventually got to the point where I did conferences on automatic pilot. Seen one, seen them all.'

'Yes, I know what you mean. Still, I have to go to these things. It is what happens at the dining table or in the bar that is important. I pick up a lot of work by networking at these events and that indirectly pays for this house, the furniture, our food, the car, and all that.'

'So it is a means to a lifestyle? To our lifestyle, even?'

'You could put it like that. I mean, I'm not entirely cynical. The actual work that I pick up is usually fine and I enjoy the challenges that it brings.'

'That's good, then.'

'Yes, it is. I'm not sure if I could actually do the work if I didn't find it interesting.'

'Let's hope that you will continue to do so, for ever and ever *Our Femme.*'

'Harold, don't be naughty. That verges on the sacrilegious.' Julia wagged her finger at Harold, with a disapproving eye.

'Anyway, how about you and Emma? How have you both been while I was away?'

'Actually, I have been more or less by myself. Emma has not been around much.'

'Oh, I hope that job of her's is not proving too demanding.'

Harold sighed. 'I don't think the problem is the job.'

'So, what is it? Do you know?'

Harold shifted in his chair and put down his cup of tea. 'I'm not shure how to put this.'

'Oh, Harold. This does not sound as though it is going to be good news. You had better spit it out, now. Come along.' Julie sat forward, looking intently at Harold.

'Well, in my capacity as general factotum here, I keep half an eye on the various waste paper baskets around the house. I like to take a plastic sack and do a round of the the rooms, just to keep everything tidy.'

'I had noticed you were a bit obsessive that way, Harold. I must admit, I rather like it.' Julia smiled.

'Yes, well, here's where it gets difficult.'

'Take a deep breath and just go with it,' said Julia.

'I emptied Emma's basket. As usual, there were a lot of crumpled up sheets of paper in it. I think she roughs out ideas and plans for the projects she is working on at the studio.'

'Go on,' Julia nodded.

'Well, my sack was getting a bit full and a rolled up sheet of paper dropped out and fell onto the carpet. So I bent down to pick it up and I just happened to notice something. It just caught my attention, out of the corner of my eye.'

'What did, Harold?'

'The words on the paper. I just noticed Penny's name.'

'So? I sometimes give her things to drop off at Penny's house on her way to the Metro. It was probably a To-Do list or something. What's wrong with that?'

'I don't think it was a To-Do list, Julia. It said '*My darling Penny*'. It was the draft of a letter. It was the start of a love letter. I am more or less sure of it.'

The blood drained out of Julia's face. 'It might not have been my Penny, though. Maybe it was one of her friends from university?'

'I suppose that's possible but a bit unlikely, don't you think?'

Julia sat back. She was breathing deeply, almost hyperventillating. 'What else did it say? Did you read it?'

'I did uncrumple it, although I felt very guilty about doing so. It did not say much. I think she had tossed the sheet in the bin after she made a spelling mistake in the first sentence. She spelled 'ecstasy' with a '<u>c</u>' at the end.'

'Where is it? Did you keep it? Can I see it?'

'I threw it away with the trash. The bin men came yesterday. It is gone.'

'Oh, Harold!'

'There was only one incomplete sentence. I can more or less remember the gist. *My darling Penny, I am still aglow from our time together last night at your house. It was for me, perfect ectacy.* As I said, the '<u>ecstacy</u>' was crossed out and then she must have crumpled the sheet at that point.'

Penny shook herself. 'Well, never mind about me. However did you feel. Did you know Emma was like this?'

Harold looked at the ceiling. 'No, I hadn't a clue. Emma never confided in me about her boyfriends. We were very close when she was growing up as a child but she grew away from me in her adolescence. I mean, I am not the sort of guy with whom she could share girlie talk with.'

Julia smiled. 'No, I see what you mean.'

'And anyway, up until she came down from university, I thought she was going to live with or get married to George. I even fantasised about becoming a Granddad at some point.'

'Well, what are we going to do about it all?' said Julia.

Harold smiled, wanly. 'You know, Julia, I think this is maybe the first time I have seen you flummoxed, without a plan.'

'I know. And I don't like it.'

'My guess is, given your intimate relationship with Penny, you will want to have words with her?'

'Well, I think maybe I ought to. But I won't do that if you don't want me to, Harold. If necessary, I can just let my relationship with Penny cool off. But Emma is your daughter. And she is living here, too. I think you have to set the pace on this one, Harold. But we must coordinate.'

Harold nodded. 'I think you should talk to Penny and explain what happened about me finding a draft of the letter. You can say it was only one sentence and that we have not read anything in detail about what they have been up to.'

'Yes. It is going to be a difficult conversation, though.'

'I'm sure it will be. I think we need to know where we stand. I think I shall have to have a parallel chat with Emma in the not too distant future, but it might be best if I let you make the first move. Penny will doubtless speak to Emma, once she knows you know. So, then Emma will know that I know, when I ask her about it.'

Julia sighed. 'I guess that is all we can do, for now. I mean, if Emma is going to stay here we have to clear this up and bring it out in the open. Maybe she will move out?'

'Maybe she will. She is a grown-up now. She will make her own decision. If you want her to go, I am sure she will not give you any hassle. She will find somewhere and move out. It might take a bit more time for her to organise the stuff she has got in the basement, but I don't imagine you would be too bothered about that?'

'No, of course not. I don't feel hostile towards Emma. She has lost her mother, and we offered her a home. I feel we should remain true to that, if we can. I feel angry with Penny but that is not directly your problem or Emma's, for that matter.'

'So, let me get this straight. We play happy families here pretending that nothing has happened until you have had your confrontation with Penny. Then we will see how things are and try to find a way forward.'

'I think that is all we can do, Harold. I'm supposed to be seeing Penny for lunch tomorrow. I'm going to her house. I assume Emma will be out, working at the studio. I don't know what I'll say to her. To be honest I'll probably be tempted to smash up her best crockery.'

'Don't go losing your temper over it, Julia. That won't do any good, you know.'

Julia looked at Harold for a long time. 'You may be right, Harold. I suppose I could make a superhuman attempt to remain civil.'

'I think that will be the best way.'

'I would only do this for you, Harold.'

Harold smiled. 'Strange, isn't it. You are the one in charge but you will allow yourself to be guided by me in this matter.'

Julia returned Harold's smile. 'Maybe not so strange. We have a very complex relationship.'

'I think we do,' agreed Harold.


The next day, Harold awoke feeling not only glum but anxious, too. When he got dressed he saw that Julia had left him a note pinned under a fridge magnet, saying she had left early to see Penny. '*Pistols at coffee,*' he thought. He made himself comfortable in the sitting room with his library book and buried himself in the trials and tribulations of a family caught up in the London blitz of WW2. Soon, he was catapulted into an alternate reality where neither he, Emma, Penny nor Julia existed. Eventually the suspension of disbelief was fractured by the sound of Julia opening the front door. She had returned.

'I'm in the sitting room,' Harold called out.

'OK. I'll just take off my coat,' Julia replied. She came in and sat down, across from Harold.

'How did it go?'

'Not so well.'

'Not a great surprise, then.'

'No.'

Harold looked closely at Julia. She appeared to be on the verge of tears. He went over to her, took her by the hand and led her to the settee. She sat close beside him, snuffling into his shoulder for a few moments. Then she pulled herself together, grabbed a tissue, blew her nose and composed herself.

'Stiff upper lip, I think. Don't you, Harold?'

'Absolutely, Julia. I mean, we are Brits!'

'I always prefer to think of myself as English, now that Scotland and Wales have gone independent,' said Julia.

'I will immediately modify my self-concept accordingly. I never did like the shortening of the term '*British*'. If you wanted to ban its use in this household, I would obey, willingly,' said Harold.

'Yes. Well, that's got the important stuff out of the way. Hasn't it, Harold?'

'Indeed. Any sort of lesbian liaison that might exist between my daughter and your lover pales into insignificance against questions of national identity.' Harold delivered a tripple head-nod to Julia, as a way of emphasising his point. A smile flitted across Julia's lips.

'Harold, I tried to be calm, like you said, but I failed miserably. I'm not going to go into the details but I shouted at Penny. I said a lot of awful things which I didn't really mean and I called her some horrible names.'

'Well done! Better out than in, as we post-Freudian folks might say,' said Harold.

'She was very spirited in her defence. It seems... Oh, this is so difficult. Harold, are you sure you want to hear about it?' Julia looked thoughtfully at Harold.

'Yes, I think so. We will never get out of the mess unless we know what's what.'

'Spoken like a true bloke, Harold.' Julia smiled at him.

'I don't think it was entirely a case of the evil Penny seducing your daughter. From what she said, it sounded like a case of mutual attraction.'

'Well, I guess that is entirely possible, on paper as it were.' said Harold.

'I don't know how serious it is. It might be one of those hot sexual passions that burns itself out after a few weeks. It might go deeper. I just don't know. I don't think I was seeing things very clearly. I was too upset.'

'So, I take it that things have cooled between you and Penny?'

'Oh, my God! The fridge/freezer is like a forrest fire compared to how Penny and I are at the moment.' Harold nodded.

'I guess I shall have to have a word with Emma, then.'

'I don't think there is any point in you pretending that you don't know.'

'What if she says she wants to move out?'

'We can hardly stop her, Harold, and it might be the best for her.'

'But if she says she wants to stay, is that OK with you?' Julia sat pensively, for a moment.

'If you are alright with that, then I would be. I'm not angry with Emma. And what was between me and Penny is of nobody else's concern. I don't think Emma had realised how close me and Penny were. She probably does now. I mean, Penny must have filled her in with at least some of the back story.'

'So, we are flexible. She can go or stay, and we don't mind either way?'

'That's how I feel Harold. But maybe you would like it if she stayed on here? After all, she is your daughter and the pair of you do seem to get on well together.'

'Yes, I would like that. But I can't hang on to her forever. I always saw her coming here, as a temporary solution to the difficult situation she was left to cope with after George went to New Zealand and her mother died.'

'*Que sera, sera*. It would seem?' said Julia.

'*Que sera, sera*.' Harold nodded in assent.

It was several days before Harold got to speak with Emma. She had returned from the city with a treacle tart. They were in the kitchen, sharing it over a cup of coffee.

'Julia was saying that you have been been getting on well with Penny, lately.' Harold's intonation indicated that he had asked a question, rather than stated a fact. Emma chortled.

'Dad! Sounds like somebody has been telling tales on me.'

Harold smiled. 'Well, I find it a little difficult to talk about these things.'

'But you're a psychologist, for heaven's sake!' said Emma.

'I know. But that just means I know a lot about what you can make rats do when you reward them with food pellets in their cages.'

'Yeah. Right,' replied Emma, dismissively.

'It came as a bit of a surprise, Emm. You know, after all that time living in the flat with George at university.'

'Well, I don't think you paid much attention to that side of my life when I was in secondary school, in that case,' said Emma.

'How do you mean?'

'Oh, come on, Dad. All those sleep-overs with my girl friends? Trying on one another's clothes? There was even three of us in my bed sometimes!'

Harold knitted his brows. He drew a deep breath. 'I had no idea. I just thought you were having girly fun. There was enough giggling going on.'

'Yes, well, maybe we kept a lid on the heavy breathing,' said Emma.

'I can't believe I am having this conversation with you,' said Harold.

'Well, you are. And you need to face up to it,' replied Emma.

'Yes, you are right. And there I was thinking I just had to get over your mother dying on us.'

'You were out of our family by then, Dad. You were living here with Julia.'

'Fair point.' Harold smiled at his daughter.

'Dad, do we have to get into a fight over this? I mean, loads of people in my generation lean a bit bisexual nowadays.'

'I suppose they do,' said Harold.

'And what about you? What happened at that horrid boarding school you are always going on about? I bet some of the boys got up to some hanky-panky there,' said Emma.

Harold laughed. 'That's my sort of phrase! I never thought you would call it hanky-panky.'

'People don't just inherit their parents' genes, you know. They pick up their vocabulary too,' replied Emma.

'Well, don't start swearing like your mother. It's not lady-like.'

'Now there's an old-fashioned phrase if I ever heard one,' said Emma, laughing.

Harold paused to pour some cream over his treacle tart.

'Not too much of that, Dad. I've just lost one parent. I don't want to say goodbye to the other one quite so soon,' said Emma.

Harold grunted.

'You are fond of Penny?' he asked.

'Yes, Dad, I am. And we have fun. It isn't all sweaty bodies, you know.'

Harold grimaced at the thought. 'No, of course not. Julia is rather upset.'

'Dad, I like Julia. She has been very kind to me, letting me stay here rent free. But if she has got a problem with this, then she must sort it out with Penny. That really isn't my business.' said Emma.

Harold nodded. 'Are you planning to move in with Penny? I mean, she has the space, I think.'

'No, I don't think I want to do that, Dad. If Julia wants to kick me out, then I'll find somewhere. I could get a room or rent a flat with one of my friends.'

'So it isn't like you are going to get married to Penny?'

Emma laughed. 'Dad, it's just a love affair. It will probably blow over. And if it doesn't, that will be nice, too. But I'm not about to enter into a civil partnership or anything like that,' said Emma.

'OK. I just wanted to get things straight in my head,' replied Harold.

'Does Julia want me to move out?'

'No, I don't think so. She was upset at first, but she is very resillient.'

'What about you? Do you want me to go?'

'Don't be silly, Emma. Of course I don't.'

Emma smiled at Harold.

'OK. I just wanted to *get things straight in my head*', Emma said, imitating Harold.

Harold gave her a friendly punch. 'So, I'll tell Julia that we have had this little chat, and that you don't want to move out. Is that right?'

'Yeah. That's fine, Dad.'

Harold nodded. He cleared up the plates and the coffee mugs and took them over to the sink. Emma went off to her room.

## Chapter 11

It was early evening. Julia was having a girls' night out with some of her business pals. Trevor had called Harold, earlier, and they had agreed to meet in the Cracked Bell. They occupied the coveted bay window seats. Trevor had just returned from the bar with a couple of delightful pints of ale. Harold sipped his pint appreciatively. He smiled as he watched Trevor wipe away a frothy moustache with the back of his hand.

'And how is the world treating you, Harold?'

Harold choked on his beer. 'Start with the easy questions, why don't you!'

Trevor looked puzzled.

'You are not going to believe this.'

'Try me,' said Trevor.

'I hardly know where to start.'

'Oh? Well, the beginning is the conventional place, I think,' said Trevor.

'Ha! Ha! Very funny.' Harold took a long swig of beer, before sitting back.

'It appears that Emma is having an affair with Penny Charlton.'

Trevor looked puzzled. 'But I thought she had a boyfriend.'

'She did. He left. Graduated, and then went to work in New Zealand.'

'So, Emma didn't go out there with him?'

'No. Apparently, the guy turns out to be very ambitious and wants to get moving on an international career in construction work, or something.'

'Hang on,' said Trevor, 'I thought you told me your Julia was having a thing with Penny What's-Her-Name.'

'Charlton. Penny Charlton,' said Harold. 'Yes, I did.'

'So?' Trevor clearly wanted beans to be spilled.

'Julia was extremely annoyed when I told her. *Livid* would be an apt description.'

Trevor nodded.

'To cut a long story short, Julia has calmed down now, although I think things are somewhat frosty between her and Penny.'

'I imagine so,' said Trevor.

'I had what might vaguely be described as a father-daughter chat with Emm. Turns out she has had bisexual leanings going way back to her early teens. '

'So how do you feel about that?' Asked Trevor.

'I can't get my head around it. I mean, look at me, Trev. I'm an ageing hipster. I screwed up my marriage. Technically, I'm a widower. I was more or less made redundant. Apart from all that, I'm living as an over-qualified manservant, cook and bottle-washer to a highly bossy woman because I can't afford to pay the rent.'

'Oh, Harold, don't forget that you are also her toy-boy!' Trevor stifled a laugh.

'Toy-Clapped-Out-Old-Wreck, more like,' replied Harold, with a chortle. 'Seriously, though, what on earth am I going to say to a sophisticated young lesbian in her twenties, who just happens to be my daughter?' Harold shrugged.

'Search me, Harold. But I think it deserves another pint, my old mate.' Trevor went to the bar and returned with fresh drinks. Harold supped up and then took a swig from the new pint mug. His mobile phone vibrated and he checked the caller ID to see who it was.

'Trev, I should take this. It's Anthea.' He stepped outside the bar to the relative quiet of the corridor. 'Hello, Anth.'

'Har-rold! Do you have anything at the clinic tomorrow, darling?'

'Mavis on holiday?'

'No, sweetie. She has a nasty tummy bug, so she is having a couple of days off,' replied Anthea.

'Oh, that's no fun. Tell her I hope she gets better soon.'

'I will. I will. But, darling, are you coming in tomorrow?'

'Just for an 11 o'clock ciggy-chuck session.'

'That's great. You can let me take you out to lunch, afterwards.'

'I can?'

'Yes, darling. And I want you to tell me how you are and how everything's going.'

'Believe me, Anth, you don't want to know.'

'Oooh, but I dooo. I shall want all the gory details, sweetie-pie.'

'If you insist!'

'Yes, darling. We can have a lovely chat over some fish and chips. How does that sound?'

'Actually, it sounds great,' said Harold. 'I'll give you a knock when I'm done. It'll be around midday.' Cutting short Anthea's protracted farewell ritual, Harold hung up and returned to the bar.

'Anth wants to take me out to lunch tomorrow.'

'Very nice too,' said Trevor. 'Where are you going?'

'She didn't say but she wants fish and chips, so it will probably be the Lobster's Claw.'

'That's a great pub for sea food,' said Trevor. He thought for a moment. 'I'm over that way, too, tomorrow. Some dreary meeting in the morning.'

'Why don't you join us? I'm sure Anth won't mind.'

'Do you reckon? Are you sure she doesn't want to talk couch business with you?' asked Trevor.

'And by that you mean Freud or condoms?'

Trevor grinned. 'Pretty much the same thing, from what I've heard.'

Harold chuckled.

'I have a suspicion that you might fancy the voluptuously vegetarian Ms. Partington, despite your antipathy towards brown rice and open sandals,' said Harold.

'No comment,' replied Trevor.

'I'll take that as a '*yes*' then.'

'Seriously, Harold, I don't want to gate-crash your lunch.'

'Actually, it might prevent Anth from digging in too much about Emma and all that stuff. I would rather just enjoy the fish and chips, if you see what I mean. I'll send her an SMS and see what she says.' Harold typed the message into his mobile phone. Almost instantaneously there was a reply.

'She's up for it, mate.' Harold smiled. 'So, we should be there by about a quarter past twelve.'

'That's great. I might even put on a clean shirt!' said Trevor.

'Bloody-hell, Trev. Don't go over the top, mate.' They laughed and elbowed one another. Harold settled back and they sat in silence for a while.

'I haven't a clue what's happening to me anymore, Trev. It feels like I have to take things one day at a time.'

'There's been too much change in too short a period of time, in my view, mate,' said Trevor.

Harold exhaled a long slow breath, slowly nodding his head as he did so. 'Let's sup-up and call it a night.'

'We might as well. Don't want a hangover if I'm meeting the buxsome Ms. Partington tomorrow,' said Trevor.

'Indeed not,' said Harold. They said goodbye and wended their separate ways home.

The following lunchtime Harold and Anthea were waiting to order lunch at the Lobster's Claw. Trevor arrived with a bulging leather satchel over his shoulder.

'Hi, guys. I didn't think I was going to make it. Haven't kept you too long, have I?'

'No, you're alright, Trev. Grab a seat,' said Harold.

Trevor deposited his bag on the floor and sat down. 'That's better,' he said.

'You do know Anthea?' asked Harold.

'Well, we have technically met, but I don't think that has amounted to much more than being seated around the same table at one of those enterprise groups that the university insists on setting up from time to time.' Trevor grinned. 'Good to meet you properly, at last, Anthea.'

Anthea blushed and swept a hand through her hair. 'Oh, it's positively lovely to meet you too, Trevor. Of course, I'm part of the enemy at those meetings. I do actually run my own small business.'

'Give me half a second and I shall tell you what it is,' said Trevor. 'It's coming. I have an image of coconuts. Wait a moment.'

'No, Trevor, she doesn't design bras,' said Harold.

'Oh, Harold, darling! You are such a naughty man,' said Anthea, giggling.

'I'm getting there. Coconuts, coconut oil, and I think I have it. Massage? Could it be a massage parlour. Maybe with some vertical sunbeds? Could I get a nice tan there?'

'He is getting warm, don't you think?' Anthea asked Harold.

'He'll be getting a bit hot under the collar if he goes much further down this path!' said Harold.

'Aroma therapy!' shouted Trevor.

'Well done! You got there in the end,' Anthea gushed.

'So how's business, Anthea?' asked Trevor.

'Call me Anth, darling. Harold does.'

'Your wish is my command, Anth.'

'Oh, it sounds like you and Harold have the same script writer. You say that sometimes, don't you Harold?'

'I do, but not to you. To you, I say that my wish is your command.'

Anthea laughed. 'Silly me! I was forgetting.'

The waitress came for their order and said she would be back with the fish and chips shortly.

'I'll try again,' said Trevor. 'How's business, Anth?'

'It's not too bad, thank you. Of course, I couldn't manage without Harold, here. He has been a great help to me.'

'I can't think why,' said Trevor, grinning.

'Well, you are not a middle-aged over-weight woman trying to give up cigarette smoking, are you.' Anthea turned her head to look directly at Trevor as she said this.

'Not the last time I looked in the mirror, Anth,' said Trevor.

'He's very good with my ladies of a certain age. I think they want to mother him,' said Anthea.

'Or smother the old sod,' added Trevor. Anthea giggled.

'But you can't let him loose with the massage oil, surely?' Trevor raised his hands in mock horror.

'Oh, no. Wouldn't let him near anyone for that sort of caper. No, he does the boring old talking cures with a bit of hypnosis thrown in.'

Harold looked up from his mobile phone. 'I heard that!'

'Get your head out of your phone, Harold. Your as bad as the kids nowadays.'

'It's Emm. I've got an SMS message here about the stuff she's got in Julia's basement. I'd better send a reply. I'll be with you in a second.' Harold's thumbs sped over the micro keyboard. The waitress brought the food. Anthea stole frequent glances at Trevor.

'And how's the world treating you, Trevor?' said Anthea.

'Call me Trev, darling. Harold does.' Trevor imitated what Anthea had said earlier, while offering a wink to Harold.

'Oh, no. I couldn't possibly call you that. I think a nice long *Trev-vee* will be much more intimate.'

Trevor laughed. 'That'll be a first, then. Nobody has ever called me that before.'

'Well, Trev-vee, how's it going? What is floating your boat, as they say?'

'One word says it all. Marking!' Trevor kicked at the bulging leather bag that lay at his feet.'

'Ah, yes. That's all you university types ever do, I know,' said Anthea.

'What? You think we spend all our time marking?' replied Trevor.

'No, Trev-vee. You spend all your time moaning about your marking,' said Anthea.

Trevor laughed. 'You might have a point, there.'

'Unless, of course, you keep all your naughty toys in there,' said Anthea, looking down at Trevor's satchel.

She smiled at Harold. Trevor began to blush.

'Oh, Harold! I think our darling Trev-vee is turning fifty shades of purple,' said Anthea.

'Stop it, Anth, or I might have to smack your bottom,' said Trevor.

'Only if you rub it with coconut oil first, Trev-vee,' replied Anthea.

Harold rolled his eyes. 'Sounds more like fifty shades of infantilism, if you ask me.'

'Oh, very interesting, Harold. So you think Trev-vee is hiding a pack of diapers in his bag?' asked Anthea.

'Anth! Give it a rest,' said Trevor.

'Alright, Trev-vee. But I think they have a baby-changing table in the girls' restroom here. So, let me know if you need anything.' Anthea gave Trevor a wink.

'Harold, this is a nightmare. Help me out,' pleaded Trevor.

'He's such a sensitive lad, Anth. You'll have to handle him with kid gloves.' said Harold.

Anthea nodded slowly. 'So, he likes a bit of leather, you think?' she said to Harold. Then, turning to Trevor, 'I've got just the outfit for you.'

'Is she always like this, Harold?' asked Trevor.

'No, I've never seen her this way before. You must bring it out in her,' replied Harold.

'Hello, boys! Talk to me, not about me,' Anthea patted the spare seat on the Chesterfield sofa she was sitting on. 'Here, Trev-vee, come and sit with me, where I can keep an eye on you.'

Harold was a tad surprised to see his friend stand up and move his pint across the table. He then went over and sat down beside Anthea. She immediately slid her arm through his, locking him close to her elbow. Harold went back to his SMS typing.

'I think Harold's ignoring us, Trev-vee,' said Anthea.

'I told you! I have to deal with Emma,' Harold replied, irritably.

Anthea turned to Trevor. 'We'll just have to enjoy ourselves without him, won't we, baby?' Anthea cuddled herself into Trevor. They both sank deeper into the sofa.

'So, Trev-vee, are you going to come and see me sometime? I think you would like that. Yes?' Anthea laced her fingers into Trevor's free hand and brought it to rest on her stomach, beneath her ample bosom.

'This is all a bit sudden, Anth,' said Trevor.

'*Carpe diem*, Trev-vee. What was that film?' Anthea had a look of concentration on her face.

'*Dead poets*. Something like that,' mumbled Harold.

'It's alive,' Anthea whispered to Trevor.

'I heard that,' said Harold, as he continued with his SMS messages. Anthea nudged Trevor.

'Visit. You to me. When?' said Anthea.

Trevor looked flustered. 'Really? You're serious?' He raised an eyebrow.

Anthea nodded.

'Tomorrow?' enquired Trevor, tentatively.

'Tomorrow. Seven. My place. Don't be late!' She let go of Trevor and extricated a calling card from her bag.

'Here's the address and my mobile phone number if you need it,' she said as she handed the card to him.

'Well, OK. Tomorrow, then.' Trevor pocketed the card. Anthea reclaimed his hand.

At this point, Harold put away his mobile phone and they all chatted for a while until Trevor had to leave.

The weekend came and went. Harold, having heard nothing from either Trevor or Anthea, decided to call Anthea. He felt he was entitled to a post-mortem and that he might get more out of Anthea than his friend Trevor. Therefore, in a quiet moment, he dialled the number and settled back for a chat.

'Anthea Partington'

'Anth! How did it go then? Did my old mate behave himself?'

'Har-rold! Lovely to hear from you. I'm not sure I should be talking to you about my darling boy, Trev-vee, though.'

'Why ever not? You always like a good gossip!'

'Of course I do, darling. But, you know, this one's a bit close. Don't you think, sweetie-pie?'

'I can't imagine why that should bother you one tiny little bit. Unless you've gone and fallen in love with the poor bloke.' Harold listened to silence on the other end of the line. 'Anth? Are you still there?'

'Mmmmm?'

'Oh, no. You have, haven't you?'

'Well, Har-old, I'm not sure that I should tell you.'

'That means you have.'

'I didn't say so!' said Anthea.

'But if it were not true, I would have got a hot denial. But I didn't.'

Harold heard Anthea giggling at the other end of the line.

'So that's it. A fat lot I'll see of my mate Trev from now on.'

'Now don't be beastly, Har-rold,' said Anthea.

'Ah! Wait a minute. It could be a case of the unrequited sort?' The degree of hopefulness that infused his voice could not be entirely accounted for by play-acting.

'I rather think not, judging by the degree of enthusiasm he put into his ministrations. Poor old Har-rold. Are you a tiny bit jealous, pet?'

Harold laughed. 'Good Heavens, no!' He blustered somewhat.

'Now, Har-rold, calm down. We had a lovely time,' said Anthea.

'Are you going to meet again?'

'Hmm. Is that really any of your business, Har-rold?'

Harold sensed that she was enjoying herself, teasing him. 'Very well, let's talk about the garden, then. I mowed the lawns today, and I think I might put a bit of fertilizer on them tomorrow, if the rain holds off.'

'Har-rold, don't be horrid. I don't want to talk about your beastly garden. Well, I suppose it is Julia's garden.'

'Indeed.'

'Well, aren't you going to ask me some more about it?' said Anthea.

'Ah, I see. I have to be your confidant. You need me, after all,' said Harold.

'Of course I do, Har-rold. And Trev-vee was gorgeous. He's so nice, too!'

'Anth, don't wax too lyrical. Remember I have seen him blind drunk, down the Cracked Bell, on more than one occasion.'

'Well, I don't want to know anything about that, thank you.'

'So, what are you going to do? Are you moving in together?' asked Harold.

'Well, Trev-vee's place is far too small, darling, and it is a bit too early to be talking joint real estate!'

'I suppose so,' said Harold.

'Mind you, I could do up one of the rooms in my clinic building.'

'Rent another floor of delapidation from daddy, you mean?'

'Yes, that's what did actually occur to me. I could do it up as a sin pad.'

'Do you mean that you see yourself as a prostitute?'

'Oh, Har-rold! You must have your little jokes. No, more like a Mistress, actually.'

'But Trev is not married. At least, he wasn't the last time I looked.'

'I know. That's a bit of a bummer. It might be more of an adventure if he was,' said Anthea, dreamily.

'And you didn't mean 'Mistress' as in whips and chains?' enquired Harold.

'Honestly, Har-rold. Your mind is like a sewer,' replied Anthea.

'I do put my hand up to the occasional coprolytic thought, Anth.'

The phone call was put on hold for some considerable time until Anthea's fit of giggles atrophied sufficiently for the spoken word to be heard and recognised, once again.

'I think it would be nice for us to have a place where we can retreat to, when we feel like it. Our own urban desert island,' said Anthea.

'I can see the attraction in that. And the rent you pay your dad is ridiculously low.'

'I know. I mean, I can see it won't be a long-term solution but it would buy us time to explore one another a bit before committing to a more permanent arrangement, if that happens.'

'God! Anth! It sounds as though you have been talking to your solicitor.'

'I have, actually,' replied Anthea.

'And all this, so soon.'

'Yes, well, once I get the bit between my teeth.' Anthea left the sentence hanging in the air.

'Back to the Mistress theme?' enquired Harold.

'Naughty Har-rold!' replied Anthea.

'Have you talked about this with Trev?'

'I vaguely ran it past him. He didn't seem very interested in interior decor.'

Harold laughed. 'No, I think that would go right over his head.'

'So I'll probably just go ahead and fix something up and then give him a key.'

'And he will keep his flat on?'

'Yes, I don't want to spook him,' said Anthea.

'But you do want to ensare him?'

'Oh, Har-rold. I wish you wouldn't put it like that! But maybe just a tiny bit.' Anthea sighed. 'Yes, maybe I do. Is that so bad of me, Har-rold?'

'Not at all, Anth. Who am I to talk? Being ensnared by Julia has been one of the best things to happen to me in a long time.'

'Yes, it does seem to have been rather exciting for you. Woken you up a bit, hasn't it?'

'I think you could say it has totally shaken up the way I was drifting from middle age to old age.'

'You mean it's made you revisit your adolescence?'

'I wouldn't go that far, Anth.'

'Oh.' Anthea sounded disappointed.

'Anth?'

'Well, it's just that I was hoping this thing with Trev-vee might take me back to mine.' They both laughed.

'Being serious for a moment, Anth, the two of you are my greatest friends. I do wish you all the best with this. I really do.'

'Oh, thank you, Har-rold. You are such a sweetie-pie!'

'Does Mavis know about your plans?'

'I've dropped a few hints. Nothing too specific. I've just told her that I am fixing up a crash-pad for evenings and weekends. I am thinking that I won't put a mainline phone connection into the new flat.'

'Good idea. Anyway, it won't matter if I mention it to Mavis, in passing, if it comes up. It's not like a secret or anything?'

'Oh, no. That's ok,'

'I'd better get going, I'll probably see you later in the week. I think Mavis told me I have a few new clients coming in,' said Harold.

'Yes, Mavis told me she had booked one or two more for you.'

'OK. Well, good luck for the future, Anth.'

'Thank you, Har-rold. Bye!'

Harold heard the phone click, as the call finished. He was smiling as he replaced the receiver. Harold was feeling incredibly lazy, and had settled himself into his favourite armchair to read his library book.

He felt the muscles of his forehead knit togther in a frown as he heard a key in the front door. This was followed by the sound of feet being wiped on the doormat.

'Is that you, Emm?' called Harold.

'No. It's me, Harold,' replied Julia.

'That's a surprise. Somehow I had imagined you were busy all day, today.'

'I cleared my schedule.'

'Was there a reason for that?' asked Harold.

'There was, actually.' Julia smiled at Harold as she entered the room. She inhaled sharply. 'That coffee smells good.'

'I just made a pot. There's plenty left. Do you want me to get you a cup?'

'Yes, that would be just what the doctor ordered.'

Harold got up to go to the kitchen. As he left he heard Julia mumbling something. He paused. 'Did you say something?'

'No, nothing much. Just that she probably wouldn't, under the circumstances.'

'Wouldn't what?' asked Harold

'Prescribe coffee,' said Julia.

Harold shrugged his shoulders and disappeared into the kitchen. He returned with the extra cup of coffee which he placed upon the occasional table next to Julia's armchair. Having done this, he sat down once more and sipped from his own cup. The room fell silent. Julia adjusted her skirt as she crossed her legs and sank back into her chair.

'Harold?' Julia uttered his name by way of gaining his attention.

'Julia?' Harold, in stating her name, implied she had it.

'I've got some news.'

'Go on.'

'It's a little bit delicate.'

Harold smirked. 'You're not usually lost for words, Julia.'

'Indeed I'm not. But, you see, I have never been in quite this situation before.'

'Sounds intriguing. Are you going to enlighten me?' asked Harold.

Julia sat quietly for what seemed like an eternity to Harold. There was something about her attitude that caused him to show patience; he made no attempt to hurry her. At last she put down her coffee cup and looked him squarely in the eye.

'I cleared my schedule because I had an appointment with my doctor at the Health Centre.'

'Your not ill, are you? You haven't got cancer or anything like that. Have you?' Harold began to show signs of panic.

'Calm down, Harold. It is nothing like that.'

Harold relaxed somewhat.

'This might come as a surprise to you, Harold, but it seems I am pregnant.'

'You're what?' Harold's jaw dropped.

'Pregnant, Harold. I'm pregnant.'

'Wow!' Harold was stunned.

Julia smiled as she lowered her head slightly and watched Harold from beneath her raised eyebrows.

'Is it mine?'

Julia laughed. 'Oh, yes. Nobody other than yourself has been inside my reproductive cathedral for some considerable time. Your seed is highly privileged, Harold.'

Harold, to put it mildly, was flabbergasted.

'But I'm old enough to be its grandfather or even its great-grandfather!' said Harold.

'This sort of thing is not uncommon nowadays,' said Julia.

'And what about you? You're in your late 30s. That's getting on for a prima gravida.'

'So you are not pleased? You don't want it?' asked Julia.

'I wouldn't say that. I haven't really thought about it. It has come as a bit of a shock,' replied Harold.

'But you might like the idea once it grows on you?'

'I suppose so. It feels a bit irresponsible for us to be entering into parent hood at our ages.'

'Stuff and nonsense, Harold.'

'It's all very well for you to say that. What happens if I pop my cloggs sooner than later?'

'None of us know precisely when our time will come. Anyway, what about your father?'

'What about him?'

'I thought you told me that he died very early on.'

'He did. It was a road accident, while my Mum was still pregnant. I never knew him.'

'And look at you! It hasn't done you much harm, has it?'

'I guess not, if you put it like that. I have never known any different. I have often wondered what it would have been like, though. To have had a dad.'

Julia nodded.

'But quite apart from me, how would you feel if I was to go earlier, than later?'

'I would have the child as a memory of you, to love and care for.'

'I don't doubt that you would cope.'

'It will be fun, Harold.'

'And quite a lot of hard work,' Harold countered.

'Especially in the early days. Of course, if I can't breast feed, you will have to do the bottle feeds at night,' said Julia.

'Thanks!' said Harold. He smiled. 'So, are my duties being extended to those of nusery maid and childminder?'

'No, Harold. The situation is even worse than you could possibly imagine.'

Harold began to look worried, in the extreme.

'You are about to become not only a father, once more, but also a husband.'

'What?' Harold shook his head slowly, in puzzlement.

'Do you want me to spell it out?' said Julia.

'I think you had better do just that.'

'Harold, you are going to have to marry me.'

'It gets worse and worse. I'm having a nightmare,' said Harold.

'I know, Harold. It'll take a few days for you to get over the shock of it all. Don't worry. Leave everything to me. Once you get used to it, you'll be fine. '

'I hope you know what you are doing,' said Harold.

'Let's have a glass of champagne to celebrate,' said Julia.

Harold dutifully pottered off to the kitchen to get some champagne flutes. The sound of the cork popping was followed by the clinking of their glasses.

'Here's to the baby,' said Julia.

'To the new baby,' said Harold.

'It seems very decadent to be drinking champagne at this time of day,' said Julia.

'Yes,' replied Harold. 'So, you are to become Mrs Hake?'

'No, Harold. You are to become Mr Rivers. We will sort out the change of name for you.'

Harold nodded. He had never been especially fond of his surname. He tried out the new one a couple of times, in between sips. 'It has a ring to it. I could get used to it.'

'Rings! You must come to the jewellers with me and I'll sort that out,' said Julia.

'Maybe I could have a black jet crystal on mine, in the shape of a coffin?' said Harold.

'You are a very naughty boy!' replied Julia.

Harold refilled the glasses and swigged back more champagne. When Julia came out with that sort of statement, he often needed a bit of Dutch courage.

## Chapter 12

The day of the wedding came blessed with a bright blue, cloudless sky. The morning was crisp. As yet, Harold had not arisen. He had decided to take up the offer to sleep over at his friend Graham Antrobus's house, given that he had felt it to be not quite the done thing to leave for his wedding from Julia's. He would have put up at Trevor's house, were it not for the fact that Trevor was in the middle of moving all his stuff into Anthea's flat. Her new pad turned out to be a far larger appartment than was originally envisaged; there was plenty of room for Trevor's furniture.

Harold's friendship with Graham, although not especially deep, stretched back across a couple of decades. They had been colleagues in the psychology department. Coming from different ends of the discipline, they did not have a huge amount in common, academically speaking, but they had made up for that with much conviviality in the Cracked Bell.

A sharp rapping on the bedroom door, accompanied by a half-decent rendition of '*I'm getting married in the morning*' sung with gusto by his host brought Harold's head sharply out of the covers.

'Alright, alright. Gordon Bennett! I'm up,' shouted Harold.

'Good to hear, Harold. I think Trevor might shoot me if I failed to get you to the church on time,' said Graham.

'And I'll shoot you if you sing any more of that bloody song!'

'Cheer up, Harold. It's your big day. You can have the bathroom. I'm all done in there.'

'Thanks, mate. I'll just get a quick shower then you can ask the butler to start robing me up.'

'I'm the only butler you'll see around here,' replied Graham. 'I hope I haven't got to help you with your bow tie knot?'

Harold laughed. 'It's OK. I ordered a ready-made one on a bit of elastic.'

'Cheat!' said Graham.

'I'm relying on you not to tell Julia. I shall hide it in a pocket, once the show's over.'

Graham laughed and left Harold to get on with his ablutions. Eventually, they caught up with one another in the kitchen.

'Looking good, Harold,' said Graham.

'Thank you, mate. You've scrubbed up quite well, too!'

'Thought I'd better pull out the stops on a day like this. Look, we've got time for a coffee or a quick tipple before we go, if you fancy one.'

'I wouldn't mind a coffee. I'd better not have a drink. Need to keep my wits about me.'

Graham fixed the coffees and they perched on kitchen stools at the counter.

'So, you never fancied getting married, Graham?'

'I won't say I have never thought about it, but it has never come to fruition. I suppose I was fairly close to Helen for a while. You remember her?' said Graham.

'Yes, I do. She used to hang out with Craig at one time?'

'Yes. I mean, nothing too serious. It was a more of a rebound situation.'

'I see. But you and Helen did not stay the distance?' enquired Harold.

'No. It wasn't as if there was a big bust up. Things got stale and we ran out of steam, I think.'

'That's a pity.'

'Yes, but it couldn't be helped. And here we are, with you about to take another leap into the dark!' said Graham.

'Leap into the dark? I suppose it is really. I have not been the instigator. You could say I have passively acquiesced to the upcomming lifescript that Julia has recently penned for me.'

'Did she make you audition?'

Harold laughed. 'I suppose she did, in a way.'

'Are you glad you got the part? Are you looking forward to the performance?'

'It should go well. The script's not too tight. Plenty of room for a bit of improvisation,' said Harold.

'So you never thought of turning her down?'

'I think the alternative would involve me sitting alone on an empty stage with no lights, no camera, and not much hope of any action.'

'Part of me envies you, but I think I need to be the owner of my future plans.'

'Perhaps that is why there would appear to be a dearth of such plans in your court, at present,' said Harold.

'Fair point, Harold.' Graham checked his watch. 'Taxi will be here soon.'

Harold stood up. 'I had better go powder my nose one last time.'

'Don't be too long, darling,' said Graham, camply.

The taxi picked up Harold and Graham. They were among the first to arrive at the registry office, although Trevor and Anthea were hot on their heels. Anthea dashed over to Harold and launched into one of her major hugs.

'Har-rold! I'm so excited. Are you? Of course you are.' She disengaged and stood back to give him the once-over, reaching out to brush an imaginary spec of dust from his left shoulder. 'There! You look stunning, darling.' She turned to Trevor placing her white gloved claw possessively on her man's arm. 'Don't you think he looks rather *distingué*, Trev-vee-kins?'

Harold saw Trevor wince slightly as Anthea pronounced the third syllable which she had taken to adding to his name, rather as a nursery school teacher might with her favourite pet of the week. He flashed a private wink at his friend.

'Got the rings, old chap?' asked Harold, with a trace of anxiety in his voice.

Trevor fished into the pocket of his waistcoat, shook them in his hands as if he were about to roll dice, and then offered them for inspection on his open palm.

Harold grinned. 'Don't stand anywhere near a drain if you do that trick again before they are needed,' he admonished. Trevor laughed. Anthea was leaning against him so hard, he had one leg set back slightly to take the strain, as it were. At this point, Emma and Penny arrived. They were both dressed in matching pale lilac skirt suits, with white lace blouses and black stockings. Emma moved across to kiss her father, while Penny joined Anthea for what looked like some serious girl talk on their respective outfits.

'How are you feeling, Dad?'

'Bit nervous. I think it is worse than the time I gave my first lecture at the university.'

'Highly romantic association, Dad.' Emma laughed and hugged her father. 'You will be great, Dad. And, anyway, the focus will be on Julia.'

'Yes, I do hope so. Is everything OK with you and Julia,' asked Harold.

'It's fine, Dad. But we don't want to be talking about that right now. Do we?'

'No, of course not. I just wanted a bit of reassurance.'

'Look, Dad, Julia has been really nice to me. It is Penny who she has given a hard time. But they seem to be much better now.'

Harold nodded. He turned to look over at the door and waved to Craig Melcheter and his wife, Tilly, who had just arrived. He went across to greet them.

'Harold! It's lovely to see you,' said Craig. Tilly gave Harold a peck on the cheek and smiled at him.

'Yes, I haven't seen you for a while,' said Harold.

'I know. Sorry about that. We've been out of the loop - working away quite a lot.'

Harold nodded. He refrained from enquiring as to what exactly work involved, since he had heard that Craig had become involved with some obscure cult after his wife died. 'Well, welcome back to the fold, then. I think you know everyone here, anyway.'

'I'm pretty sure I do. And I can intruduce Tilly to anyone she has not yet met.'

'Ah! Mavis and her husband have arrived,' said Harold.

'Oh. Is that the Mavis who runs things for Anthea at the clinic?' asked Craig.

'Indeed it is. Runs it like clockwork!' Harold went off to welcome the said Mavis. She introduced him to her husband, Jack, whom he had never before met.

'Harold! It's good to see you. You won't remember me, but I actually came to some of your gigs years ago, in the Cracked Bell,' said Jack.

'Really? I hope you enjoyed them,' replied Harold.

'I did. I loved your stuff. And the reception is there today, too.'

'That's right. You can't get away from it. The Cracked Bell is the centre of the universe.' They laughed indulgently at Harold's joke.

Eventually, Julia arrived. Given that there is little slack for arriving late at a civil ceremony, she had cut it as fine as any attention-grabbing bride could. She wore a slate grey dress with a hint of pink in the sheen. Her hair was up, a ring of neat curls supporting the base of the hive. The clerk from the local council came forward and ushered them through to the wedding chamber; the guests filed in and took their places. The civil service chuntered on. Harold noticed that it was, however, running at a much faster clip than was the case at a catholic wedding he had attended some months previously. On that occasion he had dozed off in the pews, intermittently. Today, by comparison, he was positively hyper!

Before long the deed was done and everyone was spilling out of the building onto the lawn of the courtyard. The photographer whose name, obviously, was Kevin started to round up the guests, working top down in order of importance, to cement the occasion into the annals of digital posterity. His assistant herded them onto the posing dias with the efficiency of a well-trained sheep dog. Eventually, he reported to Harold that he was all done, in terms of the formal photographs. Harold reminded him that he had been contracted to snap away more informally at the reception in the Cracked Bell. Kevin confirmed that everything was under control. Graham Antrobus then announced that there were a couple of minibuses waiting to take them to the reception. Julia squeezed Harold's arm.

'I'll just make sure my aunt Mildred is ok with the minibus,' she said.

Harold nodded. 'I'll see you in the wedding car, then,' he replied. He moved over to where Graham was standing with Craig Melcheter.

'Harold! Lovely to witness you getting spliced,' said Craig, shaking Harold's hand.

'Thanks, Craig. Where's Tilly? I'm sure I saw her inside.'

'She's gone to powder her nose, as they say.'

'Yes, I suppose they do. So, you are going in the minibuses, I take it?'

'Well, yes and no,' said Graham, mysteriously.

'Graham and I have just been having an argument about plural nouns,' said Craig.

'There should be a rule about doing that at weddings!' declared Harold.

'Graham insists that we have two 'minibi', not two 'minibuses'. What do you think, Harold?' asked Craig.

Harold laughed. 'I love it! It has to be Graham!' He walked in and around the remainder of the guests calling out at the top of his voice 'Away to the minibi, all of you. Hurry, hurry - your minibi await!' Those not having been party to the conversation with Graham and Craig looked looked wary.


Harold followed Julia into the back seat of the wedding car and let out a sigh of pleasure.

'We did it, Julia.'

'Yes, Harold, we did. How does it feel? You know, having just sworn to love honour and obey me for the rest of your life?'

'Julia, you know they don't use that line any more, especially not at a civil ceremony.'

'I know. I was only joking. Actually, I don't think I was,' said Julia.

'No, I rather thought you weren't,' said Harold.

'Who was that rather distinguished gentleman? Tall, pin-stripe suit. Looked a bit like an old-fashioned city type?'

'That was Twaggers. He is an old-fashioned city type. He worked in the city for a decade or two,' replied Harold.

'And how did you know Twaggers?'

'Boarding school. I hooked up with him when I went back to the reunion.'

'The time you had your little turn on the train and ended up in hospital?'

'That's right.'

'Maybe he has a bad effect on you. Should I keep him out of your way, Harold? I don't want you to go fainting on me at the reception.'

'No, he's OK. If anything, it was me who had a bad effect on him.'

'How so?' asked Julia.

'He was very bookish and he always followed the rules to the letter. A bit of a goody-goody, to be honest.'

'Nothing wrong with that, Harold, apart from being a bit dull, I suppose.'

'His weakness was that he loved the cinema.'

Julia looked blankly at Harold. 'And how, pray, might that be regarded as a weakness?'

'He could not go during term time.'

'And?' Julia's brows wrinkled in incomprehension.

'I showed him how to climb over the school fence and sneak into a cinema not far away.'

'Oh! You naughty boy Harold. What if that had led him into bad habits in the city, later in his life?'

'How do you mean?'

'Well, you taught him that breaking the rules could be rewarding.'

Harold laughed. 'I should think that might have been an asset, as far as working in the city is concerned.'

'Surely not?'

'We have heard of white-collar crime? No?' said Harold.

Julia laughed. Harold looked out of the window as the car slowed to a halt.

'Looks like we are here. Ye Olde Crackitum-Bellum.'

'Am I going to have to listen to your little jokes for the rest of my life?' asked Julia in mocked dismay.

'I think that is the essence of our marriage contract. You, the bride, promise to laugh at my cringe-worthy attempts at humour, while I, the groom, agree to be your cook and bottle-washer, in perpetuity.'

The driver of the car opened Julia's door and helped her out onto the pavement. Harold propelled himself there, too, but with much less aplomb. They made their way into the pub and out to the functions room at the rear of the building. The guests were awaiting them, since the minibuses had already arrived. As they walked into the room a round of applause broke out. The landlord had arranged the tables to form a square. Two vases of flowers graced the top table and Harold and Julia moved up to take their place of honour. Name tags had been put on the tables and the guests scrambled around to find their places. While the number of guests at the registry office ceremony had been kept to a minimum, a larger number of acquaintances swelled the throng at the reception. Although Trevor was doing his best to get everyone seated in their proper places, the process was slowed down by an incessant series of spontaneous conversations breaking out between guests who had not seen one-another for a while or, in some cases, for many years. Once seated, Trevor rose to make a few announcements, as Best Man.

'Hullo, and welcome, everyone. For those of you who have just joined us, I can confirm that the happy couple did indeed just get married.' A ripple of applause ran around the room. 'We asked you to sit at table according to the seating plan, partly so that the landlord and his staff can deal more easily with any special dietary requirements that were mentioned in your response to the invitation that was sent to you. I hope you don't find this too authoritarian an arrangement, although Harold tells me that Julia does like to run a neat and tidy ship at home!' A peel of laughter greeted this remark; Harold felt Julia's elbow in his ribs.

'Enjoy your meal. There is water, red wine and white wine on the table. Bottled beer can be brought out for anyone who wants it; just ask the server at your table. If you need anything more exotic, you can pop to the bar and sort that out for yourself. Enjoy your meal. And no matter how long you drag it out, speeches will follow eventually. Excessively slow mastication will provide no exemption from that torture!' Laughter and some ribald cheering followed Trevor's remark as he sat down, next to Harold. The landlord looked enquiringly over to Trevor who signalled that the meal could be started. Minutes later the servers entered bearing trays of soup bowls. Harold noticed that there was one waiter, but the rest appeared to be waitresses in outfits bearing a close resemblance to French maids' uniforms. He turned to

Julia who, he realised, had been watching him. She smiled and gave him a light kick on the shin underneath the table. Harold risked a wink in reply. Her grin broadened. He looked around the room contentedly as he began to slurp his soup. Neither he nor Julia had much family left, but that didn't seem to matter.

Harold caught Emma staring across the table at Julia.

'Everything alright, Emm...' he said.

'Fine, Dad. Just trying to think of Julia as my stepmother.'

Julia laughed. 'It sounds pretty dreadful when you say it out loud like that, Emma.'

'It's a two-way street, Julia. How do you feel about having me as your stepdaughter?'

'I think it's great. Of course the whole situation would be entirely different if you were a little girl, but you are not.'

'No, I'm all grown up and graduated.' Emma laughed.

'There is not even much in the way of a legal connection between us, give that you are now an adult. Stepdaughter or stepmother feel more like technical terms, like second-cousin once removed or something.'

'But you wouldn't say it was nothing?' asked Emma.

'No, that doesn't feel right. I think being stepmother to you, my stepdaughter, singles our relationship out as being special although perhaps for us it is a little different from how it would be if you were still a child.'

Harold nodded. 'I think you have to look to the underlying model in order to inject meaning into the terms that might be satisfying to us in our situation.'

'Oh, no! Dad's off on one of his seminars. Trevor, can you distract him or something.' Emma winked at Trevor.

'Couldn't possibly, Emm,' replied Trevor. 'After all, I'm his best man. I have to stick up for him. So, carry on, my old mate.' Trevor grinned at Harold.

'As I was saying before I was so rudely interrupted by my lovely daughter on my wedding day, you need to find the right model.'

'Whatever does that mean, Dad?' said Emma.

'By definition your stepmother is the woman who has married your father after the death or divorce of your biological mother. It is therefore a quasi-biological term. That is what shifts the meaning away from that of simple friendship or acquaintance.'

'Hang on, Harold, some stepmother-stepdaughter relationships can be characterised by hatred, not friendship,' said Trevor.

'Yes, but when you describe someone's physical attributes in terms of beauty, that does not prevent you saying that they are ugly,' replied Harold.

'So, why can't we just talk in terms of friendship?' asked Emma.

'Because it is different. Imagine you have a good friend and then you have a terrible argument. You can walk away from that person. You can declare them no longer to be your friend,' said Harold.

'So?' queried Emma.

'You could never declare that Julia was no longer your stepmother. At least, not while Julia and I remain married. And that is precisely similar to the way you can never declare that I am not your father. You will always have some of my genes whether you like it or not. And that is why the concept of stepmother is based upon an underlying genetic model.'

'Hmm... Maybe we should move on, Harold.' Trevor signalled to the waitress and pointed to their empty glasses.

Harold glanced around the room and noticed that it was not just his glass that was being refilled. Julia had told the landlord ahead of time when they booked the reception that he should not stint on the booze. Indeed, the landlord looked like the conductor of a symphony orchestra as he pointed to one waitress after another, indicating where he had spotted an empty bottle on the tables. Harold smiled as the noise of conversation began to swell, along with increasingly frequent sporadic bursts of laughter; he felt sure that this was no doubt a function of the quantity of alcohol consumed. Once the deserts had been brought to table and coffee had been made available, Trevor checked with Harold on progress.

'What do you think, my old mate? Is it about time for a bit of speechifying?'

'I guess it's just me and you, Trev.'

'Julia didn't want anyone to stand in for her dear departed father, I take it?' said Trevor.

'No, I don't think there is anyone left in terms of that role,' replied Harold.

Trevor nodded. 'Right, I'll just have a word with the landlord, so he can get the champagne sorted.' With that, Trevor slipped out of his seat and went to arrange matters. On his way back to the table, he rang the sonorous ships bell that hung from the wall by the top table. A quiet gradually decended upon the room.

'Ladies and gentlemen, it is my honour to say a few words on this auspicious occasion.'

'The fewer, the better, Trev.' called a heckler from the floor.

'There's my gravitas gone out the window!' Exclaimed Trevor. A ripple of laughter ran through the guests.

'I have known Harold getting on for thirty years, since we both arrived at the university as a couple of very green lecturers, back in the 70s. I can't remember much about how we met, although I do know the occasion. It was at the opening of a glass exhibition at the city's new arts centre. For some obscure reason, a representative from one of the European consulates had opened the exhibition and had dumped a crate full of litre bottles of vodka on one of the tables. He explained that he did not have a long speech prepared but he hoped the gift of vodka would make up for that. I think that news was greeted with three resounding cheers of the 'Hip, Hip... Hurrah!' variety. Harold and I then drank for England. A close bond was formed that night.

We have remained good mates through thick and thin. At the university, he was undoubtedly one of the best deflaters of management bullshit that I ever came across. What's more, he could even do it with a dash of humour, although that did not win him friends in high places. I very much admired the way that Harold would stand by other, possibly weaker, members of staff against the corporate bullies of the academic world. Of course, we had a lot of fun too. Mind you, I think both of us would have done better academically if we had not spent quite so much time hanging out in the bar of this wonderful establishment. However, life would have had a lot less sparkle were it not for the Cracked Bell and the company who sailed within her.' At this point, many of the older men present stood up, raised their glasses and chorused 'The Cracked Bell'. As they drank the toast, the landlord made a deep bow. Applause broke out.

'For me, one of the delights of the early years was to see Harold crawling into work, half asleep with rumpled hair and creased up clothes. This was when his lovely daughter Emma was born.' Trevor paused for the cheering and applause that went around the tables.

'That's made Emma blush, anyway!' said Trevor. 'Yes, back then one could often see the corner of a Mothercare baby cloth poking out of his pockets when he turned up very late and dishevelled for work, and I swear he used those cloths for cleaning the blackboard. Oh, a word of explanation is due to the younger members present... A blackboard was a board upon which the lecturers wrote in chalk, incredible as that might seem. At the end of the lesson, one was morally obliged to clean off one's own chalk writing so that the next poor sod had a clean board to start with. It was very bad form, not to do that. People used to nick the chalk, so sometimes you had none to write with. Partly as a result of all this, you could see Harold wandering about campus with a bag containing his own little kit - board rubber, white chalk and coloured chalks. Yes, Harold was very artistic with his coloured chalks!'

Emma and a couple of other youngsters could be seen shrugging their shoulders and smirking at one another.

'I had better move things along. After all, this is not a lecture on 20th century teaching conditions! If I start going through Harold's biography step by step we will be here for ages. I know I ought to crack jokes, but I'm not very good at that sort of thing, and I don't really want to do that today. I will just say that Harold and Veronica did an amazing job bringing up their daughter and it is great to see Emma here today, as Maid of Honour. Of course, it was sad that Veronica passed on and she will be missed by many who knew her. However, I have to say that I am pleased that Harold, as a widower, has moved on to this new chapter in his life. Some men get sort of stuck when things like that happen in their lives. I am really pleased that this did not happen to Harold. If I may say so, I do believe that

Harold and Julia are ideally suited to one another and they complement each other in many ways. It seems to me that they have been irresistably drawn together - attracted like opposing magnetic poles. With names like Hake and Rivers, you could say that they met in the estuary of life, Hake being a saltwater fish. Clearly, it is Harold who is going to have to change his spots (please excuse the mixed metaphor) if he intends to swim into the salt-free stream of Julia's river waters. Already it is possible to detect some minor differences. The man is far more smartly turned out nowadays. Beneath his bumbling exterior, he always was pretty efficient but have you seen the pace at which he bumbles about nowadays! He would appear to be doing retirement on speed! And I attribute this entirely to the good Lady Rivers' influence.' Graham Antrobus and some of the other old lags from the Cracked Bell rose to intersperse another toast on the side of Trevor's speech.

'To the good Lady Rivers,' he said. The company rose and drank the toast, in all seriousness. Julia rolled her eyes and said, 'Get on with it Trevor, or we will be here all night.'

'Ah, well, Julia... Yes. Now, of course, Harold and Julia are no longer teenagers. This is a wedding between two mature and well-rounded characters. And, if you don't mind me saying so, I think Julia's character is about to become ever more well-rounded as the months roll by. Some of the more observant among us - obviously that doesn't include Graham - may have noticed a slight bump in Julia's wedding dress. For those of you who don't know, I am very pleased to announce to you the joyous fact that Julia is in fact pregnant. I'm sure I speak for everybody present when I say that we all wish you the very best, Julia, and hope that you manage to keep the old bugger fit and in good health. Harold comes from a family of great longevity, so I think he is going to have a lot of fun too. And I know Emma is delighted by the fact that she is going to have a baby sister.' Once again, Graham Antrobus rose to his feet. 'Let's drink to the upcoming sprog.' Everyone rose. 'The Sprog,' they cried, and drank their toast.

By this time the landlord was looking a bit frantic. Harold noticed him passing whispered messages to the staff. Waitresses began circling with reinforcement bottles of champagne to top up the thirstier guests before there were any more improvised toasts.

Trevor paused for a moment, looking around the tables at all the guests.

'My friends, I have been to a few weddings in my time.'

'It's about time you went to your own!' interjected Graham Antrobus. Trevor looked down at Anthea who was seated next to him. He smiled at her and then responded to Graham.

'I might well do that, sometime. But today belongs to Harold and Julia, not to me. As I was saying, I have seldom been to a wedding characterised by such a feeling of optimism. Everyone I have met and talked to seems so happy with this state of affairs. So, I am sure you will join with me in hoping that they have a lively and interesting marriage for many years to come. I therefore give you the toast. To Harold and Julia!' The company rose and toasted the happy couple.

Harold looked round the room and noticed one or two folks had sidled out, presumably to go to the bathroom or stock up with some double fire-power from the bar downstairs. He decided to get on with his speech, nonetheless. He rose and stood behind his chair, and beamed around the assembled company. He shuffled some loose sheets of paper in his hand, raised his head in a gesture calling for silence and proceeded.

'Psychology was born of a merger between experimental physiology and the philosophy of mind.' He paused. 'Bugger! I seem to have brought my old lecture notes for Psychology 101.' Hoots of laughter resounded around the room. Harold pocketed his notes.

'I shall just have to improvise without notes.'

'Why change the habit of a lifetime, Harold,' shouted Graham Antrobus, who now occupied the role of principle heckler.

'Where's my board rubber? Anyone seen my blackboard rubber? I need something to throw at Graham!' Everyone roared with laughter.

'I would like to say a brief word relating to Veronica, who passed away not long ago. Although my marriage to her could be described as a tad astringent at times, we succeeded in bringing up our daughter, Emma, and I feel very proud of that. However, as some of you know, while Emma was away at university things were not so good.

Sometimes, marriages run out of steam. One way or another, I became involved with Julia. I see my relationship with Julia as a completely different chapter, phase, or era of my life, in whatever way you want to put it. I have discovered what it is like to fall in love, as a middle-aged man. I do not think that Julia had any idea that things would come to this, although she sometimes tells me that it is all working out according to her Master-Plan. Perhaps the terminology should be updated to the post-feminist Mistress-Plan?' One or two of Harold's friends smiled, knowingly.

'I would not say that I was exactly destitute, but I went to Julia more or less begging for a place to stay. Having been kicked out of the university in a sacking dressed up as an early retirement, I was short of cash. Julia is a very busy and successful business consultant. I could not afford to pay her rent, so we agreed that I would earn my keep, as it were. I did the cooking and kept the place neat and tidy. The strange thing is that what might have been a straightforward contractual relationship, admittedly with a bit of sex thrown in, blossomed into a deep and mature love affair. Falling in love later in life is not the same as being in love in your teens. Clearly, we each have our own histories to bring to the table, or should I say, to take to the bed, and these histories are stuffed with far more content of a varied nature than anything a couple of teenagers could offer one another. It is as though our separate autobiographies have become joined (and joined officially, today) like two strands of spiralling DNA. One of our tasks will be to stitch them together retrospectively as our understanding of one another becomes ever deeper and ever more profound. Another task will be to explore how we shall view and experience the world and our own emotional existence in the future, so completely and irrevocably entwined. It is between these two tasks, the understanding of our past and the creation of our own future, that our happiness will lie in the experience of the present moment. We are, and shall always be alive to one another in those moments, as they come and go ephemerally, creating our own new history. I have nothing more to say, except to thank you all for coming to our wedding and to wish you all happiness, too.' At this point, Harold sat down. A slightly stunned silence ensued. There was no clapping. Trevor arose.

'Profound, as ever, Harold. Thank you for that, my dear friend.' Trevor took a sip of wine and then clapped his hands in a business-like fashion. 'This concludes the formal part of the wedding. You are welcome to stay for as long as you like. The waitresses will be coming around to clear off some of the debris from the tables. They will be able to bring you more coffee or wine, if you need it. Have fun!' Trevor sat down.

'Thanks, Trev,' said Harold.

'It's been a pleasure,' said Trevor.

Julia leaned over to Harold to whisper in his ear, 'Harold, I don't think we should stay too long. We need to get back home and get changed for the trip. I have the taxi booked for five-thirty to take us to the airport. You're sure everything is packed?'

'Absolutely,' replied Harold.

'Let's do the rounds in a minute, but we can't rush. We must take time to say goodbye to everybody and we have to thank them for the presents, too.'

'I have a list of those, if you need reminding.' Harold laughed.

'What would I do without you, Harold?'

'As of now, Julia, that is an empty and meaningless question.'

'Yes, it is. You're right!'

'Do we tell people where we are going for our honeymoon or not?'

'Definitely not. That can be our little secret. I have never been to Copenhagen before, and I must admit that I am looking forward to it very much.'

'Do you remember how we talked about going away for a trip, at some point?' asked Harold.

'Yes, I do. We never did,' said Julia.

'So, maybe this is it,' said Harold.

'Yes. And we would never have dreamed that it would be a honeymoon trip, back then,' said Julia.

'Do you know one of the most interesting things about getting married, Julia?'

'I expect you are going to tell me, Harold.'

'I think it is a pronoun shift in our personal identity.'

'What the fuck do you mean by that ?' asked Julia.

'The first person pronouns, the *I* and the *me*, gradually fade in use and importance. They are taken over by the existential *we* and *us*.'

Julia reached up and put her hand over Harold's mouth to gag him into silence. Then, kissing him, she said 'I'll take your word for that, Harold, but right now we have to thank our guests and say our farewells.' They rose from the table holding hands and, with confidence, took their first small steps into marital entwinement.

www.ingramcontent.com/pod-product-compliance
Lightning Source LLC
Chambersburg PA
CBHW051503170626
46811CB00002B/615